EBURY PRESS

OPERATION HAYGREEVA

Born in 1960, Prabhakar Aloka grew up in Bihar. He is a postgraduate from Delhi University. He joined the Indian Police Service in 1986 and was allotted the erstwhile Andhra Pradesh cadre. After a brief stint in the state, he joined the Intelligence Bureau, India's premier intelligence agency with over 125 years of history. In nearly three decades of service in the IB, he was rigorously trained in covert operations. The fiction he writes reflects his extensive experience.

OPERATION HAYGREEVA

PRABHAKAR ALOKA

EBURY
PRESS

An imprint of Penguin Random House

EBURY PRESS

USA | Canada | UK | Ireland | Australia
New Zealand | India | South Africa | China

Ebury Press is part of the Penguin Random House group of companies
whose addresses can be found at global.penguinrandomhouse.com

Published by Penguin Random House India Pvt. Ltd
4th Floor, Capital Tower 1, MG Road,
Gurugram 122 002, Haryana, India

First published in Ebury Press by Penguin Random House India 2021

Copyright © Prabhakar Aloka 2021

ISBN 9780143454410

Typeset in Bembo Std by Manipal Technologies Limited, Manipal
Printed at Thomson Press India Ltd, New Delhi

www.penguin.co.in

To the Almighty,
for his benevolence in my enduring struggle to render selfless service
to society

To my parents,
who sowed the seeds of human values, humility and righteousness

To my teachers,
who inculcated the philosophy
'Atta Dipa Viharatha'
(dwell as a lamp unto yourself)
as the guiding principle

न त्वहं कामये राज्यं न स्वर्गं नापुनर्भवम् ।
कामये दुःखतप्तानां प्रणिनां आर्तिनाशनम् ॥

(Neither do I desire kingdom, nor heaven, nor do I long
for rebirth. I yearn for being able to alleviate
the sufferings of those in sorrow.)

—*Bhagavatam, the story of King Rantidev*

'Spies descending from the skies glide the entire world around;
Their thousand eyes, all scanning, sweep the earth's remotest bound;
Whatever exists in heaven and earth;
Whatever beyond the skies . . .'

—Atharvaveda, Hymn XVI

Prologue

Mumbai, 11 July 2006

Birdsong punctures the stillness of dawn, merging to the chatter of the early risers who were already out on the streets of Virar to rouse Sullu from her sleep. 'Earlier than usual,' she thinks to herself, as she sits up in bed, scratching at the skin under her anklets. She has recently been dealing with strange itchy sensations over her body. They disappear just as suddenly as they appear. She isn't entirely sure if it is because her doctors have just confirmed she is pregnant, or is it something else? Something she is too afraid to articulate, even within the safety of her own mind.

She looks at Madhav. His half-open eyes silently implore her to let him stay in bed for just a little longer. She smiles at him affectionately. They have been married only for two years, but in that short period, they have learnt to recognize what these little gestures mean.

She walks over to their street-facing window and gently draws the curtains. She stands there for a while, absorbing the early morning atmosphere. A grumpy chaiwallah pushing his cart, a municipal worker sweeping aside the previous day's litter, and stray mongrels basking in the bright light of dawn. This is Mumbai.

Eventually, Madhav sits up and yawns, even as Sullu continues to stare unmindfully outside. It is a habit she has recently picked up. For some months now, she unfailingly stands at the window each morning, taking in every little detail. It is almost as if she isn't sure if things will be the same the next morning. Madhav is convinced it isn't just the pregnancy, for the window-gazing had begun well before. Something else seems to be weighing down on her.

As the clock ticks closer to 6 a.m., the demands of the day begin to drift through Sullu's mind. There is tiffin to be prepared, chores to be done. Shrugging her shoulders with a sigh, she moves away from the window and walks towards the kitchen. The filter coffee that they share each morning is usually accompanied by a conversation. They discuss each other's plans for the day or decide what they will eat for dinner. But recently, even this had changed. Without warning, Sullu would suddenly bring up matters completely unrelated to the day's business, as she did this morning too.

'Madhav,' she begins, gently running her fingers over her belly, 'do we really have to continue staying in Mumbai? I mean, wouldn't it be better for our child, and for us, to move to a smaller city? Somewhere nondescript, where things are not so . . .'

Madhav looks at her with a puzzled expression on his face.

'Sullu, we've had this conversation before. It's not possible. Where will we go? Even if we move, it has to be to another metro. My career will be over before it even begins if we move to some unknown small town. We have to stay here, for the sake of our child's future,' he responds, fully aware that she won't be convinced.

Sullu lets it be for the moment, for she can't deny that he is right on all counts. Perhaps this feeling is a result of the anxiety and paranoia of being pregnant. Although she doesn't bring it up again this morning, and silently helps Madhav get ready for work, he senses her worry. On the rickshaw ride to Virar station, he finds his mind returning to Sullu's concerns. He knows she is right to some extent. Mumbai has its fair share of problems and is by no means the ideal place to raise their child. But leaving isn't an option. He is due for a promotion any time now, and the last thing he needs to think about is the prospect of shifting.

He is so thoroughly immersed in these thoughts that the rickshaw driver had to call out several times to let him know that they had reached the station. Apologizing for his absentmindedness, he hastily reaches into his pocket for the fare. He hands over a hundred rupee note, but the rickshaw driver gestures that he has no change. If he waits for the change, he will miss his train. Cursing his luck, he tells the driver to keep the change. 'So much for a good start to the day,' Madhav thinks to himself, as he darts towards the station to join the steady stream of commuters all rushing to get to work on time.

The chaos and the crowd are just the distraction he needs to turn away from his own worries. Everybody seems to be in a frantic hurry to get somewhere, at all times of the day. For Madhav, the sheer size of the crowd and its hurried pace always come as something of a relief. Amidst them, his worries don't loom so large.

As he waits for the train at his usual spot by the fruit stand, he takes out his phone. He has missed two calls from Sullu. He is about to call her back when his train pulls into the station. It is usually packed well beyond its capacity, but somehow it always manages to chug along. It is weighed down not just by the number of people it carries, but also their outsized ambitions. In many ways, the Mumbai local is a microcosm of the country and its aspirations.

No sooner had he reached his office than Sullu texted, 'Reached?' Madhav wants to get started with his day and doesn't want to focus on her worries right now. He sends her a quick reply and puts away his phone. As the day goes by, he immerses himself in his work. At 3 p.m. he realizes that he has completely lost track of time. It is a message from Sullu—'How was the palak paneer?'—that alerts him that lunchtime had passed, and he had forgotten to eat. To admit that to Sullu would only make matters worse. So, he replies with his trademark playfulness, 'Out of this world. You'll win *MasterChef* at this rate.'

The rest of the day passed uneventfully. But at 5 p.m., just as he is trying to wrap up work, she sends him another message—'Dhoklas and coffee are waiting at home. See you soon!' Madhav wonders why she is bombarding him with so many messages. This is unusual, even by her recent standards. Whatever it is, he has to return home immediately to make sure everything is all right with Sullu. He will just have to come to the office a little earlier than usual the next day to finish the pending work.

While the day went by in a blink for Madhav, it trudged along slowly for Sullu. All through the day, she paid little attention to the contents of Madhav's messages. She cared only about the notification on her phone, indicating that her husband has responded. As evening approaches, she restlessly awaits his return. When he finally gets back, he does not even have to ring the doorbell. She has been anxiously watching, first through the window and then the peephole, and opens the door as soon as he reaches it.

As she serves him a cup of coffee, she breaks the uneasy silence most unexpectedly.

'Did you hear, Saddam Hussein's trial took a strange turn today.'

Madhav looks up from his coffee at her, surprised. What has happened to his wife? They usually discuss their favourite *saas–bahu* serials, but today she has jumped straight to international news.

* * *

About an hour after Madhav reached home, train number 90831 on the same route leaves Churchgate station yet again, packed to the brim with people returning home after a long day's work. The first-class compartment is also jam-packed with barely any standing room. The regulars, like the group of government employees who are discussing office politics, have long mastered the art of keeping a conversation going even amidst the deafening commotion that is a constant both inside and outside the train.

'Boss, this Palkar no, I tell you. He sits in his office till eleven every day, but never decides on a file. Every time it's the same thing. Returns it with the same remark, "Please see me." I am telling you he is an expert at playing the *nigyysob* game,' one of them says.

'*Nigyysob?*' his colleagues respond in unison, puzzled by the word.

'Don't you know N-I-G-Y-Y-S-O-B? Now I Have Got You, You Son of a Bitch! Palkar is like the Tendulkar of this game. Without even looking at the file, he will ask you to see him. And then he will grill you on all kinds of things that have nothing to do with the matter at hand. Some small thing that you haven't done, or something you've neglected, he will make sure you confess regardless and apologize. Then, if he thinks you're sufficiently ashamed, he will return the file, asking you to bring it back after you've completed your unfinished work.'

'Don't worry, yaar. He's retiring soon anyway.'

'Arrey, I'm telling you. He'll keep getting an extension, and we'll probably retire before him.'

The uproarious laughter that erupts from the group is so loud that it nearly drowns out a conversation that a woman in an adjacent seat is trying to have with her daughter over the phone. She looks up at the men with mild contempt before returning to her call, covering her mouth with her tightly curved palm to ensure that her daughter can still hear her. 'As I was saying, if you finish your homework quickly, there will be chicken for dinner. Kohlapuri chicken, your favourite. But only if you finish it. Deal, Nanna?' The little girl at the other end exults in excitement as she promises to finish her homework on time.

Elsewhere in the same compartment, a group of amateur crooners have broken into song as they always do on their way back from work. They sing the popular song 'Jeena Isi Ka Naam Hai . . .'

It is a crowd favourite, and an unspoken bonhomie quickly emerges in the compartment. In no time the five government employees abandon their discussion. Their briefcases turn into tablas, and the gossip on their lips gives way to joyful whistling. The woman in the adjacent seat feels her contempt towards the men disappear. Even as she continues to speak to her daughter, she chuckles at their childlike enthusiasm. A young couple standing close to the footboard remove their earphones to join the spontaneous revelry. They look into each other's eyes and smile. What was only moments ago a suffocating ambience has transformed, just like that, into one of liberating joy. It is just another day in Mumbai.

And then, just like that, everything is snuffed out.

A loud explosion rocks the train, throwing it off the tracks. There is fire everywhere, and thick clouds of smoke engulf the compartments. The government employees, the woman on the phone, the singers, the couple, all lay lifelessly at varying distances from the compartment that was only an instant ago full of life. Now Palkar will have no one to play NIGYYSOB with. The woman's daughter will not eat chicken for a very long time. The singers have unwittingly rendered their final performance. The young lovers will have to await another lifetime to put the song's philosophy to the test.

In the next ten minutes, six other such explosions throw several trains across Mumbai off their tracks. Hundreds of people lay dead, and with them, millions of dreams. If the trains represent a microcosm of the country and its aspirations, the bomb blasts are an attack on it.

* * *

Back home, Madhav and Sullu are still watching TV when news of the bombings breaks. Sullu gasps. Her uneasiness through the day seems justified now. Madhav is left dumbstruck. If he hadn't decided to come home earlier than usual, he would most likely have been on one of those trains. Their child would have been left fatherless even before its birth.

* * *

Even as the south-west monsoon rains lash in fury at the dense and pristine hills of north-east Kerala, a group of about twenty men huddle together in discussion under a large canopy they erected some months ago. With their large binoculars, professional camping gear, and camouflaged outfits, one might easily mistake them for being wildlife enthusiasts on an adventurous sighting expedition in Thrikkaipatta. But one glance at the dangerous explosives their tents harbour, or the slightest whiff of the grave conspiracies they are plotting, will immediately allay any such misconception.

They appear to be in a celebratory mood. All of them, except their leader, Tabrez, who is reminding them that it isn't wise to rejoice too early. He speaks in impeccable Malayalam, and his words hold their attention like a magic charm. Although the camp is very dimly lit, with only a weak bonfire and a few solar lamps, the scars on Tabrez's face are clear.

They add an aura to his hardened face and an unmistakable edge to his words.

'Even if we successfully pull off a hundred attacks like this, nothing will fundamentally change. Yes, we will kill many infidels, but we will also end up killing many of our own brothers and sisters. Collateral damage is fine. This is a holy war we are waging, and Allah will judge these martyrs fairly on the day of reckoning. But we cannot forget that our core mission is something more than just killing infidels. We need to get at the nerve centre, kill the people that truly matter, only then will they sit up and take notice.'

He pauses several times in between, not just for emphasis but also to discern the reaction among his men.

'Western culture and science have destroyed our values, but we cannot afford to completely disregard them. We must make the most of what modern technology offers, to hit them where it hurts most. Like I have reminded you all through your training, this is not just about inflicting reckless violence. It is a complex game of information and misinformation . . .'

Even as his voice trails off into the darkness, his gaze settles on one man in particular. His name is Shafeeq, and he has very recently joined their ranks. Tabrez's searing gaze is discomfiting and Shafeeq shuffles nervously.

* * *

New Delhi, Early Hours of 12 July 2006

The clacking heels of the prime minister's security detail pierces the grim silence of the night and can be heard across the Secretariat building. They follow him as he moves swiftly through its tense corridors, accompanied by a small army of bureaucrats and assistants. For over an hour now, statements have been issued, redacted, and revised. It is almost as if the government's response is mirroring the confusion and chaos that is quickly taking hold of not just Mumbai, but the rest of the country as well.

An emergency meeting has been called at the Ministry of Home Affairs to take stock of the rapidly evolving situation. It is 12.20 a.m., and most of the attendees were in bed when the call came. But this was the kind of meeting that one could miss only at the risk of, at worst, instant dismissal, and at best, the lingering reputation of incompetency and irresponsibility.

The prime minister walks into the briefing room to find a curious combination of drowsy eyes and anxious faces awaiting him. These are the most important people in the country on matters pertaining to internal security. With frustration and anger written all over his face, he takes turns looking at each person in the room. His gaze finally settles on Vinayak Pant, the home secretary. The bags under Pant's eyes are so dark that one could be forgiven for assuming that he had been punched in the face. Pant looks away immediately, pretending not to have noticed that the prime minister is looking straight into his eyes.

'Officers, how kind of you to have gathered here in the middle of the night. I want you to picture this in your tired minds. It's 10 p.m. and I'm sitting down to have dinner with the Kuwaiti general. It is perhaps the most high-level meeting with the region in the last ten years, something that we've really struggled to put together. We're not even past the first course, and I am ushered out. Yet another bomb blast, they tell me. Can you imagine how embarrassing that was? Let me tell you more. Next week, I am scheduled to attend a very important investors' summit in Europe. I was going to speak about how India is the economic destination of choice for the twenty-first century, and how we've put aside the conflicts and uncertainty of the past and ushered in a new age of stability. And today, we've allowed not one but seven bomb blasts in the heart of our financial hub. And even if we forget international opinion for a moment, think about what this will do to people's perceptions within our borders. People will live in fear—for their lives, and for their loved ones.'

The home secretary appears to mumble something, only to quickly check himself. But nothing escapes the prime minister's sharp gaze.

'Is there something you wish to say, Vinayak? Please go ahead.'

'Sir, from the information that we have, the blasts in Mumbai seem to be part of something larger. And that's not the only worrying news. This appears to be the handiwork of a new organization, something outside our current intelligence penetration. We need to come up with new strategies immediately. I recommend that we recruit . . .'

'Don't jump the gun here, Vinayak. We can talk about who you want to recruit much later. Even the man on the street knows that it's part of something larger. What I'm asking for is concrete information. What exactly do you know? Who are these people, where are they based?'

The home secretary shuffles nervously in his seat, unsure of what to say. Sarita Sanyal, the chief of the Intelligence

Bureau, jumps to his rescue. The only woman in the room, she has overcome great odds to rise to this post in an otherwise male-dominated field. When she speaks, people usually pay attention.

'Sir, if I may interrupt . . . what Vinayak sir is saying is true and a fair summary of what we know at this point. Today's attacks are part of a larger operation. We strongly suspect that attacks are being planned in other major cities as well. A hitherto little-known organization called the Lashkar-e-Hind has claimed credit. We don't even know at this point if their claim is credible, and our current sources provide us only a limited picture. But the modus operandi appears to be entirely unprecedented, and it is therefore entirely plausible that a new organization is behind this. Unlike in the past, whoever executed this attack did not come here from Pakistan. They were only sponsored and guided from across the border. We have enough reasons to believe that our own citizens are being radicalized through the Internet. What is even more worrying, sir, is that their training is also happening over the Internet. How to manufacture bombs, how to evade security checks, all of it . . .'

The prime minister takes a deep breath. He remains silent for a few moments while everyone else prepares themselves for yet another lambasting.

'What you are effectively saying is that you have no clue whatsoever. Please say it the way it is. We have no time for eloquence.'

'But, sir . . .'

The prime minister brushes her aside with a wave of his hand.

'Just one question. What do I tell our fellow countrymen?'

Nobody dares to meet the prime minister's eyes.

'Very well, then. Let us meet when you have an answer.'

With that, the prime minister walks out of the room, with the home minister in tow. A cool breeze wafts into the room as the doors shut. The officials in the room heave a deep sigh, but the relief is only momentary. There is a mountain of work ahead of them. Decisions to be taken, tasks to be delegated, statements to be released. It is unlikely they will be returning home any time soon.

Sipping on a cup of tea that had just been brought in, the home secretary takes a few moments to regain his composure. He then turns to address the officials, 'New intel teams, new networks, new strategies. We might still be dealing with our old nemeses, but their methods appear to be completely new. At this point, we can only speculate, and you all heard the PM. We need concrete information, and so the IB will take the lead on this. How soon can we get cracking, Sarita?'

'Sir, we have started working on it. There is still a lot to be done, but we've made some headway. We believe mobile phones are central to the new modus operandi, and that's our entry point. The brightest of our officers are working on this even as we speak, and we're expecting to make more progress soon.'

'Okay, good. That's something to start with. And who is leading it? I don't have to tell you this, but it doesn't matter how talented the team is; it does not work unless you have a head who can harness their talents effectively and put everything together. If you were to just go by seniority, then Anil would be the man. But I'm not so sure, you know . . .'

'I completely agree, sir. Which is why I've decided to assign it to one of our very best. You know him all too well . . . Ravi Kumar.'

The home secretary nods in approval. He looks somewhat reassured for the first time all evening.

* * *

As he does every single day, Ravi Kumar arrives at his office at 9.30 a.m. sharp. A large man, Ravi's size exists in unusual harmony with great agility and dexterity. It suits his personality well. No older than forty-five, and yet Ravi is already in charge of the Central Counterterrorism Command, an important wing of the IB. C3, as it is more widely known, is the country's premier counterterrorist agency. It is on the back of sheer talent that Ravi has come to head it, upstaging many senior officers in the process.

Those who know Ravi often speak of his two outstanding qualities. On the one hand, he is a no-nonsense officer who values precision over everything else. After having worked in the field for over two decades, he knows that the slightest error could have disastrous consequences. On the other, he is also something of a maverick. He excels at using highly unorthodox methods that are difficult to predict, even for his closest aides. In his personal life, it manifests as irreverent humour that few can resist. But on the whole, he is a highly principled man who understands the importance of his position and spends almost every waking moment working. He has only one vice—tobacco. He claims it helps him calm down and focus.

As he sits in his office, filling his pipe with tobacco—this too, with meticulous precision—he begins to mentally go over the day's business. Ravi then presses a rusty old-fashioned call bell on his desk, summoning an orderly who, in turn, summons Subramanyam, his personal secretary.

'Anything important?' Ravi asks, putting aside the pipe in a drawer, as Subramanyam walks in.

'Yes sir, something very important that you cannot ignore. Mars is debilitated in your fourth house. Jupiter is in transit in your twelfth house and sir, don't take this lightly, but you are in Rahu *mahadasha,* an unlucky phase. You may have tough times ahead. You need to perform a *havan.*'

Ravi looks at his secretary with amused affection.

'And sir, I have completed your tax returns and calculated your tax liabilities for the next year. I've put the papers in this folder for you to sign. And yes, I have spoken to the vet. He will examine Ranger at 4 p.m. tomorrow.'

Without bothering to look at the contents, Ravi signs each of the papers Subramanyam places on his desk. He shares little of Subramanyam's enthusiasm for astrology but tolerates his advice nevertheless, for he is efficient and has proved to be extremely loyal and reliable. Indeed, he even looks forward to Subramanyam's daily predictions. It lightens the otherwise serious and often dreary nature of their work. In general, Ravi has nothing but respect for Subramanyam. Out of respect for his secretary—who is at least ten years older and more conservative—he never lights his pipe in his presence.

After Subramanyam leaves, Ravi pulls out his pipe and calls for a coffee. He puts on the TV and surfs through the news channels. There is only one thing on the nation's mind that morning—the deadly bomb blasts that killed and maimed hundreds of Mumbai's innocent citizens. Something catches his eye on ABN News. It is showing a video clip he has already seen of the chief of the Lashkar-e-Taiba (LeT), a global terrorist organization based in Pakistan, openly calling for Jihad against India and lauding the Lashkar-e-Hind (LeH) for its contribution to the cause.

The clip is followed by an angry monologue by the anchor. Ravi does not focus on such outrage. It is his job to bring down organizations like the LeT and LeH, so that the country can turn its focus towards other concerns. He sits staring at the TV, pipe in hand, thinking. Just the fact that they had managed to hoodwink the combined might of India's internal and external intelligence agencies, and their international partners, was enough indication that there was radically something different about the modus operandi of these attacks. They had to catch up quickly.

The buzzing sound of the intercom interrupts these thoughts. Subramanyam is on the line.

'Sir, the chief has summoned you for a meeting to her chamber at eleven.'

'What is on the agenda?'

'No idea, sir.'

'Who else will be at the meeting?'

'Only you, sir.'

Ravi does not have to guess what the meeting will be about. As he walks into the chief's chamber, he is almost certain where this conversation is headed.

Sarita is cordial yet business-like in her manner.

'Ravi, please come. I will take less than a minute. The PM had called for a meeting last night to take stock of the Mumbai blasts. He is of course not pleased and wants us to get to the bottom of this at the earliest. I have decided to put you in charge. You will report directly to me.'

'Ma'am, and Anil Sir?'

'You do not have to report to him for this particular assignment.'

'But . . .'

The sudden awkwardness and hesitation in Ravi's manner is all too evident to Sarita. Anil is the second-in-command at the Bureau, and technically Ravi's immediate superior. Although Anil as deputy chief is at a higher rank on paper, Ravi's position as head of C3 was more coveted for the autonomy and influence it offered. The resulting tension between Ravi and Anil is not exactly a secret within the Bureau.

'I understand your hesitation, Ravi. I might not be directly privy to your relationship with Anil, but I have my ears to the ground at all times. Don't worry, you will not face any interference. The home secretary is also in the loop.'

Ravi nods, sure that Sarita's assurance notwithstanding, Anil is not the sort to let go of any chance to create trouble. But it is not the sort of accusation one would make in front of the chief.

'Thank you, ma'am. So, about this case . . .'

'Yes, what about it?'

'For quite some time, I have been planning to bring in some fresh recruits to work directly under me. I know this is not how we do it, but the Mumbai blasts have only strengthened my conviction that we need young minds working at higher levels. Older assumptions won't work anymore. It is clear that our enemies are increasingly entrusting the younger generation with important assignments. Unless we do the same, I have the uneasy feeling that we may find it hard to keep up with the changing times.'

Sarita nods in approval.

'You're right. It's quite clear that we haven't really kept up our pace.'

'There is just one problem, ma'am. The next batch of officers only graduates in four months. But I can't wait that long. I'll have to pick them out of training immediately.'

Sarita pauses. She shakes her head, then nods, then shakes again. Finally, she looks up at Ravi and says, 'You do what you have to, just be discreet about it. In the delicate position you are in, you wouldn't want to feed the trolls any further, if you get what I'm saying.'

As he walks out of the chief's office, Ravi can swear that there was a mischievous glint in her eyes as she uttered the last sentence.

The Fort

Ravi drives slowly through thickly forested fringes on the outskirts of Gwalior, taking in the sights and smells of untouched nature that gradually give way to the unmistakable stamp of civilization. It is an old palatial estate simply referred to as the Fort, for it is so ancient that nobody knows anything of its original history, or its historical name. It had been abandoned a long time ago by the local tribals who believed that the premises were haunted by the ghost of a British officer who had died there in pursuit of a new *shikaar*. With the exception of self-proclaimed *tantriks* and godmen who showed up from time to time, seeking to exorcise the area, nobody usually dared to venture in the direction of the Fort. That being so, the bureau had encountered no trouble in securing it for their purpose. It was a perfect cover and allowed the bureau to operate without the fear of intrusion. They used it primarily to house research units and to train newly recruited officers.

As his car enters the Fort, Ravi's spirits lift seeing the young officers passionately perform their training routine. Although the official reason for his visit—an interactive session with the trainees—is scheduled for the afternoon, Ravi has arrived several hours in advance. He is intent on observing each of the trainees as closely as possible.

At lunchtime, Ravi politely declines the principal's invitation to join him for a meal and sends Subramanyam instead. He sits quietly at a corner table in the trainees' mess eating the same food as everyone else. There are twenty-five recruits in all, each of whom have been picked through a highly selective process that involved, among other things, a notoriously difficult examination. Nobody has the slightest clue as to who he is. They will find out in an hour's time, but they will still have no idea what exactly has brought Ravi here. As far as everybody else is concerned, he is merely there to interact with the trainees and offer a sense of what it is like working in the field. Such visits are fairly routine.

At exactly 2 p.m., the young trainees clear out of the mess with clockwork precision. There are no proctors, no bells going off, nobody to tell them what to do. The schedule for each day is posted on the notice board at the end of the previous day, and it is the responsibility of each trainee to ensure that they are at the designated venue at the designated time for each session. Punctuality and discipline are a significant part of the evaluation rubric, and nobody wants to risk being unfavourably graded.

However, it is not a game of one-upmanship, except in rare cases. For the most part, the trainees look out for each other and work in tandem. Indeed, friendships forged at the academy are often said to last a lifetime. There is an unspoken code of solidarity. If one forgets to do something or is lagging behind on an assignment, somebody or the other is always around to help. Punctuality being the essence, it is not out of the ordinary when trainee officers are found seated in the seminar hall ten minutes ahead of schedule. They all rise as the principal enters with Ravi, walks up to the podium and begins addressing the cadets.

'We are fortunate to have with us today Mr Ravi Kumar, the head of the Central Counterterrorism Command. He is one of the bureau's most decorated officers and has been awarded every medal worth aspiring for. The Indian Police Medal, the President's Police Medal, the Police Medal for Gallantry, to name only a few. He has taken time out to speak to all of you about the organization that you are soon going to be part of. Without any further ado, please welcome him. The class is yours, sir.' With this, he escorts Ravi to the podium and leaves the hall.

Ravi spares no time for introductions or pleasantries and starts off with an unexpected question, 'How many of you noticed me at the academy earlier?'

Some hands go up.

'Good,' Ravi remarks. 'Who amongst you can tell me with certainty how long I have been watching all of you? Would you say it's true that I've been around for the last two days? If you're sure, keep your hands raised.'

The recruits are perplexed. They can't be sure. Ravi scans the room. All hands have dropped down, except one.

'What's your name?'

'Mihir Kaul, sir.'

Mihir is tall, well-built and wears a look of unusual seriousness. Ravi had already noticed him earlier in the day and is impressed by what he has seen so far.

'Tell me, officer, when did I start watching all of you? Yesterday, the day before, a week ago?'

'This morning, sir. You were at the training ground, and then you were also at the mess.'

'How sure are you?'

'Very sure, sir. I saw you driving in this morning.'

'Yes, you saw me driving in this morning, but what you didn't see is my driving in yesterday. I had gone out early in the morning, and returned later in the day, which is when you must have seen me.'

'I don't think so, sir. Your car was not here yesterday. I am certain of that.'

'So, you do not trust me? You think I'm lying?'

'Of course, I trust you, sir. But with all due respect, I think you are lying. I think you are just testing me.'

Ravi smiles. He is impressed by the boy's spunk.

'Well done. You may sit down. One of the most important demands of this job is the ability to keep your eyes and ears wide open at all times. You are at the academy now, and you are protected. But you must hone your senses, sharpen them as you would sharpen a pencil. Because the moment you step out on the field, you realize that most of the time, it is something as simple as keeping track of who's coming and going, who's meeting who that will offer the most valuable leads. There will always be attempts to deceive, attempts to create the impression of something else being the case, the simplest example of which is what I just tried to demonstrate through Mihir. If you have sincerely paid attention, you will not be fooled. It was easy this time to make out that I was lying because I had no malicious intent. I was just trying to test him, and he was quick enough to sense it. But that will not always be the case.

'Deception on the field is a different ballgame altogether. The agenda will not be to test you but to break you. Failure to see through all of it will have disastrous consequences not just for you but for the citizens of this country. Even as I speak, vested interests are trying to infiltrate our country with the aim of disrupting the most cherished values of our constitutional and social fabric. We are a country united in our diversity—cultural, religious, social, linguistic, economic— and these elements are out to tear apart this unity. You have been recruited to take on the privileged responsibility of safeguarding this unity.'

Even as he speaks he looks at each face in the class, taking in their reactions. Some are copiously taking down notes, while others seem to effortlessly register everything mentally. Some just sit and stare, stifling yawns as they strain to appear as if they are following each word. After a brief pause, he continues, 'But make no mistake, you are not alone in being assigned this enormous responsibility. You will be a small part of a massive network of individuals and organizations, each contributing in their own distinct way. I am here today to talk to you about exactly what will be expected of you, and what distinguishes your role from, say, the brave jawans guarding our borders.

'I'm sure you have heard of the late Karam Singh, one of the most outstanding individuals to have served our country. He patrolled the Chinese border under the harshest conditions, out in the wilderness for months at a time, with no links to the outside world. His unit was ambushed by

Chinese troops, and many of our jawans were martyred. They are our heroes, and we strive to emulate them. Their work is demanding and unforgivingly strenuous, but it is at the same time straight forward and the boundaries are clearly drawn. Their identities are well defined from the very beginning. But in our line of work, nothing is straightforward. You will be expected to switch identities and assume an entirely different persona. You must be prepared to let go of your roots and ground yourself in a different history and culture. Sometimes, you might even be expected to join hands with the enemy and be one with them.'

The audience is spellbound, though they are not sure of where Ravi's talk is headed.

'I can see that some of you are confused, which is all the more reason to pay careful attention to what I have to say. Let me tell you a story. This will make it easier to understand what I am driving at. A man is out to destroy a shop, let's assume he is a disgruntled employee of the shop. He is really no match for the shop owner who wields more resources and might. But at the same time, the owner knows that the employee spells trouble and will not let him get anywhere close.

'Nevertheless, the employee stands at a safe yet threatening distance, keeping close watch. Over a period of time, he cultivates a small army of flies and mosquitoes. Even though the shop owner continues to keep an eye on him with dedicated security guards round the clock, nobody understands what the employee is up to. As long as he does not come close to the shop, he is seen only as a passive threat. The man, too, is well aware of this. He knows that he will be driven away or killed if he goes anywhere close to the shop.

'Then one day a bull is walking down the street unmindful of any of this. The staff at the store are used to feeding the bull every evening. They do not think of it even remotely as a threat. As the bull nears the shop, the man drives the flies towards the animal. They enter its ears. The bull, in a sudden fit of rage, goes charging into the shop and knocks down everything inside. Taken aback and desperate to protect the shop from further damage, the security guards start beating the bull. They try to chase it away. But this has the opposite effect, and the bull is further infuriated. It charges at the rest of the store in retaliation. The flies and mosquitoes have by now quietly buzzed away. The man did not have to come anywhere close to the shop. Through his flies, he gets the innocent bull to do his bidding.

'What I'm trying to suggest is that the age of conventional warfare is slowly coming to an end. We are now faced with very distinct and increasingly treacherous modes of hostility from enemy interests. Knowing very well that they are no match for the sheer might of our armed forces, like the ex-employee knows he is no match for the shopkeeper, our enemies are now operating at a distance. While we continue to successfully keep them away physically, they nevertheless continue inflicting damage. They do so like the man in the story, who builds a network of flies and mosquitos to trick an innocent bull into charging into the shop. Let's assume that you've been hired by the shop owner to investigate the bull's attack and to come up with a plan to prevent such incidents in the future. Who would you focus your efforts on, most logically? The man, the bull, or the flies?'

The recruits are silent. A lone voice from the back responds, 'The flies.' Ravi asks him to stand up.

'What is your name?'

'Cyrus, sir.'

'Cyrus what?'

'Cyrus Bandookwallah, sir.'

There is a look of recognition on Ravi's face.

'So, Cyrus, tell me. Why do you think the man or the bull should not be targeted?'

Cyrus speaks with a calculated casualness, almost as if he is not intimidated by Ravi's stature, 'The man is at a distance and was never directly present at the scene of the incident. Even if it is clear that he is responsible for it, it would be beyond the legitimate authority of the shop owner to target him.'

Ravi nods attentively.

'But why not the bull since the bull was at the scene of the incident and directly carried out the action that you are tasked with thwarting?'

'If we punish the bull, we will have done nothing to prevent the man from getting his flies to get into the ears of some other bull, or cow, and lead them to do the same thing. Of course, now that the bull has its own score to settle, we cannot let it go either. But that will not fully solve the problem. We need to prevent the flies from getting into the ears of the next bull that walks past the store.'

Ravi walks around the hall, surveying each face closely as he listens to Cyrus.

'Fair enough. But how would you go about doing that? Someone else, please.'

Eager to impress Ravi, many raise their hands. Ravi picks out one trainee at random, a young turbaned Inderpal Singh.

'Fumigate the surroundings of the store so that no flies or mosquitoes will breed in the vicinity.'

Ravi shakes his head.

'It does sound like a good solution on paper. But I can think of many operational hazards that would disqualify it from the very outset. The others who raised their hands, did you have anything else in mind?'

Nobody volunteers.

'Okay. Can somebody in the room think of what the operational hazards might be? And yes, if you're asked to speak, start by introducing yourself.'

A bespectacled boy of lean build raises his hand.

'Jose Cherian, sir. Indiscriminate fumigation would be a disaster. Since the flies don't always hover around and only enter the scene when the man instructs them to. Round-the-clock fumigation would make no sense. We need a more targeted strategy. One that would monitor the traffic of the flies very carefully and create barriers only in the routes that they are known to take. Indiscriminate fumigation would simply drive away all business prospects. Who would want to shop in an atmosphere that is constantly polluted by fumigants? Not only would it be unsafe, but by driving away customers we would have unwittingly helped the enemy achieve his goal of bringing the store down.'

Ravi is impressed and lets it show.

'Very well put. Now can somebody translate this into the terms of our field, keeping in mind what I said earlier about the end of conventional warfare?'

Mihir and Cyrus raise their hands. Ravi waits to see if there are other hands, but nobody volunteers. He decides to speak up himself, 'Since nobody else is volunteering, and these two have already spoken, let me say this myself. Our enemies now seek to sow seeds of distrust within the country, by exploiting our social and religious differences through carefully orchestrated propaganda. Something like the flies that get into the bull's ears, leading the bull to turn against the hand that feeds it. But the story of the shop and the flies is only a metaphor, one that is far too simple to capture the messiness of real-world intrigue. Here, there is no one single thing that we could compare with the flies. We are talking about tangible networks of human and material resources that are often camouflaged to the extent of being nearly invisible. Your job is to uncover these networks and disable them with as little collateral damage as possible.

'Sometimes, these networks are intertwined with networks already engaged in organized crime, smuggling, and drug trafficking. But sometimes, they are neatly embedded in very ordinary streams of business and are nearly undetectable. Your job is to identify the conduits and sometimes become one of them. You cannot go in there with a gun to their head and expect to defeat the enemy. The goal is not to kill or arrest recklessly. It would be akin to punishing or killing the bull. Rather, the goal is to paralyse these strategies by creating barriers in the intermediary route between foreign controllers and domestic actors. And it will not be easy. You have joined an organization that prizes only those who are selfless in their service to the nation. You will be expected to work under extreme physical and mental duress.'

The session goes on for a full two hours, and even those who were uninterested at the beginning have come to be fully engrossed by the end. Ravi is an exception among officers of his rank and cadre. Most are too immersed in their work to find time to engage at length with junior officers, particularly trainees. But Ravi has always thrived in the presence of younger officers. He has carefully sought to strike the right balance between teaching them from his experience and paying sincere and serious attention to their fresher perspectives. It is not a universally popular strategy. Many of his detractors within the department often cite his penchant for bypassing hierarchies and engaging junior officers on important missions as evidence of his poor leadership abilities.

In fact, Ravi's appointment as chief of C3 was itself seen by many as a circumvention of the time-honoured procedures of succession. He had been picked over many officers who were technically senior to him, and they were not very pleased to find themselves placed below him in the chain of command.

* * *

Later in the evening, Ravi spends several hours going through reports and reviews put forth by other officers. He compares with his own observations from the day. Mihir Kaul and Cyrus Bandookwallah are on the top of his list. They have consistently been the highest-rated trainees, and they had made a strong impression on him. But his plan is to hire three officers, and there are three or four candidates with comparable credentials. Unable to arrive at a conclusion, he decides to look closely into Jose Cherian. On the surface, there is nothing impressive. He is physically not the strongest and is seemingly not very good at sports. Ravi had barely noticed him before he had spoken up in the lecture hall. But as he looks through Jose's file, Ravi learns that he is an extremely proficient programmer who had given up a lucrative job as a software engineer at a global corporation to join the service.

While Jose would make a great fit for Insomnia, the agency's surveillance and monitoring wing, Ravi is here to recruit those who can work in the field. Although he has some of the most advanced surveillance and communication technologies at his disposal, Ravi is somewhat old-fashioned in his methods. He believes strongly in the irreplaceable value of cultivating a human-centric approach to intelligence and espionage. But recent developments have shaken up his long-held assumptions.

Struggling to make up his mind, he decides to ask Subramanyam, who can always be counted on for a fair assessment. By now, it is rather late, inching close to midnight. But Subramanyam is accustomed to being woken up at odd hours by his boss and is always eager to offer his advice. Ravi explains the dilemma to Subramanyam, who asks a few follow-up questions before offering his view.

'Sir, it is not just Jupiter that is in transit in your twelfth house. Everything in the world is going through a great transition. I don't understand these things too well, but my elder son does. As you know, he is an engineer in Germany. He was telling me just the other day that the Internet is no longer just a mode of communication. He was talking about how people will soon be leading a large part of their lives virtually. I don't understand these complex things, but I know it is possible. I gifted my granddaughter a computer for her last birthday, thinking it would help her studies.

But she spends hours and hours on the computer, not studying, but talking to and playing games with strangers from all over the world. Nothing we say or do deters her, and she never tells us what she is talking to these strangers about. Finally, my poor daughter-in-law had to create a fake account online to get into my granddaughter's circles and see what is happening.'

Ravi listens intently, amused by Subramanyam's typically eccentric yet valuable perspective.

'But we know all this already, Subramanyam. Insomnia is there precisely to keep a watch over all of this. I'm here to recruit field operatives. This boy, Jose Cherian, has none of the grit and suave that a field agent needs.'

'Sir, you are making the same mistake that my daughter-in-law made initially. She would discreetly find out what my granddaughter was up to, and then give her long explicit lectures on discipline and valuing time. Finally, she realized that she was looking at it the wrong way. Instead of giving lectures, my daughter-in-law began to use the fake account not only to see what my granddaughter was up to but also to subtly manipulate her in the direction that she wanted her to take. Instead of stupid car racing games, she now plays chess and scrabble because her close online friend kept pulling her in that direction. Now she is hooked. Little does she know that this 'friend' is actually her mother!

'There was a time when surveillance and fieldwork were separate, but the Internet has changed things, sir. And it is like astrology. It doesn't matter if you believe in it or not; it is what it is. But the point of astrology is not to prove that what is bound to happen will happen. Rather it is to prove that you can change what is bound to happen if you take the right steps, modify your behaviour and perform the correct rituals.

'Think about the story you narrated, sir, about the man, the bull and the flies. You will, of course, need men to keep the man away. You will also require men to keep the bulls in check. But after you've realized that the culprits in the middle are the flies, what you will need is a fly that can keep track of what the other flies are up to, and when feasible, lead them in more worthwhile directions. You are in Rahu mahadasha, sir, don't forget. You need to keep up with your fate if you want to change it.'

Ravi chuckles, 'Subramanyam, I keep thinking how lucky I am to have you as my secretary. But now I realize that it is true the other way round as well. I think I'm the only person in the world who can follow your cryptic meanderings.'

Examiner

Cyrus, Mihir, and Jose are in an official car that takes them through the tree-fringed streets of Chanakyapuri in Delhi. They do not have the slightest clue as to why they are being summoned to the headquarters. They take turns speculating, if only to pass the time. Cyrus, who possesses the sharpest humour among the three, jokes, 'I don't know why Jose and I are being summoned, but Mihir, you are definitely going to be suspended for your cockiness in Ravi sir's class.' He then proceeds to imitate Mihir, 'With all due respect, I think you're lying, sir.' They burst out laughing, while the driver struggles to maintain a neutral expression.

Like the Fort, the headquarters too is located in a nondescript setting. But far from being on the outskirts of Delhi, it is situated within the most affluent locality in the capital. But it is not very easy to find. Past the embassies, luxury hotels and elite residences lies a surprisingly expansive stretch of forest land that serves as the perfect cover for one of the most secretive organizations in the Indian security establishment. Here too, local rumour keeps unsolicited visitors at bay. To get to the offices of the bureau by the regular route, you have

to make your way past an old crumbling hunting lodge that is
thought to be several centuries old. The present inhabitant of
the mansion, allegedly a descendant of the Nawab of Awadh,
is infamous for his unsparing contempt towards trespassers. He
is known to be unafraid to let his bloodthirsty hounds loose
on unsuspecting visitors, and nobody goes that way. The only
other way to get to the Bureau's headquarters is strictly out of
bounds for all civilians as it passes through a monitoring station
of the Indian Space Agency.

As the surroundings quickly transform from posh opulence
to disconcerting wilderness, Mihir—who has spent some part
of his adolescence in Delhi—remarks to the others that he
would have never suspected such a place exists in the heart
of the capital. As they alight from the car, they thank the
driver. The trio take a few moments to compose themselves,
straightening their collars and combing their hair with their
fingers. They collectively take a deep breath before walking
through an unassuming side entrance into the building that
presumably houses the nerve centre of the country's covert
intelligence operations.

The driver takes them to meet Subramanyam, who they
recall having seen at the academy with Ravi. Subramanyam,
in turn, wastes no time leading them straight into Ravi's
office. Cyrus immediately takes note of its stark neatness.
The meticulously organized desk, with not a single inch of
clutter, takes him back to memories from his childhood. His
father and grandfather, who had both served as covert agents,
had drilled into his mind the idea that a clean workspace
was the first step towards efficiency. In their long-winding
tales about excitement on the field, they had never failed to

point out that being organized was essential to being able to change according to the situation and even assume different identities. As they stand facing Ravi's desk, Cyrus wonders if it is just a coincidence that Ravi seems to share the same idiosyncrasy or if it is endemic to the profession as a whole. Even as he entertains this train of thought, the other two look on awkwardly, trying not to meet Ravi's stern gaze.

Ravi clears his throat, as if to bring Cyrus back to earth. He has no time to waste.

'I have a task for you, gentlemen, and it's a little different from the sort that you're used to. You may be wondering why you're here, and why only the three of you. We'll get to that later. But first let's get straight to our task. Come with me.'

He takes them to his computer and opens a face-mapping program.

'This is CCTV footage from one of the train stations that was attacked in Mumbai,' he tells them, zooming into a blurry image.

He then scrolls through a series of images, each almost indistinguishable from the other.

'And here are pictures from the two weeks leading up to the blasts. Look at it for a while, look carefully, and tell me what you find in common. You are free to discuss with each other. Take your time, and let me know.'

The three men stare intently at the screen as Ravi steps aside to give them room. They cannot believe that they are in the office of the head of C3 and are actually looking at material from a real ongoing investigation. Fighting hard to suppress their excitement, they exchange ideas in hushed tones. It does not take them too long to come up with an answer. Cyrus and Jose are hesitant to speak up and urge Mihir to summarize.

Mihir speaks up, 'We got it, sir. It's the man wearing the kurta pajama. This man, here. He is at the station every day at exactly the same time as the explosion, but on the day of the attack, he is nowhere to be seen.'

'Excellent. Now that you have identified this, what else do you notice?'

The three confer with each other again, but this time they can find nothing. They look up at Ravi and shake their heads. The disappointment is evident on their faces.

Ravi laughs.

'Don't worry. You've done well. There's nothing else that you will find here. I was just trying to see if you would get carried away and overreach in your deductions.'

They stare at him in disbelief before heaving a collective sigh of relief. Ravi leads them back to his desk and pulls out a few pages from a folder. 'Take a look at this,' he says, pointing to marked out places on a map, 'Mahim, Bandra, Virar, Borivali. All these are stations on the western line of Mumbai's suburban rail. And at each of these stations, CCTV footage indicates a similar pattern. Individuals who are consistently found at the same time in the days leading up to the blast, are nowhere to be found on the day itself.'

Ravi put the papers back in the folder and asks them to take a seat.

'We do not have a trail yet. That is, we haven't managed to identify all these individuals. But we have a scent. The man you identified is Saifullah. Motivation, modus operandi, backers, all mostly unknown. You've been summoned here because I need you to track this man down and be my eyes and ears. Do you think you're up to it?'

They look at each other nervously. This time, it is Cyrus who speaks up.

'But sir, aren't we still some months away from finishing our training?'

Ravi's nostrils flare up. On the inside he is tickled but is intent on continuing to put up a stern exterior.

'The most important rule you must never forget is this: Do not respond to a question with another question, particularly if it has nothing to do with what you have been asked, and most particularly if it is none of your business. All I asked is if you're up to the task I'm assigning you to.'

'Yes sir!' the trio call out in unison as they line up in salute.

'Good. This is a very rough map of where he lives. I will let you decide what you have to do. This is your chance, and I expect you to do your very best. I believe I do not have to tell you about the need for absolute secrecy, discretion, and finesse. Subramanyam will give you my personal number, but do not try to get in touch with me until you have made some concrete progress.'

As they leave Ravi's office and walk down the corridor, the three of them wonder if they should stop to ask Ravi for more specific instructions. Mihir reminds them of the rule about asking questions. Cyrus nods, but Jose is unconvinced. He tells them in a hushed whisper, 'The rule is that you don't respond to a question with another question. We aren't going to respond to a question. Besides, it is entirely our business to know how we are to do what we've been asked to do. Also, if they already know who it is and where he lives, why don't they just apprehend him?'

Cyrus and Mihir laugh. Cyrus taps him on the head with playful affection and says, 'You and your logic-chopping will drive us crazy or get us all killed someday. Didn't he also say that we are not to speak to him until we have something concrete?'

* * *

Cyrus keeps his head down as he makes his way through the narrow lanes of Dharavi, where Saifullah is known to live. He has spent the last month hanging around Saifullah's building, even renting a small room in the vicinity, seeking to learn as much as he can about Saifullah's immediate neighbours. He has learnt that they are a group of students, who mostly stay at home, only occasionally going to college. He has shadowed them for quite some time now, paying careful attention to their behaviour, style of dressing, and lingo, while also learning that they studied physics.

As he prepares to climb the narrow stairway that leads into their apartment, Cyrus casts a quick sideward glance. From one corner of his eye he spots a green telecom service van pull into the next lane. He pretends not to have noticed it and runs up the stairs. Dressed as any ordinary college student, in a pair of jeans and a plaid shirt, he knocks at their door. Even from outside the door, the strong stench of marijuana is unmistakable.

The door is opened by a lanky man with long curly hair. Cyrus already knows that his name is Shashank.

'Hi, I just moved in recently. Just a couple of buildings away, and I've been looking for people to chill with and find out the easiest way to get to St. Andrew's College. I was told that you guys are also students, so I thought I would just come by and say hi.'

Shashank looks at him sceptically, but Cyrus catches on immediately.

'And um, also,' he says, with a sheepish wink, 'I . . . I was wondering if you could tell me where I can score around here.'

The suspicion on Shashank's face gives way to a grin of recognition.

'Well, well. A man after my own heart. Please come in.'

It is a cramped apartment that looks like it hasn't been cleaned in months.

'This is Asif,' Shashank says, pointing to his friend who is busy rolling a joint.

'What's up, brother?' Asif says, stretching his hand out.

After he has settled down, they end up talking about what he studies, what they study, how many papers they have failed in, etc. Cyrus knows it would be strange if he were to straightaway ask about their neighbour. He will have to watch out for his chance and take it when it comes.

The joint is lit and passed around. Cyrus sits uneasily, his eyes occasionally darting towards the thin wall that separates the apartment he is in from Saifullah's. When it is his turn, he is careful not to inhale, but nevertheless feigns pleasure. 'This is great stuff, man,' he says to the two men who look at him with an expression of befuddlement.

'Are you for real, bro? This is some shit stuff. It's all we can afford, unfortunately.'

Cyrus grows slightly anxious. He has to be more careful.

'Umm, it's just . . . it's just that I started smoking up very recently. So, I can't really tell the difference, bro.'

Shashank and Asif look at each other and laugh.

'Ah-hah! An innocent. A virgin. We have so much to teach you then,' Asif announces triumphantly.

Cyrus smiles along even as his mind jumps at the opportunity to take the conversation in the direction he desires.

'Absolutely, dude. Like, tell me one thing. How do you manage to smoke without the neighbours finding out? I mean, the walls in this area are all so thin.'

'Nobody cares here, man. There's just this weird middle-aged fellow who lives next door. He's probably crazy or something,' Asif replies, passing the joint to Cyrus.

Cyrus passes the joint on without indulging. 'I'm good man, thanks. Just a few drags get me really high. Anyway, you were saying about your neighbour. What's his scene? Like, what does he do in life?'

Shashank responds, 'No idea, bro. He only goes out at night, and sometimes doesn't return for like an entire month. We've bumped into him only a few times, but he refuses to even smile. He has this strange look on his face.'

Cyrus pretends to laugh along with the two. He knows there is not much else to be found out. He decides to make an excuse to leave.

'My neighbours are also weird, man . . .' he starts, before pausing to glance at his watch. 'Oh wait, that reminds me. I had asked a plumber to come. Half the taps at my place don't turn properly. I'm so sorry I have to go but thank you so much for the joint. I'll be back soon. Let's hang out more often.'

* * *

Dressed in khaki overalls and wearing a workman's yellow hat, Jose alights from the green van he has driven into the lane next to Saifullah's. As he unfastens a ladder from the roof of the van, nobody on the street pays any attention. It is an everyday sight in these parts where something or the other is always in need of repair. Jose looks into the tea shop opposite him and calls out for help. Almost as if he had been waiting to be summoned, a man quietly sipping his tea on a bench outside the shop jumps up. It is Mihir, disguised as a middle-aged businessman.

Jose shouts out to him, 'Telecom department, saab. Here to fix some wires. Just need some help holding this ladder.'

Mihir walks towards him and holds the ladder as Jose climbs up with great deliberation. Up there, he begins to fiddle with some wires and a generic-looking black box that is already mounted atop the pole. After checking that it is firmly in place, he gets down. Mihir helps him place the ladder back on the roof.

After they have done that, Jose tells Mihir, 'Saab, you'll have to get inside the van. The rope has to pass through a few times for the ladder to be tied securely.'

Quickly looking around to ensure that nobody is watching, they both enter the back of the van, which is fully sealed off from the front. The windows are painted over with thick green paint, and as they seal themselves shut, they find themselves enveloped by darkness. Jose rummages through his toolkit and retrieves a small torch, before pulling out a laptop to check if the device he has just affixed is up and running.

'So, what was it that you fixed up there?' Mihir asks Jose, in a hushed voice that can barely be heard over the furious sound of typing.

'Just checking if the scanner was configured properly,' Jose responds, not for a moment looking away from the screen.

'Scanner?'

'It's not one thing, but a contraption of many bits of hardware and software. I'll explain it to you some other time, but basically, I've been trying to access Saifullah's computer all these weeks. I finally managed to do that yesterday. I just wanted to make sure I hadn't made any mistakes.'

Mihir has questions but holds back. He is impressed by Jose's immersion in the work at hand and watches quietly. Still not averting his gaze from the laptop, Jose finally breaks the silence, 'How's it going for you?'

'Not all that bad, I would think. I mean, I've been around here for three weeks now, and I've finally managed to befriend the owner of this stall here. Was a tough nut, didn't yield to any of my advances. It took me a while, but I could finally make some progress a few days ago. His wife is very sick and he can't afford the medicines that can save her life. They're quite expensive, and I had to almost clean out my account. But what else could I have done? Ravi sir said we're not supposed to get in touch with him, and I know nobody else at HQ. Let's just hope I'll get reimbursed when we finally can get in touch with him.'

'The sooner we figure this out, the sooner that can happen. I'll get going. I have to give him those medicines later. And I'll let you continue with your work. If all goes well, we can go back tomorrow. Cyrus said he'd hit a roadblock when I bumped into him at the tea shop. But that's okay. Between the two of us, I think we'll have enough information to report to Ravi sir. But yeah, put away the laptop for now, I'm opening the door.'

* * *

Mihir's task has been the least straightforward of the lot, not to say anything of the potential dangers. It had been decided that he would cultivate an informant in the vicinity, which would mean exposure at least at some minimal level. After scouting around for a week, he had decided that the tea vendor in the lane next to Saifullah's house was ideal. When he learnt of the man's difficulty in buying medicines for his wife, it only cemented his decision. From his training at the academy and the dossiers he had read, Mihir knew that to convince someone to become an informant, it was essential to find their vulnerability or what they wanted desperately. It was crucial to go ahead if the value of the potential information was worth the expense.

As the day comes to an end, the tea vendor wonders what Mihir is still doing at his shop. As far as he knows, Mihir is a broker who manages many properties in the neighbourhood. He has been coming every day for the last month but never stays longer than twenty to thirty minutes. After the day's final customers have cleared out, Mihir walks up to him with a package in his hand.

'Here, the medicines you need for your wife. An entire week's supply.'

Tears well up in the man's eyes.

'You have saved my wife's life. What can I possibly do in return?'

Mihir recalls his instructor's advice to not beat around the bush if the target is overwhelmed by your gesture. He turns to the tea vendor, 'The man in the house in that building. I want you to give me updates twice a week on his whereabouts. And if there is anything slightly out of the ordinary, I want you to call me immediately. In return, you will have these medicines delivered to you every month. Agreed?'

The man falls silent as he wipes his tears.

'That's all, saab? I will do it. Why twice a week? I will give you daily updates. And my boys go around the neighbourhood delivering tea. I can ask them also to keep watch.'

'No, twice a week is enough. And don't involve your boys. Nobody should know about this. You will do what I ask in complete secrecy. Even your wife can't know. Cook up some story to explain the source of the medicines. Do you have it in you to do what I'm asking?'

The man nods enthusiastically.

'Anything you say, saab. Nobody will know, don't worry. The illness has sucked all curiosity out of my wife, and she won't care either way. But what has that man done? Why are you so interested in him?'

Ravi's parting advice at the headquarters the previous month flashes in Mihir's head, and he proceeds to repeat it verbatim.

'The most important rule you must never forget is this: Do not respond to a question with another question, particularly if it has nothing to do with what you have been asked, and most particularly if it is none of your business. All I asked is if you're up to the task I'm assigning you to.'

'Please forgive me, saab. I don't want to know. As long as you take care of the medicines, I don't care about anything else.'

Mihir pats the man on his shoulder. 'Good, I will come back tomorrow morning, so you can tell me everything you already know about this man. Open your shop an hour before usual.'

Mihir walks away with his head held high, his face shining with pride and satisfaction.

* * *

The next day, the three return to Delhi by separate flights. They are bursting to talk to each other but cannot decide on a meeting place. Restaurants are out of the question, and while the headquarters is the most obvious option, Jose insists that they meet elsewhere. Mihir suggests that they meet at his house near Karol Bagh. He tells them that he himself hasn't returned since joining the academy and reminds them that his mother and grandmother are under the impression that he works in marketing. He asks them to dress up as business executives and pretend to be his colleagues. They are all in Delhi on a quick visit to meet clients. Cyrus is amused by the elaborate ruse that Mihir appears to have concocted but decides against pressing further when Mihir insists that it is a long story for another day. 'Just think of this as another undercover mission,' he tells them.

At the end of the busy street on which Mihir's house is located, they reconvene, dressed in ill-fitting business suits and bearing briefcases, all procured hurriedly from a costume store. Mihir's mother and grandmother are thrilled to see him. It is a surprise visit. He explains to them that he is on an unexpected business trip, and the two men with him are his colleagues. His mother is eager to lay out an elaborate feast for them, but he tells her that they need to urgently work on a presentation. His mother protests, insisting that he has returned after such a long time and must spend some time with her before diving into his work again, but he pays her no heed.

He leads Cyrus and Jose—who have been standing awkwardly at the door—into his room, and asks them to wait for a few minutes. He goes back to the living room and assures his mother that he will be staying for a couple of days and that he will be free to catch up at length once his friends leave. She is somewhat relieved and lets him go. Mihir returns to his room and bolts the door from the inside, only to find Cyrus fiddling with his old toys. His cheeks turn red with embarrassment, and he asks Cyrus not to go through his things. Cyrus withdraws his hand. All the while, Jose sits in a corner, shaking his head vigorously as he stares at his laptop screen.

Cyrus starts by telling them what they already know about the unproductive encounters with Saifullah's drug-addled neighbours. Jose has already filled Cyrus in on Mihir's recruitment of the tea vendor as an informant. It is only Jose whose exploits they know nothing about, except for Mihir's brief encounter the previous day. Jose remains silent, his eyes glued to his laptop screen. Cyrus and Mihir are puzzled. After much prodding, he begins to speak.

'It just doesn't make sense, or rather, I don't want it to make sense.'

He pauses. Mihir and Cyrus exchange looks.

'It was quite difficult to get into Saifullah's computer. Very solid encryption protocols, military-grade, as they call it. But when I did . . .'

Jose falls silent again. After a few moments, he continues, 'When I finally got into his computer, I had to make my way through some more layers of encryption—routed through several virtual private networks—before I could access his emails and files. Saifullah knew all along that we were trying to spy on him. He'd been informed of our arrival, and he had surreptitiously taken pictures of us hanging around his neighbourhood and sent it back to somebody codenamed Md.S Mohammed something, I would assume. He seemed to know exactly what we were up to each day.'

There is an uneasy silence that hovers over the room. Cyrus tries to defuse the tension, 'It shouldn't be that surprising, you know. If he has been in that locality for a long time and is as dreaded a terrorist as we believe him to be, then it's possible that he's cultivated his own network of spies who kept tabs on us. I've heard stuff like this from my dad. Don't worry, we did our job, I'm sure we won't be asked to go back there. Let's just be glad that we escaped unharmed.'

Jose is unconvinced.

'That's what I thought too, until I decided to trace the recipient of these emails. And . . .'

They are interrupted by a knock on the door. Mihir opens to find his mother bearing a tray loaded with tea and snacks.

'Mauji, I told you not to bother. Why did you have to take all this trouble?'

His mother ignores him and steps into the room. As she sets down the contents of the tray on the table, she says to Mihir, 'I am not here to disturb you, Nechu. Just something to refresh your brains and bodies. I'm sure you and your friends must be tired.'

Jose and Cyrus rise to thank her, but she brushes them off, 'Do children have to ever thank their mothers? Think of it as your house, please don't feel conscious of anything.' They smile awkwardly, before Mihir rushes her out of the room and bolts the door. He tells her that they are short on time to finish a presentation. Turning back towards his colleagues Mihir begins to apologize profusely, but he stops when he notices that his mother's interruption has eased Jose's tension.

They sip their tea in silence, until Jose continues, 'I tracked down the recipient, but the encryption at his or her end was the most sophisticated I've ever seen. I couldn't get in despite my best efforts. All I could manage was the exact location. Can you guess why it was so difficult?'

Mihir shrugs his shoulders, while Cyrus contorts his face as if to say, 'You're the expert, how would we know?'

'The same reason why I asked to meet somewhere outside the office. This Md.S, whoever he or she is, works at the bureau. I traced every email back to the Chanakyapuri headquarters. The network's impenetrable unless you're in very close physical proximity.'

'A-and h-how sure are you of this?'

'One hundred per cent. I checked everything repeatedly, including the hardware, which is what you saw me doing yesterday. I thought initially that I was making some basic mistake that was leading me back to our own networks, and for once, I wish I was indeed making a mistake. But this is what it is. Somebody at the bureau is stabbing us in the back. I don't know who exactly . . .'

Cyrus interrupts him. 'It would have to be somebody at the highest level because nobody apart from Ravi sir and his staff knew about this mission. But who could it be?' As always, it is Mihir who chimes in with sober words of advice, 'I don't think there is any point speculating. I think we should go to him immediately.' The other two nod in agreement. Much to Mihir's mother's disappointment, they decide to leave immediately, citing an urgent meeting. Mihir promises to return soon. They hail a taxi and head towards Chanakyapuri. It is a fairly long journey, but there is grim silence throughout, each lost in private speculation.

At Chanakyapuri, when the taxi driver asks them for a specific address, they realize that they have completely forgotten about the difficulties that come with accessing the headquarters in an unaccredited vehicle. They decide to get off at the closest junction and call Ravi. Mihir volunteers but realizes when he pulls out his phone that it is already well past office hours. The three briefly confer and decide that they have no option but to disturb him. Ravi does not pick up at first but calls them back after a few minutes.

'Hello, who's this?'

'Sir, this is Mihir Kaul.'

'Mihir Kaul, of course. I've been waiting to hear from you, but you do realize that you could have waited until tomorrow morning, don't you?'

'I'm terribly sorry, sir. But we had to get in touch with you. Something big has emerged from our investigation. You have to hear this immediately.'

Ravi remains silent for a few moments.

'Is it something you would have disturbed me for even at two in the morning?'

'I think so, sir.'

'Is it something that has direct implications for national security?'

It is now Mihir's turn to remain silent for a few moments.

'In all likelihood, yes, sir.'

'All right then, meet me at my residence. I will send you the address immediately. This better be good, or you'll pay dearly for interrupting the little time that I get for myself.'

The Scent of a Mole

The three pay no heed to the opulent sights that greet them on all sides as their taxi zips past the streets of Lutyens's Delhi. Crammed together in the back seat, they have their eyes glued to Jose's laptop, as he desperately continues to follow the trail, hoping to find employees at the bureau corresponding to the mysterious initials Md.S. As the car slows down, signalling that they are almost at their destination, Jose opens up a new document and types out for the others to see, 'It's a dead end. Either the bureau doesn't maintain an online registry, or it is impenetrable. I don't think there's anything else to do. Let Ravi sir take it from here.' The others nod, as they get out of the car onto the sidewalk outside Ravi's bungalow.

The guard posted outside the gate is busy chatting with a guard from a neighbouring bungalow. They survey the three from top to bottom with scepticism. Only Mihir appears somewhat assured, while the other two seem uncomfortable in their rented blazers. The guard asks for their IDs and calls Ravi over the intercom. Although Ravi asks him to let them in, the guard insists on inspecting their briefcases, if only to satisfy his curiosity. He is confused to find all three briefcases completely empty, except for Jose's, which contains his laptop. The other guard scratches his head for a while until a look of understanding comes over his face. He nods his head as if he knows.

While Ravi's guard opens the gate and gestures to the three that they may enter, the other guard remarks, 'I understand everything now. A lot of this happens at my saheb's bungalow. But I didn't expect your Ravi saab also to turn out like this. What can I tell you is power is like that, it corrupts you no matter what.' Mihir, who overhears this, freezes in his steps. He turns back to correct the guard's misplaced impression. 'It's not what you're thinking. Ravi sir is not like that, nor are we. The briefcases are not even ours.' He pauses for a moment, wondering whether to elaborate further.

'It's a long story, never mind,' Cyrus tells the guard, and they walk briskly towards the door where Ravi is already waiting. With Mihir out of their earshot, Ravi's guard turns toward the other guard, and begins to berate him, 'Why say all that? What do you know about my saab and his work? These are all James Bond-type people. They are patriots and cannot be corrupted. Not like your saab who does nothing but count money.'

At the door, Ravi makes no effort to conceal his amusement at their appearance. He greets them with hearty sarcasm, 'Well, well. Look at what one month in Mumbai has done to my boys. Which of the two sucked you in?' The trio exchange looks of puzzlement. Ravi laughs out loud and proceeds to settle their confusion, 'I meant, Bollywood or Dalal Street? Can't think of anything else that would demand such outfits.' They let out a forced round of laughter, as Ravi ushers them in with an affectionate pat on their shoulders. He leads them through the living room into his study and asks them to be seated.

Even in the disoriented state he finds himself in, Cyrus cannot help but note that the study is as impeccably organized as Ravi's office. It is an old high-ceiling bungalow with Victorian-era chandeliers. The walls are lined with bookshelves, and the room is tastefully appointed with a large three-sided desk on one side, and a sofa, a reclining armchair and a coffee table at the other end.

Adopting a more serious tone, Ravi tells them, 'This better be good. You caught me at a really bad time. I was catching up with a very old associate when you called. I will just go and fetch him. I'm sure he'd love to hear of your exploits. Please feel free to sit down or browse through the books while I'm gone, but just don't look at anything on my desk. The bar cabinet, you can look at from a distance. But don't touch anything. It's a prized collection gathered over many years.'

Mihir gets up.

'Sir . . .'

Ravi turns to him.

'Sir, we'd rather speak to you privately. It is very sensitive information.'

Ravi brushes Mihir off with a wave of his hand.

'Whatever it is that you want to tell me, you can tell him. He's not just an associate but my mentor. Almost like a father to me, to tell you the truth.'

Mihir shakes his head profusely.

'With all due respect sir, we really insist that we speak to you in private. Please . . .'

Ravi looks at Mihir with amused curiosity.

'Very well then, if you insist. I'm all the more intrigued now. To be honest, I wonder what it is that three semi-trained rookies have found that exceeds the intelligence clearance of somebody who's been at the bureau since even before they were all in their nappies. In any case, let me just go tell him that I will take a while. Won't be longer than a minute. And yes, what would you like to have? Coffee or tea, or something else?'

Ravi pauses, having caught Cyrus's glance slipping away ever so slightly to the well-stocked bar cabinet neatly ensconced between two bookshelves behind his desk.

'By something else, I meant juice, milk or water. You have a long way to go, and a lot to prove before I let you even catch a whiff of . . .'

Cyrus turns red in embarrassment.

'I w-wasn't going to . . . I wouldn't dare. I was just . . .'

'So, tea or coffee or . . .'

Mihir jumps to Cyrus's rescue.

'You don't have to take the trouble, sir. Really, we are fine. We just had some before coming . . .'

Ravi chuckles.

'If I had to take any trouble, I wouldn't be asking at all. Tea, it shall be.'

Saying so, Ravi walks out into the living room, smiling to himself.

Cyrus and Mihir look around and idly fidget with their briefcases while Jose pulls out his laptop. Never the type to be content with silence, Cyrus taps Mihir on his shoulder and begins to tell him in a hushed tone, 'Is it just me or do you think that Ravi sir isn't taking us seriously at all. He's acting like we've just returned from a vacation, or like we're here to invite him to a wedding. I mean, even after you told him that it is something that you would wake him up at two in the morning for, something with direct implications for national security. And especially knowing that we wouldn't dare bother him like this if not for . . .'

'If not for what, gentlemen?'

Looking up to find that Ravi has returned already, Cyrus jumps in his seat. He smiles awkwardly, eager to deflect attention for the second time in two minutes. As he settles into his armchair, Ravi chuckles lightly and puts Cyrus at ease, 'Don't worry about it. I really did sneak up on you. Just goes to show that in our world the old saying about walls having ears is to be taken quite literally.'

A man enters the room and diligently sets out tea and biscuits on the coffee table. Ravi takes a sip and turns towards him, 'Thank you, Shabbir. Please close the door on your way out. If there's anything, just call me on the intercom.' As the door gently thuds to a shut, Ravi gets up, and walks towards his desk to fetch his pipe, which has already been filled. He settles down in his chair again, lights up and takes a few puffs before finally looking up at the three men who seem all too eager to get down to business.

'So, to what sensational information do I owe the pleasure? And please get to the point.'

Cyrus and Jose remain silent. It is an unwritten rule by now that collectively directed questions will be answered by Mihir.

'Sir, Jose has uncovered very credible evidence that somebody at the bureau is directly colluding with Saifullah and his organization.'

For the first time all evening, a look of surprise and concern takes over Ravi's face. He shuffles in his seat and asks Mihir to go on.

'Sir, we don't know who it is. All we know is that this person goes by the initials Md.S'

Mihir, who is unusually perceptive of even the slightest change in demeanour, catches a brief look of recognition dawn on Ravi's face, but it is immediately replaced by a more neutral expression.

'And how do you know this?'

'Sir, Jose managed to . . . what's that word . . . it's almost like a, I don't know how else to put it, like a tantric term.'

Ravi laughs.

'A tantric term?'

Mihir is mildly annoyed by Ravi's continuing lack of seriousness but is careful not to let it show. He looks at Jose, who promptly responds, 'Penetrate.'

'That's the word. So, Jose managed to penetrate Saifullah's internet network, and uncovered emails sent to an anonymous email ID that he managed to trace back to our Chanakyapuri headquarters. Saifullah seems to have figured out that we were onto him and had been sending this Md.S person pictures of us taken while we were there.'

'Can I take a look?'

Jose almost drops his laptop in his eagerness to show Ravi what they've uncovered. Ravi swiftly scrolls through the images. He pauses for several seconds at one picture that shows Jose in khaki overalls atop a telephone pole while Mihir holds a ladder in place. Quite unexpectedly, Ravi erupts into raucous laughter. It is all the more disconcerting, for it lasts only a second. He eventually sets aside the laptop and looks away. He remains that way for over a minute, absorbed in thought. Cyrus finds it hard to conceal his annoyance and gestures to Mihir to speak up.

'Sir . . .'

Ravi turns to face them.

'Yes?'

'Sir, what do you think?'

Ravi gulps down the remainder of his tea and places the cup on the table.

'What is there to think? You've clearly failed. Why would you make the elementary mistake of being seen together? It mustn't have been very difficult for this fellow Saifullah to put two and two together. I'm sure he had cultivated his own network of informants who would have tipped him off about you three hanging around his house. Do you realize what a grave error you have committed? We'd tracked him down with so much difficulty. Now that he knows we're on to him, he's going to disappear again. I mean, I understand a chance encounter, like when Jose asked Mihir to help with the ladder. But you, Cyrus, how could you be foolish enough to talk to Mihir at that tea shop on such a regular basis? If you can't resist the temptation for just one month in such a low-risk setting, I don't think you have what it takes to go deep.

'But I also can't blame you. It's my fault. Clearly, this was an ambitious experiment that made me place greenhorns in field. I suppose its best that all three of you return to the academy.'

Mihir and Jose bow their heads down in shame, almost as a reflex action, but Cyrus continues to look straight ahead. The anger on his face is evident as he punctures the silence, 'But sir, what about the fact that we uncovered concrete evidence of somebody at the bureau colluding with a dreaded terrorist organization? Yes, we made some mistakes and Saifullah got away, but with a mole in our midst, it wouldn't matter if we caught a hundred Saifullahs.'

Ravi scoffs at Cyrus's insinuations, 'Evidence? What evidence do you have? All that you have evidence of is Saifullah being aware of your identities. How can you be so sure that he was reporting to somebody in the bureau?'

Cyrus prods Jose to speaks up.

'Sir, I tracked down the recipient's email ID, and it clearly pointed to an IP address originating at our headquarters.'

Ravi dismisses this immediately.

'Do you remember nothing of what I said at the academy? Do not take our enemies for mindless fools. They are just as adept at playing this game as you. You should know these things better than me. Even small-time crooks manage to pull it off these days. Just the other day, when I was away on official travel, my brother received an email from a fake ID set up in my name, claiming that I had been robbed of all my belongings and was stranded without money. It claimed that I had been locked out of my bank accounts and needed him to transfer money to a kind Samaritan who had bailed me out. They were trying this scam on a mass scale and hadn't bothered to find out that I am a senior IPS officer who would never land up in a situation like that. Now they're cooling their heels in Tihar.'

Jose tries hard not to shake his head in dismay.

'But sir, it wasn't the email ID that alerted me. It was the IP address that led me to the HQ . . .'

Ravi signals that he is in no mood to listen, 'We're dealing here with terrorist organizations with deep pockets, and sharp brains working for them. Many are computer engineers like yourself. I'm sure it's not that hard to set up a false trail if you know how.'

Jose is unconvinced by Ravi's attempt to explain away his discovery and persists, 'That is true, sir. And there indeed was an elaborate attempt on their part, and it took me weeks to work my way through it. I went past every layer of encryption and finally arrived at this conclusion. You are absolutely right about the false trail, sir, but I followed it all the way to the real one. And that trail ends at our own headquarters.'

Ravi chuckles again.

'At least I have an answer to the question I asked you at the door. Bollywood, it is.'

Even the perennially cool-headed Mihir is unable to contain his frustration any longer.

'With all due respect, sir. I don't think you should be treating this matter so lightly. You probably know this already, but my father . . . h–he died because his own colleague from the bureau, b–b–betrayed him. And we could have easily met the same fate because somebody at the headquarters had compromised us. I just met my mother for the first time in years, and it could very easily have never happened. We could have been dead weeks before. Jose could be wrong, and I hope he's wrong, but shouldn't we look into this thoroughly before dismissing it so lightly. Again, I say all of this with utmost respect.'

A deafening silence suffuses the room. Jose and Cyrus had no clue until now about the real circumstances behind Mihir's father's death. He had never said anything, and they had never thought it appropriate to ask. A lot is suddenly beginning to make sense. Ravi too feels squeamish. He wonders if he has pushed them a little too far.

'I'm sorry, Mihir, if I upset you in any way. You must know that I am very sorry for your father's unfortunate demise. It came as a terrible shock to all of us. The only reason I will not jump to conclusions before we find a real smoking gun is that the circumstances here are different. Your father had been betrayed by a field agent. What you seem to be suggesting in this case is something a little different. You have to know that every piece of data, every alphabet that leaves the headquarters is closely monitored, and nobody could possibly carry on with something like this undetected. But in any case, I will look into this with all seriousness.'

Mihir finds himself feeling a little vulnerable and embarrassed at his sudden outburst.

'I'm sorry, sir. I didn't mean to . . .'

Ravi brushes his apology aside and continues, 'Jose, what would you need to confirm beyond all doubt that the emails had indeed been sent to somebody at the headquarters?'

'Sir, I need physical access to the headquarters. I can even tell you exactly which computer it originated from. Then, there won't be any room for doubt.'

Ravi nods in approval as he gets up.

'Wonderful. That is all there is to it, then. We will find out tomorrow. If you're right, not only will you be fast-tracked into the bureau, but also amply rewarded. But if you're wrong, you'll be off to the academy, and it is unlikely any of you will work directly under me ever again. I will ensure that all three of you have boring desk assignments in the remotest corners of our country for the rest of your career. Now that this is out of the way, I suppose there is nothing else to discuss. If you'll excuse me, I have kept my guest waiting too long. I will see you all at the headquarters at 9 a.m. tomorrow. Have a good evening, gentlemen. And yes, please finish your tea before you leave. Shabbir will heat it up for you.'

* * *

The taxi ride back to Mihir's house is a tense one. The meeting had sowed more doubts than it had resolved, and they find themselves somewhat disoriented. Jose is carefully going through the images again, while Mihir and Cyrus are brooding over the sudden and most unexpected prospect of their careers being permanently thrown into jeopardy. When they are close to Mihir's house, Jose taps them both on their shoulders and types into his laptop for them to read, 'My worst fears have come true. I checked, double-checked, triple-checked. None of the photos sent by Saifullah show the two of you together. How did Ravi sir know?'

Cyrus and Mihir are shell-shocked. Not for the first time this evening, there is absolute silence for several minutes. Finally, Mihir asks for the laptop and types out for the others to read, 'And to think that I tried to correct the guard's impression of Ravi sir. Who knows? Maybe he was right after all.' Cyrus snatches the laptop, and deletes the words 'Ravi sir', replacing it with 'the mole'. Jose looks at Cyrus and shakes his head, as if to suggest that perhaps it was unwise to jump to such a drastic conclusion. Mihir nods. He takes the laptop from Cyrus and types, 'Maybe he had somebody watching over us in Mumbai.'

* * *

Ravi is on the terrace with his guest. It is dimly lit, and the two men appear as little more than silhouettes. Ravi tells his companion, 'I knew these boys were smart, but I underestimated just how smart they are. They are on to us, sir. I see no point in keeping it from them any further. That kid Cyrus, he's a particularly difficult one. He reminds me so much of his dad. So forthright and unfearful in the face of power. Unless we take care of this situation immediately, things can easily spiral out of control. If we continue bluffing, what is to stop him from going to the chief, or even worse, Anil? It's all very unnecessary. I know you had a different plan in mind, but we'll have to ditch it. Tomorrow has to be the day, we can't delay it.'

The guest nods in silence as he gazes into the smoggy Delhi sky.

* * *

The last time they were at the headquarters, it was a different sort of anxiety that had filled Mihir, Cyrus and Jose. It has been a little over a month since, but so much has changed. As their car makes its way past the space agency's station, there is none of the innocent excitement of the previous time. There is only dread and fear now. At 8.47 a.m., the car pulls up outside the headquarters' foyer. Unlike the previous occasion, the driver speeds away immediately leaving the three to fend for themselves.

It dawns on them that they do not quite remember where Ravi's office is. The last time the driver had taken them through a side entrance, but they cannot remember where exactly it is. They realize that they have to go through the main entrance. They hurry up the stairs, and make their way past security screening when a receptionist asks for their IDs and purpose of visit. They hand in their academy IDs. Mihir speaks on their behalf, 'We're here to meet Mr Ravi Kumar. We have an appointment for 9 a.m.' The receptionist looks at them with wide eyes, as if to suggest that she has no idea what they are talking about.

'I'm sorry, but this is a very large department and our appointment registers are linked to designation and not name. Unless you can give me the exact designation of the person you intend to meet, I cannot help you.'

'The chief of C3, Mr Ravi Kumar.'

'I'm sorry, mister. There is no such department here. I'm afraid you might be at the wrong address.'

'Wait, what? Are you sure? This is exactly where we met him last time. A-and, and an official vehicle dropped us off here just now.'

'I'm sorry, it must be a mistake.'

The three of them exchange puzzled looks as they walk back towards the door. Jose looks around and notices that the signage all around them indicates that they are at the Central Bureau of Statistics. He points it out to the other two. Cyrus lets out a sigh of recognition. He tells the other two in a hushed tone, 'How foolish of us, really. Surely everything is coded. Wait, let me try.' He runs back to the receptionist and tries his luck, 'We're here to meet the chief statistician.' The receptionist smiles and looks at her computer. She quickly scans through the screen and looks up at Cyrus, shaking her head.

'I'm sorry, the chief statistician has no appointments at 9 a.m.'

Cyrus glances at his watch. It is already 8.52 a.m. They have only eight minutes left. The last thing they want is to be late.

'I think we should just call him on his phone. No point playing this guessing game.'

Jose nods and pulls out his phone. There is no network. Again, something they should have expected. He curses quietly under his breath and runs out of the door and down the stairs. Outside, the phone immediately picks up a signal. He hurriedly calls Ravi, who picks up after only a few rings and tells Jose to ask for the chief of the poverty-eradication department. Jose pants his way back to the receptionist, who struggles to mask the fact that the three have ensured a rather entertaining start to her day.

'The chief of the poverty-eradication department, that's who we want to meet,' Jose tells her, struggling for breath.

She quickly looks at her screen again. Without shifting her gaze, she reads out, 'Jose Cherian, Mihir Kaul and Cyrus Bandookwallah. Very well, you may go on. C-335.

Third floor. Please take the visitor's entrance, which you will find at the end of the hallway if you go through this door.' He thanks her profusely, and signals to Mihir and Cyrus that they can now go in. As they make their way through the long corridors that lead to the visitors' entrance, they realize that in all their excitement, they had barely paid any attention the last time around. The headquarters' non-descript façade is highly misleading. The building is enormous, they realize. It is the sort of intricately laid-out complex—like a large multi-specialty hospital with a hundred different wings—that one could easily get lost inside. While the reception area is eminently populated with all sorts of signage, there is nothing once you go past, except for miniscule numbers on each of the doors. Unless you know where to go, it is highly likely that you will get lost.

They take the elevator to the third floor, where yet another perplexing discovery awaits them. The numbers are not sequenced in linear order. C-300, for instance, is followed by C-458. Mihir glances at his watch. It is 8.57 a.m. They look around, desperately trying to remember from last time. But it is a hopeless search for all corridors look alike. With not much time left, they decide to follow their instinct and walk through the south-west corridor, hoping to find somebody who may be able to direct them to the right office.

They are fortunate. Only a minute later they catch a glimpse of Subramanyam walking through the other end of the hallway towards a water cooler, chanting mantras under his breath. They begin to run. Subramanyam hears their loud footsteps and turns towards them. He signals to them to slow down and begins to walk in their direction. They meet halfway.

There is no need for explanations. Subramanyam already knows.

'Sorry, sir. It's just . . .'

'Relax, relax. Just follow me.'

Subramanyam leads them through a formidable maze of hallways, doors, and junctions, before finally ending up at the corridor in which Ravi's office is located. 'I hope we remember every turn, or we'll be just as hopelessly doomed next time,' Cyrus whispers to Mihir and Jose. 'If there'll be a next time,' Mihir reminds him. Subramanyam asks them to wait outside as he enters Ravi's office. After a minute or two, but what seems like eternity to the three, he returns and asks them to go in. Ravi's office is just as spotless and organized as they remember it. Similarly intact is his inexplicably out-of-place enthusiasm, 'Well, if it isn't the sensational three musketeers again. Please, sit down.'

They awkwardly take their seats.

Looking into Jose's eyes, Ravi immediately asks, 'So, whizz-kid. What is the plan of action?'

'I just need to get access to the bureau's network, sir. Wired access, preferably.'

Ravi rolls his fingers over his desk, as if he were playing the tabla and gets up from his chair. They all follow suit. Ravi signals to Mihir and Cyrus that they may remain seated.

'Same rules as in my house. You can look at anything you want while we're gone, except my desk. Flouting the rule at my house would have incurred my displeasure, but here, it might invite charges of treason and inciting war, so rein in your curiosity.'

Before Mihir can clarify that they have no such intentions, Ravi has already walked out of his office. Clutching his backpack in one hand, Jose walks briskly to catch up with him. They go through yet another maze of corridors, not a single word exchanged all throughout until they reach an unmarked door guarded heavily by four uniformed personnel bearing guns. They rise in unison to salute Ravi, who stops to inquire about their well-being. They seem happy to see him, and shake their heads vigorously, indicating that all is well. Although the guards signal to him that there is no need to do so, Ravi insists on logging his entry in the biometric system. As he places his thumb over the scanner, he turns towards Jose and asks, 'Did you sleep well last night?'

Jose is taken aback. He takes a few moments to respond.

'Y-yes, sir. I-I mean, actually . . . not really, sir. To be honest, not a wink of sleep, sir.'

Ravi smiles.

'Excellent. You're in the right place then. Welcome to Insomnia. Just one word of advice, although this should be needless to say by now. Play along with whatever I say, don't act surprised no matter what. And whatever you find, say nothing. Say out loud that you've come unprepared and will come back some other time, and that will be the sign that you've found what you're looking for.'

The door swivels open with a whooshing sound, and Jose follows Ravi into a long, dimly lit room. Ravi leads Jose through a seemingly unending row of servers and computers before they arrive at another guarded door. Another round of salutes, another login, that leads into another long room with computers and servers. The only difference is that this room is better lit and is split into cubicles with people manning the computers. Jose looks around with fascination but has no time to pause as Ravi hurries past this room too.

He finally stops at the end of the room, at what appears to be more of a chamber than a cubicle. Inside, a scruffy middle-aged man—who looks like he hasn't slept in days, if not weeks—rises to greet them.

'This is Jyotirmoy Saha. He heads Insomnia, which you would have realized by now is our electronic surveillance division. He's an extremely accomplished computer scientist, with a PhD from MIT. The real one.'

Jose and Jyotirmoy awkwardly shake hands.

'Saha Saab, this is Jose Cherian. He's doing some research on cybersecurity at the bureau, and the home secretary has granted him all-access clearance to inspect our networks. So, if you could just grant him the necessary permissions, he can do the needful.'

Both Jose and Jyotirmoy look at Ravi with incredulity. Jose remembers Ravi's advice at the door, and quickly amends his reactions. Jyotirmoy knows all too well that the home secretary granting such clearance to a research scholar is an outright fabrication—even those at the bureau don't usually have complete access—not to mention the implausible fact that the chief is escorting him personally. But after all these years at the bureau, Jyotirmoy knows the game all too well. Whatever it is, it is not for him to know, and so he must simply play along.

Ravi sits in a corner, lost in thought, while Jyotirmoy helps Jose obtain access. Jose quickly goes about his business, and the room remains entirely silent except for his frantic thumping on the keyboard. Not more than five minutes later, Jose clears his throat loudly and turns to Ravi, 'Sir, I'm really sorry, but I think I've come a little unprepared. My other laptop has the necessary tools installed. If it's all right, may I come back another day?'

Ravi shakes his head furiously as he rises. He turns towards Jyotirmoy and comments, 'If this is the future of our computing talent, then we'll have to import more people from MIT. I'm sorry for wasting your time, Saha Saab.'

* * *

Although Ravi had told them that they could look at anything except for his desk, Mihir and Cyrus do not dare rise from their seats. Nor do they speak to one another. They simply sit there, gazing at an obscure painting on the wall behind Ravi's desk, lost in separate trains of thought. Their long contemplation is interrupted by the creaking sound of the door. An orderly enters with cups of tea, followed immediately by Ravi, who walks in hurriedly with Jose diligently in tow. Mihir and Cyrus look at Jose expectantly, but he does not meet their gaze. Ravi settles into his plush leather chair and sips on his tea. He opens his drawer and pulls out his pipe. Before reaching for his tobacco pouch, he looks up at Jose and asks, 'So? What did you find?'

Jose takes a deep breath.

'I can affirm with one hundred per cent certainty that Md.S is somebody at the bureau, sir.'

Ravi lifts his eyebrows.

'I see. And who is it?'

'I don't know, sir. The encryption's too complex.'

'So, you will need more time?'

Jose shakes his head.

'The computers here share the same IP address, and the encryption within the network is impenetrable. Only the network administrator, which is Saha Sir, I would assume, can have access to it. Unless I can have the same level of access as him, I'm afraid the trail ends here, sir.'

Ravi thinks for a few moments as he fills his pipe.

'Unfortunately, I cannot involve Jyotirmoy. For the same reason that I had to lie about who you were. Is there any other way?'

Jose fumbles as he replies in the negative. The silence that then follows is interrupted by Mihir, who chimes in, 'Sir, there is a way. We have the initials, Md.S. If we can run through the rolls of the bureau and shortlist names that match these initials, it would be a start at least.'

Ravi laughs.

'Rolls of the bureau? Do you realize what you're asking for? The registers that we do have are all highly coded, and only the higher cadres are explicitly named on our rosters. Md.S could stand for anything. I need you to be more specific.'

Mihir replies, 'Sir, if you could give us a list of all rostered employees whose first name is Mohammed, and the second name starts with the letter S, I think we will have a fair shortlist to work with.'

Ravi's nostrils flare up as he puts his tobacco pouch back in its place.

'Explain. Why Mohammed? And how sure are you?'

Mihir looks baffled.

'Do I really have to? I mean, it's a no-brainer. Md.S, Mohammed something starting with S. We were tracking a man named Saifullah, an Islamic fundamentalist. He was in contact with somebody at the bureau who goes by the initials Md.S. I cannot think of any name other than a Muslim one that would conform to these initials. I am completely sure, sir'

Ravi appears utterly displeased, although his unflinching eyes seem to indicate that this is exactly what he has been expecting. Lighting his pipe, he rises from his chair.

'If you're so sure, then you've perhaps chosen the wrong line of work. A position in the media might have suited you better. If I had to pick one thing and one thing alone that comes in the way of effective intelligence work, then that is prejudice. You have absolutely nothing to go by, and yet you have already decided that it is a Muslim man. And you say you're completely sure. You should be utterly ashamed of yourself. Let me make this clear once and for all. I will not bat an eyelid if you tell me that our biggest threat as a nation comes from extremist Islamic groups. That is a fact I cannot deny. But if you will deduce from that the conclusion that anybody working with these groups is necessarily a Muslim, or even worse, that anybody who is a Muslim is involved in terrorism, I will have to disagree in the strongest of terms. But if you're so sure, let me give you just one name. Do you remember the kind man at my house who served you tea and snacks yesterday? His name is Mohammed Shabbir. You might as well suggest that he is a terrorist. That's how flimsy your grounds are.'

Mihir feels a tinge of guilt but decides to stand his ground.

'I'm terribly sorry if you took it that way, sir, but I'm not suggesting that the cook at your house is our mole. I'm talking about somebody in a higher position. I'm not insinuating anything, just suggesting that this is our most tangible route. With all due respect, sir, I don't see anything wrong in believing that extremist Islamic groups work in tandem with Muslim individuals. It is the most obvious thing.'

'Please explain. How is it obvious?'

Mihir pauses for a few moments. He takes a deep breath.

'I'm sorry to bring up my own life yet again, sir, but you would know better than me the circumstances that led to my father's unfortunate death. He was betrayed by his own colleague, in service of some deluded ideology . . .'

Ravi scoffs as he cut Mihir off.

'Let me tell you about your father's tragic death, young man. The colleague that you are referring to was not a Muslim but a Sikh named Gurbinder Randhawa. He was honey-trapped, blackmailed, and paid off to ensure his betrayal. He did not care in the least about ideology. If you are naïve enough to assume that it is only ideology that drives people to do wrong, then you most certainly do not belong here. Human beings are complex, and all sorts of motivations drive them. I'm terribly sorry to be breaking this intimate piece of information in front of these two, but that is only because I want it to be a lesson for them as well. If I had my way, this is the sort of case study you would be reading at the academy.'

Cyrus and Jose appear stunned as Mihir struggles to fight back the tears. Ravi pauses to puff on his pipe, before continuing, 'Md.S could very well stand for mad serpent or Madhav Sarkar or whatever. What makes you think that somebody trying to evade detection would use their actual initials? Indeed, Md.S could very well be me, under some other alias. You have no way of finding out.'

A deafening silence fills the room until Jose intervenes, 'Then we have no option but to access Saha Sir's workstation, sir.'

Ravi chuckles, in an eerily menacing tone.

'If we go that far, or if Saha finds out anything, then I could be in deep trouble.'

More silence. They realize there is nothing more to be said. Ravi sets his pipe down and begins to address them, 'What if I told you that last evening, before you came and after you left, I was having a drink with the mole you seek so desperately to find? Would you like to meet him?'

The three exchange puzzled looks, not for the first time in the last twenty-four hours.

Haygreeva

Cyrus, Mihir, and Jose do not know what to expect when Ravi introduces the man walking into his office as the mole they've stumbled upon. He introduces the man as Madan Singh. If not for the faint scar on his forehead, which accentuates the wrinkles around, one could easily mistake Madan Singh for a forty-something-year-old. The carefully dyed hair, trimmed moustache, and a well-built frame altogether work well to disguise the fact that he is sixty-eight years old.

Before Ravi can say anything further to the three of them, Madan pulls out a packet of cheap beedis from his pocket and lights up. Seemingly to nobody in particular, he announces, 'Unless you're careful, you can completely lose yourself out there on the field. Midway through my career, at the height of the Khalistan movement, I went undercover as a landless labourer in rural Punjab. I had never smoked all my life but had to pick it up then because it was over beedi and lassi breaks that the other labourers would bond and sometimes discuss the sort of information I was seeking. My assignment ended after some years, the Khalistan movement is more or less done, but I could never stop smoking beedis.'

Ravi laughs. Although he has heard the story several times, it never ceases to amuse him. The trio connects the dots in their head. Md.S, Madan Singh, it fits. But there is a lot that makes no sense. Is Ravi also involved? Why else would he continue to be so nonchalant?

Ravi begins to speak, although if he had the time, he would have preferred to let the three simmer in doubt and confusion for longer.

'This, gentlemen, is the mole you have been seeking. Md.S, Madan Singh. He was the one in contact with Saifullah.'

Mihir, in particular, is utterly flustered. He speaks up, 'H-have you known all along?'

Ravi smiles.

'Not only have I known of this, but have also been most directly involved in . . .'

Cyrus butts in, 'I'm sorry, I just don't follow. The chief of the Central Counterterrorism Command has been actively colluding with a terrorist? Y-you put our lives at risk?'

Madan Singh rises from his chair. He walks around the office as he speaks. He pauses after almost each line, to puff hard on the perennially dying embers of his beedi.

'We hadn't intended for you to find out. If not for your discovery, it would have all gone on smoothly. This is why you rookies were assigned to the case in the first place over someone with more experience. But now that you have found out, you have a decision to make. Ravi sir, would you care to explain to these meddling fools?'

Ravi rises from his chair and begins to walk around as he speaks. There is a studied seriousness to his movements and intonation, something the trio hasn't seen since their first meeting almost a month ago.

'It's very simple. I leave you two options. Join hands with us, and not only will your careers be secure, but there is also a lot of money to be made. Ten times your measly salaries. Refuse our offer, and try to blow the whistle, and I will personally ensure that not only will you be out of the bureau, you won't ever find employment anywhere. And don't for a moment think that anybody will believe your audacious claims, even if you decide to blow the whistle.'

The three of them remain silent. There is too much to process, too many shocks to absorb. They remain that way for over a minute. Madan looks at Ravi and shakes his head with a wink, as if to suggest that they shouldn't be wasting any more time. Ravi glances at his watch, sighs and returns to his chair.

'Okay, you can relax now. We were just fooling around with you. Neither is Madan Singh a mole nor is the person you were assigned to track in Mumbai a terrorist. This was all just part of an elaborate simulated exercise, orchestrated by Madan sir on my instructions.'

The trio is partly stunned but also partly relieved. They are full of questions, and Ravi can see it on their faces.

'I pulled you out of formal training, which is not usually how we do things here. Having done that, I needed to know if you were ready for the demands of the job, and this was the only way to do it. You can think of it as a final examination in some sense. Now, unlike academic exams, advanced simulation exercises such as this one work best only when you have no clue that this is what it is. And I had no intention for you to find out, not now, not ten years down the line. But you forced my hand.'

Mihir asks, 'So there is no Saifullah? Who was that person then? Another agent? And what about the neighbours, the tea vendor? They told us that the man had been around for a long time. Were they also a part of the set-up?'

Ravi looks at Madan, inviting him to respond.

'That's none of your business, kid. What you need to know, you now know. The rest of it doesn't concern you. Agents, informants, could have been anybody. It's not that difficult to find unemployed actors in Mumbai anyway.'

'So, did we pass this . . . this exam of yours?', Cyrus asks.

'Jose, with flying colours. You two, just about barely, but . . .' Ravi is interrupted when his phone rings. He picks up, listens for thirty seconds or so and hangs up without saying anything.

'I don't have all day. Madan sir will take it from here and facilitate your formal induction. Not a word of this training exercise to anybody else. And gentlemen, brace up for Operation Haygreeva.'

'Hay . . .?' the three rookies ask in unison.

'Lord Vishnu assumed the body with a horsehead to kill a demon. A prophecy said that the demon would die at the hands of someone with a horsehead. Hay means horse, and Greeva denotes neck. In our profession, we have to take different avatars according to situations. And that is exactly what shall be expected of you in the months to come, gentlemen.'

* * *

Over the next ten days, Madan takes Mihir and Cyrus through a rigorous set of training exercises to help them intimately understand the nitty-gritties of fieldwork—established modes of clandestine communication, techniques of infiltration, exfiltration, disguise, cultural assimilation, and so on. Through case studies and anecdotes from his own colourful career, Madan demonstrates to them that espionage is not an exact science but an ever-evolving craft honed through observation, resolve, and patience. Mihir and Cyrus take it all in with awe. Only a few days into their training, they come to conclude that if espionage is a craft, then Madan is a master craftsman.

In the meantime, Jose begins working at Insomnia. He responds to the demands of his job like a fish thrown into water, picking up the tricks of the trade with surprising ease and swiftness. Even Jyotirmoy, who had been a world-renowned cybersecurity researcher before joining the bureau after losing his wife in the World Trade Centre bombing in 2001, is baffled by Jose's intuitive grasp over tech.

Mihir and Cyrus do not directly interact with Ravi during their training, but Jose is regularly invited over to Ravi's office for long discussions. Ravi is eager to acquaint himself with the cutting edge of cybersecurity and digital surveillance. He found discussions with Jyotirmoy not very helpful as Jyotirmoy tends to struggle with translating technical matters into ordinary language. On the other hand, Ravi finds Jose to be blessed with the ability to explain sophisticated technological methods to even an absolute beginner. Faint murmurs grow within the department of Ravi having found his blue-eyed boy.

* * *

Given its location at the heart of Lutyens's Delhi, Nehru Park is typically thronged mostly by rich businessmen, senior bureaucrats, politicians, and their families. It is an eclectic bunch of activities that the park hosts every morning. In addition to the regular walkers and joggers who go about their business quietly, there also are laughter clubs, meditation groups, and yoga classes to be found scattered across the vast lawns. There is even a space for live music, where each morning a fairly eminent classical Hindustani singer, Pandit Prakash Kumar Ji publicly undertakes his daily practice. To him, it is a rehearsal, but to the enthusiasts who flock to listen to him, it is like a mini concert each day. With a flair for showmanship and storytelling, he keeps his audiences thoroughly engrossed by interspersing his songs with gleeful anecdotes and aphoristic musings on subjects as profound as life and death, but also trivial matters such as the weather. Of particular delight to the onlookers is his oblique and convoluted commentary on the latest political rumours in Lutyens's Delhi, which typically tends to spawn further discussion and gossip over post-workout tea.

Today, as he finishes off a long-winding recital of a Marathi Abhang, Pandit Ji catches in the corner of his eye the unmistakable figure of Ravi briskly walking up the path with his dog Ranger and another young man he doesn't recognize. It is Jose, who has, for the last week, been accompanying Ravi on his morning walks. Ravi thinks it would be easier to pepper his daily exercise with a dose of learning rather than have it eat into his schedule separately.

After sipping on some water to clear his throat as his audience enthusiastically applaud, Pandit Ji announces, 'The next is a Nirgun Bhajan set to tune by my Guru, the great Kumar Gandharva Ji himself. This is addressed to all those under the delusion that celestial deities have forgotten about them and have lost all interest. To them, I say, pay attention. If you know where to look, you will find what you're looking for.' Then closing his eyes, he begins to sing soulfully, '*Awadhoota, gagan ghata gehrai* (O disinterested one, the clouds are thickening in the sky).'

As soon as Pandit Ji begins to sing, Ravi gets up and walks away as quietly as he had settled down amongst the audience, almost as if the words themselves have given him what he needed. At a considerably safe distance, even as Pandit Ji's singing faintly echoes in the background, Ravi ties Ranger to a nearby bench and begins stretching, while Jose sits down.

After finishing his workout, Ravi fishes out a piece of chewing gum from his pocket, puts it in his mouth, and walks towards an unmarked trash bin a few feet away from a locked side entrance. After disposing of the gum wrapper, he realizes that he has accidentally dropped a few notes into the dustbin. He lets out a loud sigh and puts his hand into the bin. Along with the notes, he retrieves an envelope securely taped to one side and discreetly puts it into his pocket. It takes all of two seconds. He unties Ranger, walks out of the park, and gets into a waiting car, Jose following closely behind him. Ravi asks the driver to take them to the headquarters. As the car gets moving, Ravi fishes out the envelope from his pocket and retrieves its contents, a single sheet of paper. He hands it to Jose, asking, 'What do you see here?'

Jose looks at the paper, which is blank on both sides. Ravi carefully studies Jose's blank expression and chuckles to himself. 'What is it?' Jose asks. Ravi chooses not to respond and instead hums softly, '*Awadhoota, gagan ghata gehrai,*' before gently pulling the sheet out of Jose's hands and placing it back into the envelope.

Inside the privacy of his office, Ravi opens the envelope and carefully places the blank sheet on his desk.

'From you, these past weeks, I've had the wonderful honour of learning all about cutting-edge technologies and their applications. Today, it's my turn to teach you something. Very low-tech, very old school, but highly effective.'

Saying so, Ravi reaches into his drawer and pulls out an ordinary-looking pen. He places the blank sheet on a retractable document holder that sits innocuously on his desk. Jose watches intently as Ravi performs each step with the calculated relish of a magician. He turns on a small switch on the pen cap, and a thin beam of blueish light emerges from the back. He points the pen at the sheet, and suddenly words appear.

'Invisible ink,' exclaims Jose in a tone of wonder, 'straight out of a spy novel.' Ravi smiles. 'Indeed. Back when I started, we'd use candles and matchsticks. But the underlying principle . . .'

His voice trails off, and his expression acquires a sudden seriousness as he looks at the encrypted message and writes the characters down on a separate sheet of paper. With the cipher hardcoded into his memory, Ravi takes no more than a few moments to decode the message. He writes down in all caps, 'EXPECT FIREWORKS SOON. BIG GIFTS BEING SENT', and shows it to Jose. 'What do you think this means?' he asks. It is, of course, a test, for Ravi knows exactly what it means. Although he is not privy to the exact code, Jose has a hunch, 'A warning about an impending terrorist attack, and money or arms being sent across?'

'Money. The code for arms is sweets,' Ravi replies.

Jose is yet to connect the dots. He does not, in the first place, know where Ravi got the envelope from. Ravi senses Jose's confusion and begins to explain, 'As much as computers and all of that are going to be increasingly important in our line of work, you must know that it is and will remain a fundamentally human endeavour. The singer at the park, why do you think we've been stopping to listen to him every day? It's not because I like to start my day off with classical music.'

'Yeah, I did think that was odd. You never actually listen.'

'Exactly. He looks out for my arrival each day, and if there is something to be communicated, he begins to sing a Nirgun Bhajan, like he did this morning. That tells me that there is an envelope to be found in that particular waste bin into which I pretended to have dropped money. What is important to remember, considering all that I've told you about intelligence being a human-centric endeavour, is that the singer himself didn't drop the message. Somebody else dropped the message, that person himself or herself being only a node in a larger and more complicated network of clandestine communication, and then sent a pre-determined email to the singer last evening, which was his cue that he had to sing a Nirgun Bhajan this morning upon seeing me.

'That's all the singer knew. He didn't know about the dustbin, or the message in it, nothing. Just what his job was. And even if somebody were to accidentally stumble upon the message, and somehow figure out that it contained a message written in invisible ink, there is no way you could decode it unless you had access to the cipher, which only I and the source of this information have.'

Jose is amazed but also bursting with questions. This is exactly as in the spy novels he had grown up reading, but so much more exciting.

'So, is this tied to some particular agent on the field, or the singer and the trash bin are generic conduits for any intelligence that has to be passed on to you?'

Ravi looks at his watch.

'The trouble with you is that you ask too many questions, and the trouble with me is that I have too little time. When was the last time you met the rest of the musketeers?'

Jose is taken aback by the unexpected shift in topic. He pauses for a few moments before replying, 'Not since that day when we were all in your office together.'

Ravi smiles.

'Great. Save your questions until they get here because you're all about to be assigned your first real task. It's time to transition.

Octopus

Mihir and Cyrus cast curious glances at Jose and Ravi, who are both in their trackpants. Subramanyam is also in the office. He is, of course, sharply dressed but is in another corner filing away paperwork.

There has been no indication of what the meeting is about. The message from Ravi had been rather abrupt, 'See me in my office ASAP.'

Ravi rises from his chair and addresses Mihir and Cyrus, 'The three musketeers reunite. How wonderful! Please sit down.' Mihir and Cyrus take their seats beside Jose without comment. Ravi continues, 'I've been hearing good things about you two. Just yesterday, the mole . . . I mean, Madan sir, was telling me that you're ready to be on the field. And this morning, Jose and I were on a walk when the opportunity to send you there came up. I want you to listen very carefully to what I have to say. One of our field agents, codename Octopus, has made contact after a long gap. What we know is that a large sum of money is being funnelled through the hawala route to fund a major terrorist attack on Indian soil. It is very limited information, but it is an invaluable start.

Your job is to take it from here and find out exactly where the money is coming from, who is receiving it, and so on. And it won't be enough to find out, you need to neutralize the entire network and terror module.'

The three pay careful attention to each word as Ravi goes on to describe the elaborate workings of the hawala system. It is notoriously difficult to intercept given that it works entirely on trust, and no records of any sort are maintained. Each transaction, he explains, has its own predetermined code, and it would take a very narrowly defined strategy to break through. He tells them that he is convinced that the transaction will be routed through the hawala market in Delhi, right under their noses. He explains that the other important markets in Srinagar, Gujarat, and Punjab, have long been compromised, and the enemy will not take the risk.

Although Jose is also a part of the meeting, it is clear that it is Mihir and Cyrus who will be directly assigned. Questions flood their mind. Who will do what, and how? Displaying his uncanny gift for anticipation yet again, Ravi begins to address their questions without waiting for them to ask.

'Now, there are two key components to an operation like this. The first is having your ears to the ground. Mihir, you will do what you did with the tea vendor in Mumbai. I want you to penetrate the hawala market in Delhi. The money we're talking about is being sent from Afghanistan. Identify a key broker who deals with Afghan transactions and win over his trust. If this transaction is as large as I think it will be, then it most certainly will be something all the big players in the market might have some knowledge of. Until you completely win over somebody's trust, do not do or say anything that may blow your cover. One whiff that we're on to them, and the enemy will cancel the transaction, and it's game over for us.'

'Why is it game over? Isn't that what we want? That the transaction doesn't happen,' Mihir asks.

'Only under carefully designed circumstances. If all we want is to thwart the transaction, we might as well go into the hawala market with guns and threaten all the brokers. But that won't do us any good. They'll just find another way of funnelling the money, and we will be left fumbling in the dark. We won't know anything about the people involved, or their agenda. We need to let the transaction happen so that the second component of our operation can come into play. And that will culminate in neutralization of the entire terror outfit.

'Cyrus, you will coordinate with Mihir and come up with a strategy to apprehend the receiver after the transaction has taken place. Again, subtlety is key. You can't just walk into the market and apprehend him right there. That way, too, the enemy will know that we're on to them and may alter their plans. You need to execute it in such a way that the enemy has no clue that we have their man. It is a high-risk game because if we let the transaction happen and then fail to apprehend the receiver, the consequences might be tragic. At the same time, if we just thwart the transaction and do nothing else, we won't know anything about the larger picture, which is what we want ultimately. And sooner or later, we will pay the price for it.'

* * *

Mihir makes his way through the crowded bylanes of the Kashmere Gate area in Old Delhi. He draws more attention than the others in the crowd. Hawkers and touts keep coming up to him every few metres, offering everything from balloons to earphones and even female escorts. It is his appearance that has them convinced he's a person to sell to. He is wearing a silk shirt, leather shoes, has rings on all fingers and a fairly heavy chain around his neck. His hair has been dyed grey in some parts, and he looks like a middle-aged prosperous trader. He wants to convince the operators that he is someone who relies on the hawala route for cross-border transactions.

If there is one thing that Mihir has learnt from Madan Singh, it is the importance of playing the part so convincingly that one's identity completely dissolves under one's assumed cover. And so, Mihir had asked Cyrus to scout the peripheries of the hawala market for a few days and observe the general characteristics of those who frequent it. Based on Cyrus's description, Mihir has carefully transformed his appearance and mannerisms so as to fully blend in.

Outside the hawala market, there is a large, dilapidated haveli. Mihir stops at a small stall nearby to buy himself a paan. He pulls out his flashy leather wallet, replete with a fake voter's ID, driving licence, and visiting cards that identify him as Parimal Virani, a diamond trader from Surat. He sifts through a crisp wad of currency notes and stretches his hand out to give the paanwallah a ten-rupee note. He checks himself midway and hands him a twenty-rupee note instead. He brushes aside the paanwallah's move to return the change. 'This is for you, enjoy yourself,' he tells him. With his mouth fully stuffed with the sticky juices of the betel leaf, Mihir's fake Gujarati accent sounds even more authentic. The tip has little to do with the put-on generosity of Parimal Virani but is Mihir Kaul's attempt to deflect attention from the fact that he had almost committed a grave error. Without that particular ten-rupee note, the transaction he hopes to carry out is dead in the water.

The haveli is large and multistorey, yet very plain and nondescript. It would be easy to mistake it for an abandoned building waiting to be bulldozed. At the entrance are several men. They keep their eyes open at all times and can tell familiar faces from the new ones. Presently it is just after lunch, which is not a particularly busy time. Some of the men are engaged in a game of cards, while some others lay sprawled lazily, fanning themselves with discarded newspapers. They take note of Mihir walking in. Signalling to the others to continue their game, one of them gets up to inquire.

'Hello boss, building is under repair. You can't go in,' the man says, even as he sizes up Mihir from top to bottom.

Mihir knows from local informants that this is to be expected. It is their way of warding off unwanted visitors.

'I know. That's why I'm here. The contractor sent me here to pick up some leftover material,' Mihir replies confidently. It is the standard response of the code that allows the touts to decide who can be let in, especially when it is an unfamiliar face.

'Understood, boss. Do you know where to go? I can help you find the best material. Gulf, Africa, South-East, which material do you want?' the man asks Mihir. In addition to keeping away unwanted intruders, these men also serve as touts, each employed by particular brokers to enrol unaffiliated customers in exchange for a small commission. For although it is impossible to enter the market unless one already knows an existing customer who communicates the protocol, not every new customer who walks in is already affiliated to a particular broker. Besides, the market is sub-divided along specific geographical lines, and one's referee might be dealing with a broker specializing in a completely different region.

But Mihir already knows exactly which broker to meet. 'Just tell me where I can find Ismail Seth, Afghanwallah,' he tells the tout, who nods in recognition, wakes up one of the sleeping men, and asks him to direct Mihir to the right place. The man struggles to open his eyes, having fallen fast asleep in Delhi's afternoon heat. He yawns as he lazily stretches out his arms. Mihir Kaul would have, of course, waited in decent silence, but Parimal Virani is a busy man with no time to waste. 'Get up fast, you lazy crook. I don't have all day,' Mihir snaps at the man who immediately springs up and apologizes. It is evident from Mihir's clothes, jewellery and arrogance that he is a very rich man. In any case, Ismail Seth is one of the most senior brokers in the market and only deals with very select clients.

The tout leads Mihir up an old creaky staircase onto the first floor, which is divided into several cubicles of varying sizes using cloth curtains. The arrangement reminds Mihir of the cloth markets of Chandni Chowk. Within each compartment is a large white mattress on which a broker sits with large briefcases—in some cases, piled all the way up to the ceiling— along with note-counting machines and multiple telephones. Some of the larger compartments even have television sets and air-coolers. The tout walks Mihir past the row of brokers to another staircase at the end of the room that leads to the second floor. Here, unlike the first floor, the hallway is empty. And while the rooms on the first floor appear unused, except for storage, all the rooms on this floor—about six in total—look to be occupied. Presumably, these are reserved for the more elite brokers, like Ismail Seth.

The tout leads Mihir to a room at the end of the hallway and asks him to wait outside while he goes in. After a few moments, the tout returns and tells Mihir that he can enter. Just as Mihir is about to do so, the tout clears his throat loudly. 'Boss, some money for *chai-paani*,' he tells Mihir. Mihir reaches into his wallet and pulls out a hundred rupee note. The tout, unaccustomed to such large tips, is overwhelmed with gratitude and thanks Mihir profusely. In his mind, Mihir knows that if he is unable to win over the broker's trust, it might not be a bad idea to cultivate this tout as a back-up source of information.

Mihir walks in to find a fairly well-adorned room, replete with air-conditioning and a flat-screen television on the wall. Ismail Seth, who is talking to someone over the phone, gestures to him that he may sit down. Mihir discreetly scans the room as he waits, hoping to pick up even the slightest hint about the Seth's personal life. He notices that the Seth is wearing a rather expensive-looking watch and that there are several such watches lined up on the table. There are several large and formidable almirahs behind him. The walls are bare, with the exception of three garlanded pictures and framed verses from the *Quran*. Two of the pictures are of an old man and a woman, who are presumably the Seth's parents. The other picture appears to be much more recent and of a middle-aged man. From where he is seated, Mihir can only make out that the year of death is 2006.

The Seth finishes his phone conversation and turns towards Mihir.

'You have the code?' he asks, wasting no time on introductions.

Mihir nods and pulls out the ten-rupee note from his front pocket. He presents it to the Seth, who compares the serial number of the note with some entries in a small diary on his desk. Scratching off an item on his list, he takes the ten-rupee note and places it into a machine that shreds it into unrecognizably small fragments. He then asks Mihir, 'Do you want it in apple flavour or mango flavour?' Mihir is momentarily flustered. He hasn't been taught to expect this question. But eager not to come off as an amateur, he quips in response, 'Apple or mango, how does it matter, Seth? Fruits are what I'm interested in. Mix it up, whatever you wish to feed me.' The Seth chuckles, swivels around in his chair and turns to face one of the almirahs. He pulls out a large bunch of keys from his front pocket and opens it. In the top compartment are crisp currency notes of large denominations, while the bottom has smaller denominations. Mihir is awestruck, for he has never seen so much money at once in his life. But Parimal Virani, of course, has, and so he betrays little of Mihir's amazement.

The Seth pulls out a precise number of bundles from both compartments, removes the rubber bands around them and feeds them into a note-counting machine on his desk. Mihir guesses in his head that apple flavour refers to large, and mango to smaller denominations. The Seth quickly counts the bundles by hand one more time before handing it over to Mihir who puts it in his briefcase. Mihir thanks him and is about to leave when the Seth remarks, 'This is an unusually small amount by my standards. I only did it because my man in Kabul said that there will be bigger consignments if you are satisfied. I hope he's right.' Mihir replies, 'You just wait and watch, Seth. This was just a trial transaction because the IT department bastards have their eyes on me at all times in Surat and that route is not very feasible anymore. You see, I deal in diamonds.'

The Seth cuts him short, 'I'm not interested in the details. It's none of my business whether you deal in diamonds or guns or women. As long as you don't waste my time on loose change next time.' Mihir smiles as he responds on his way out, 'Don't worry, Seth. Even I don't like wasting my time on loose change.'

Two days later, after conferring with Ravi and Cyrus, Mihir returns with a clear strategy. The bureau's man in Kabul, undercover as a prosperous international trader, has been instructed to transfer a large sum of money. In addition, Ravi has also helped him procure a high-quality counterfeit Rolex for the Seth. The touts at the entrance recognize Mihir and do not stop him this time. Some even rise in salute, presumably having heard of his generous tip from the last visit. He walks straight to Ismail Seth's room on the second floor.

Without saying a word, Mihir places the watch on the Seth's table. The Seth looks up at him with puzzlement. Mihir tells him, 'I got out of here undetected last time, Seth. Like I told you, I've been looking for a discreet channel, away from the prying eyes of the IT department, and after trying so many things, this has worked. This watch is a small way of expressing my gratitude. You can think of it as a token of my loyalty. I told you, I don't like wasting my time on loose change either.' The Seth is impressed but is hesitant to accept the watch. Mihir insists on it, telling the Seth that the watch is of no value compared to the amount he is saving because of him. The Seth gladly accepts, and he slowly opens up a bit and becomes friendlier. As he is about to leave with two briefcases filled with apple flavoured notes, Mihir tells the Seth, 'It's close to lunchtime, Seth. I am new to Delhi and want to eat at the right places. Why don't we go out for lunch together?'

The Seth is not exactly eager, and points to a tiffin carrier on his desk, indicating that he usually eats in his office. But Mihir insists, and the Seth, who is worried about coming across as cold even after having received such an expensive gift, gives in.

Mihir keeps this up for a week, and the frequency of transactions increases. He is careful to visit the Seth only close to lunchtime and makes it a point to insist on having a meal together. Mihir realizes that the Seth is a thorough professional, who will reveal nothing about the deals he brokers or his customers, no matter what. He is, in that sense, rather incorruptible.

About ten days later, while they are having lunch at the Paranthe Wali Gali, Mihir stumbles on an unexpected breakthrough. Talking about his family, and how they had been in the hawala business for several generations, the Seth mentions his recently-deceased brother—the man in the picture on the wall. He had been handling the family's operations in Mumbai and some months earlier, had died in the serial train blasts on his way back home. Mihir is tempted to reveal immediately that he is working precisely on preventing such deaths in the future, but holds his cards, deciding to confer with Ravi before making any such move. Ravi is thrilled by this most unexpected turn of luck, and gives him the go-ahead, but advises him to tread cautiously in any case.

The next day, although there is no pending transaction, Mihir visits the Seth in his office. The Seth is happy to see him.

'Right on time, Virani Seth. Look, I haven't even brought my tiffin today.'

Mihir is in a more sombre mood than usual. 'We will of course have lunch together, Seth. But before that I would like to discuss something here, in the privacy of your office.'

The Seth asks him to go ahead.

'Do you remember the first time I came here, Seth? You told me that it is none of your business whether I deal in guns or diamonds or women? You are an absolute professional and do your job with sincerity. But what if I told you that it does matter, that it is your business to know what happens with the money? What if I told you that the terrorists responsible for your brother's death are planning yet another series of strikes targeting innocent civilians, perhaps on a deadlier scale than last time? Would you prevent it, if you could do so?'

The Seth is taken aback, and wonders where Mihir is headed with this. With hesitation, he responds, 'Y-yes, of course, there is no question. In the name of Allah, these heartless men commit such grave sins. Nobody deserves to die in this manner. B-but I'm sorry, I don't understand. What is the connection? How will I prevent it?'

'I knew you would say yes. It has only been two weeks, but I have come to realize that you would never willingly cause harm. I'm sorry for having misled you all this while Seth, but I am not a diamond trader, nor is my name Parimal Virani. I am a government agent tasked with the responsibility of preventing terrorist attacks on our soil. We have solid intelligence that the enemy will be sending in large sums of money from Kabul via a hawala channel to finance these attacks. And because the enemy is aware that we have the other markets under constant surveillance, we are convinced that the transaction will be routed through this market. We don't know exactly when this transaction is going to happen, but we will soon. And when I find out, I will let you know. All you have to do is let me know when the transaction has happened, so we can apprehend the receiver.'

The Seth looks at Mihir with the expression of a man staring at death. The blood has been sucked out of his face.

'B–but even if I wanted to help you, which I want to, don't get me wrong . . . How will I know exactly which transaction? Besides, there are many others in this market who deal with Afghan networks. It could be routed through anybody.'

'Remember the other thing you said on the first day I came here, Seth? You don't deal with loose change. This is crores of rupees we are talking about. Nobody else will have the immediate liquidity to deliver on such a large transaction. And you will know immediately because it won't be a familiar face who comes to collect it.'

'B–but if word gets out that I helped you, then my business will be destroyed. The other brokers are like hawks, waiting to eat into my slice. If you come in and arrest this man, then everyone will know.'

Mihir places his hand over the Seth's shivering palms and reassures him, 'I promise you, Seth. You will not get into any trouble, and nobody will find out that you've tipped us off. We won't apprehend him here, or outside, or anywhere close to Kashmere Gate. All you have to do is alert me as soon as he's left your office, and we'll figure out what is to be done. Do us this favour, and you will have not only helped save countless innocent lives, but you will also have made some very powerful friends.'

* * *

It is unusually cold and misty, the sort of Delhi winter morning that makes one want to stay under one's blanket. Except that it isn't winter, but only the early days of autumn. While it is welcomed with relief by most others, Ravi couldn't care less. Regardless of what the weather is like, and however late he might have gone to sleep the previous night, he pulls himself out of bed each morning at 6 a.m. sharp. For the last month or so, Jose, too, has unwittingly found himself becoming attuned to an early start to the morning. At the academy, he had found himself frequently getting into trouble for turning up late to morning assembly. His classmates' best attempts to wake him up would often fail. But the conversations with Ravi are by themselves rewarding enough to motivate him to wake up early.

Having grown up with a fascination for spy novels, Jose finds these conversations to be invaluable in helping him calibrate his fanciful impressions with the ground realities of espionage. The prestige attached to walking with the chief of C3 each morning, a singularly unending source of envy within the department, does not strike Jose as being of any significance. Ravi likes Jose precisely for this reason, apart from his inexhaustible knowledge of digital technologies.

After several years at the highest levels of bureaucracy, if there is one thing that Ravi has a vehement distaste for, it is the propensity for sucking up to those in power. It is a trait that is all too familiar. In Jose, however, he sees something markedly different and tends to view him almost as an intellectual equal.

As they walk briskly around the park, very little is visible through the thick smog that engulfs their surroundings. But Pandit Ji's intricately layered vocals cut through the smog and land on their ears even from a distance.

'*Ud jaayega hans akela* (the swan will fly away alone) . . .'

'About time,' Ravi remarks to Jose, as he begins to walk even more briskly towards the trash bin near the entrance. It has been well over a fortnight since the last message from Octopus, and Ravi's impatience tells Jose that fresh information has arrived.

Back at the headquarters, Ravi allows Jose to have a go at deciphering the message. Beaming with pride at having engaged in his first act of non-digital decryption, Jose reads out to Ravi, 'Gifts shipped. Receive tomorrow.'

* * *

Everything is as usual outside the hawala market. The pan stall, the hawkers, they are all there. Except for a minute detail, so insignificant that even the most regular visitors might perhaps fail to notice. The regular paanwallah is nowhere to be seen. In his place is a taller, better-built man, who is however just as shabby and unkempt as his predecessor. The sub-brokers, who are the paan stall's most loyal customers, find nothing particularly suspicious when the new man explains to them,

'Brijesh's child suddenly took ill, and he had to take her to the hospital last night. I'm his cousin. He'll be back by the evening.'

It is close to lunchtime when the new paanwallah's phone rings. 'Yes, Brijesh Bhaiyya, your child is getting discharged? Great news, God is great indeed.' As he hangs up, he catches sight of a police jeep zooming past the main road, not for the first time in the last hour. Two minutes later, a clean-shaven bespectacled man, fairly young, emerges from the hawala market bearing two large briefcases. He begins to walk towards the end of the road, where he has his car parked. But before he can get there, a speeding motorcycle with two fully jacketed men zip past. Before he can realize what has happened, he is on the tarmac, and the briefcases are missing. The paanwallah runs to his rescue and helps him up. He points out that the motorcycle is stuck in traffic, and that they can chase it. The paanwallah's eyes fall on the police jeep, which has been circling around the area for a while.

'Police! Police!' he begins to yell out in their direction.

The man is not happy at the paanwallah's effort to summon the police. 'Why are you calling the police? I have a car, I can chase the motorcycle myself,' he says. 'Arrey bhaisaab, just thank your fortune that the police jeep was right here . . .' the paanwallah responds. The man appears to be in half a mind to get away from the scene and chase the bikers himself. But it is too late. The police jeep has already turned around in their direction.

Without alighting from the jeep, the constable in the driver's seat asks them what the problem is. The paanwallah explains the sequence of events and points to the motorcycle still stuck in traffic at a distance. The constable quickly confers with his superior, who is seated beside him, before asking the man to sit in the rear of the jeep. The paanwallah too follows suit.

'Eh, who asked you to sit?' the constable scolds the paanwallah.

'Please, saab. Let me also come. It's always been my dream to be a part of a police chase,' the paanwallah pleads.

'Okay, okay. Make it fast,' the constable says, and both men get into the rear of the jeep where another armed policeman is already seated. As the police jeep closes in on them, the two bikers realize that they're being chased and make a dash through the traffic. It turns into a long and winding chase that takes them through the busy bylanes of Old Delhi all the way into Lutyens's Delhi. Although they manage to consistently keep the police vehicle at bay, the bikers never fully disappear from view. The chase ends at what appears to the man to be a deserted farmhouse. Here, the bikers seem to suddenly lose their desire to escape the police, and wilfully surrender.

As the policeman pats the paanwallah on his shoulder and says, 'Well done, Cyrus,' the man turns around and begins to run. But the paanwallah has a gun pointed at him.

'Where do you think you're going? You're under arrest.'

The Two-Sided Mirror

In an unmarked room buried somewhere within the many labyrinths of the C3 headquarters, the hawala recipient sits on a cold steel chair. He wears a stone-faced expression as a doctor subjects him to a thorough medical examination. It has been six hours since he was apprehended, but he has all along insisted that they have the wrong man. From his wallet, they have retrieved a driving licence that identifies him as Satwinder Singh from Mohali. A quick inquiry with the regional authority that had issued it reveals that the driving licence is indeed authentic, but that the picture affixed on it is not. To completely eliminate all doubt, Ravi instructs the Punjab station of the bureau to track down the actual Satwinder Singh. He turns out to be a tractor-driving farmer who does not have the slightest idea how his driving licence has been duplicated, not to mention his complete ignorance about the man who has been flaunting it as his own. At the end of the exercise, it is clear they don't have the wrong man.

On the other side of a two-way mirror that encloses one end of the room, Ravi is talking to Mihir and Cyrus. They have asked him for permission to engage in physical coercion.

'For the hundredth time, we're not policemen or thugs,' Ravi tells them. 'Physical intimidation is never very effective. Sure, in the short run, you can give him a sound thrashing, and he might spill a few beans, but we're not after a few beans here. We're after the entire goddamn plantation. For that to happen, gentlemen, I need you to think more intelligently. There's a reason our work's called "intelligence".'

There is a knock on the door. It is the doctor who has finished examining the man. 'Thank you, doctor. You will be informed if there's anything else,' Ravi tells him as he collects a file and shuts the door. As he runs through the file quickly, a wicked expression creeps up on his face. Turning to Mihir and Cyrus, he says, 'You heartless fellows, you wanted to beat up a poor diabetic man when a few biscuits might have just done the trick.' Having let the others have their shot at the man for the last six hours, Ravi finally decides to swing into action. He walks into the pantry, picks out a pack of sugar-free biscuits and sweeteners, two steaming cups of tea dispensed by the vending machine, and sets them all out on a tray. As he runs through these motions, he also runs a quick simulation in his mind.

As he walks through the partition that separates the officers from the suspect, Ravi puts on a smile and begins to address the man in chaste Punjabi, '*Satwinder Paaji, tussi theek aan* (Satwinder, are you well)?' On the other side of the mirror, Mihir and Cyrus exchange looks of surprise. 'Our boss knows Punjabi?'

Clearly flustered, the man posing as Satwinder Singh struggles to muster a coherent response. His bluff is immediately caught. As he places the tray on the table and invites the man to help himself, Ravi adds, 'It's okay, it's okay. You don't have to carry on with your poorly rehearsed act any longer. We know everything already.' Gobbling up two biscuits like a malnourished child, the man reveals just how vulnerable he is. Ravi is pleased. He knows it will be very easy.

'Look, we know, for instance, that you're diabetic. Why did you have to keep that from us and put yourself through all this torture? And I understand what torture it can be. Trust me, I'm diabetic myself and have been through a similar situation. Many years ago, I was captured by some people who you might be familiar with. Friends, colleagues, well-wishers, in one or the other capacities you might know them. Anyway, when I got captured, and they realized I was diabetic, they starved me until I was nearly dead. But my men surrounded the abandoned safe house I was being kept in, and I escaped.

'We're not evil people, you see, although your masters might have drilled it into your head that we are. Instead of letting you suffer, we are giving you food, and diabetic-friendly food, mind you, even before you've said a single thing. But where are your people today now that you're in trouble? Don't for a moment think that you'll escape the same way I did. You're currently being held in one of the more secure facilities in the country, and it would take nothing short of a full-scale military invasion to get you out of here. Knowing this, your people would rather kill you than risk having their entire operation ruined. I know you're not going to trade loyalties just over diabetic biscuits but think of it as a token gesture of better gifts to come.

'If you help us out, not only will you live you might also live comfortably. Diet of your choice, a private and

well-furnished cell to live in. We'll even throw in a TV and
fridge if you prove your worth. On the other hand, if you
refuse to comply, or worse still, if you give us the wrong
information, you will suffer a fate worse than death. In fact,
you'll be begging us for death. Think it through. All I'm
proposing is a deal. I'll give you some privacy to think it over.
You can finish the tea, the second cup too, and the biscuits by
the time I'm back.'

The man is clearly shaken. He hasn't stopped eating his
biscuits, a clear sign that he is giving Ravi's offer serious
consideration. Bearing the same sheepish grin that he had
entered the room with, Ravi walks out. He quips to Mihir
and Cyrus, 'The cookie quite literally has crumbled.' The two
look on with admiration.

'Sir, just one question . . .' Mihir says, speaking evidently
on behalf of Cyrus as well. Ravi asks him to go ahead.

'The story you narrated to him of your escape from
confinement. Did that actually happen?'

'Let me ask you a question in turn. Tell me, what is
common to all successful gamblers?'

Taken aback, but not exactly surprised by Ravi's cryptic
response, Mihir ventures forth a guess, 'Um . . . luck?'

Ravi laughs.

'That is what every unsuccessful gambler believes. Let me
tell you what is actually common to all successful gamblers. It
is the ability to hold your cards close to your chest, pay very
careful attention to your opponents' body language, and bluff
with all the confidence in the world when you know that your
opponents are at their most vulnerable. And the work we do
is in many ways just like gambling. Give the man an hour, and

he'll begin to sing even better than Pandit Ji at Nehru Park. I'll be on my way for now. I trust you to take care of the rest. Gamble as your please, but bluff sensibly. If you go around promising him a life of freedom and a private jet, he'll catch your bluff immediately. If you need me, and I hope you won't until you have all the facts at your disposal, you know how to reach me. Good day, gentlemen.'

True to Ravi's words, in a little over an hour, Mihir and Cyrus begin to extract crucial information from the man, including, of course, his real identity. He is Omar Rasheed, formerly a full-time software engineer in the Middle East, and until seven hours ago, a part-time lieutenant of the Lashkar-e-Hind.

* * *

'Gifts received. Awaiting further instructions on Diwali preparations,' reads the email that Omar types out in front of Mihir and Cyrus. Jose sits in another corner of the same room, monitoring the proxy connection that he has set up to ensure that no red flags go up at the receiver's end. After finding out that Omar is himself a trained software engineer, Ravi insists on Jose being around to ensure that he tries no dirty tricks.

'Now, what?' Cyrus asks.

'Now we wait,' Omar responds, 'they usually reply within a few hours.'

But only ten minutes later, a response lands in his inbox. It contains a satellite phone number. 'Call the number,' Mihir instructs him. 'It's not that easy,' Omar says. 'Do you even know how satellite phones work?' Cyrus and Mihir instinctively turn towards Jose, who asks immediately, 'Yes, what about them?'

'My organization and others like mine use satellite phones not just because they're impossible to tap, but also because the location of either party can be determined by the other in real-time, to a very precise degree of accuracy. If I call from here, and that too from some random number, they'll immediately know that I've been compromised. It has to be from my own satellite phone, and it has to be from my apartment. And it has to be me. Otherwise, it's all over. You won't get what you want.'

'Give us your address, and we'll have the satellite phone brought here. We'll figure out the rest,' Mihir tells Omar.

'It's two crores that I'm supposed to have received. Do you really think they wouldn't be tracking my SatPhone constantly? If you move it outside of a hundred-metre range from where I live, they'll be alerted. And then, it's all over,' he points out.

Cyrus is annoyed.

'Stop saying "it's all over, it's all over", and just do as you're told. Don't try and act smart with us. Give us your address, and we'll figure out what to do,' he snaps.

Omar gives them his address, an apartment in Hauz Khas.

As soon as he hears of this, Ravi calls for a meeting.

'Any ideas, gentlemen?'

'I think I can clone his phone without having physical access to it. But it would be tricky, and not just for technical reasons,' Jose speaks up.

'What do you mean?' Ravi asks.

'Well, satellite phone networks are controlled by private operators, about a dozen of them, based all around the world. I looked up Omar's satellite phone number, and the operator is a Kuwait-based company. From what I could gather, they're not particularly receptive to requests from intelligence agencies,' Jose says.

'Can't you just hack into it?' Mihir wonders.

'I'm not the expert here, but I don't think you could do that unless you had an army of Jose Cherians working for weeks on end. We simply don't have the time or the resources,' Ravi replies. Jose nods vigorously, evidently impressed by how quickly Ravi has understood the situation.

'And even if we did, I don't think we could do it without the risk of inflaming diplomatic tensions with the entirety of the Arabian Peninsula. Cyrus, I want you to find out everything you can about this company. Jose, you figure out what needs to be done at our end once we secure the company's cooperation. And Mihir, you continue with the interrogation, don't leave the man alone even for a moment. You know what they say about an idle mind being a devil's workshop. Let us reconvene at 7 p.m. Cyrus and Mihir, you have seven hours to get him to talk. Find out everything you can, squeeze him dry. As for myself, I have some phone calls to make right away.' Ravi tells them as he leaves the room in a hurry.

Back in his office, Ravi calls Sarita and briefs her on the situation.

'A Kuwait-based company you say . . .'

'Yes, ma'am.'

'Well, I wouldn't have my hopes high up. It's diplomatically very tricky, and given how little time we have, perhaps there is no point even trying. Figure out another way. But Ravi, whatever you do, don't make the mistake of sending the man back to his apartment. God knows what he might have stowed away inside. If he blows himself up in the middle of goddamn Hauz Khas, then you and I will both be crucified.'

'Of course, ma'am.'

'And Ravi . . .'

'Yes, ma'am.'

'Well done. Keep it up.'

'Thank you, ma'am.'

On Ravi's advice, Cyrus and Mihir have been very sparing with the food and water they've been providing Omar. A few biscuits and a cup of tea and then nothing for a few hours. It yields a curious result. It appears to them as though they are interrogating two people, and not one. When hungry, Omar is cooperative and even expresses deep remorse from time to time. But as soon as he has eaten, even if it is only a few biscuits, his responses acquire a marked tinge of sarcasm. At times, he even declares his pride at being complicit in the mass murder of innocent civilians, or infidels, as he terms them. He gives them important information about the Mumbai train blasts and other impending designs, but Cyrus and Mihir do not believe much of what he says. There is something about the man that compels them to doubt his claims.

'The problem with this country, you see . . .' Omar is lecturing them, after having just eaten a few biscuits, when the phone rings. It is Ravi, asking to meet in five minutes. It has been six hours since that last meeting. 'Save your crap for later,' Mihir snaps at Omar, before following Cyrus into the adjacent room, where Jose is still busy at work.

'Gentlemen, we need to come up with an alternative plan. The chief, in consultation with other senior officials has ruled against the possibility of seeking Kuwait's assistance. There are complex diplomatic reasons underlying this, and it does not concern you. What we need to do immediately is follow through on plan B.'

'I didn't know we had a plan B,' Jose interjects.

'There always is a plan B. And it doesn't end there. The rules of this game aren't always set by us, and so you must ideally have plan Z as well, somewhere at the back of your mind. I have spoken to a dear friend of mine who heads the National Disaster Management Authority. They will stage a full-fledged mock fire drill around our man's residence, during which the two of you will go in as firemen and retrieve the satellite phone from his residence. Mihir and Cyrus, can I count on you?'

'Yes, sir,' they respond in parade-like unison.

'Good. Now, after you retrieve the phone is where it gets slightly tricky. We have an extremely short window of time. If the call isn't placed by tomorrow, his handlers will know something is up, and might pull the plug. And because we can assume that the SatPhone is being tracked, it cannot be moved beyond a hundred-metre radius. Which means that Jose and whatever gadgetry he needs to clone the phone will need to be stationed in proximity. You take the phone to him, he clones it, and then you put it back exactly where it was. Any questions?'

All three hands go up. Ravi gives Jose the first shot at asking.

'Sir, how can we be sure that they don't have the place under surveillance, in addition to just tracking his SatPhone?'

'That is a most pertinent question. And the answer is that we cannot be sure. As a precaution against physical surveillance, the fire drill will cover a one-kilometre radius around Omar's house. As for electronic surveillance, hidden cameras or whatever it might be, we will cut off power supply to the entire zone for the duration of the drill. Nevertheless, we can never be sure. Which is why, the whole thing will have to be done very tactfully.'

* * *

The next morning, a public-announcement van goes around Block M of the affluent Hauz Khas area, announcing a mock fire drill that is to begin in fifteen minutes' time. Although the residents grumble about the short notice, they are beholden by law to do as told, and have no option but to comply. Amidst the row of fire engines that line the streets is a decoy. From the outside, it looks exactly like any of the other fire engines, but there is a crucial difference known not even to the firemen on duty. In lieu of the compartment that stores water is a mobile miniature of Insomnia, outfitted with all the tools Jose will require to clone the SatPhone upon retrieval.

At the exact hour marked out on the schedule, loud sirens begin to wail, and the residents pour out onto the streets. They are then escorted, by foot and vehicle, to a pre-designated point of safe assembly—an open ground at the edge of the one-kilometre radius. It is a massive exercise by all standards, and close to two hundred fire and police personnel are on duty.

'This is the thing that always amazes me about Delhi,' Mihir quips to Cyrus as they wait for their target building to be cleared out, 'you'd imagine that a few hundred people might be living on a road of this size, but it's several thousand people. It's quite the sight.'

It takes fifteen minutes for the evacuation exercise to be completed, after which Mihir and Cyrus swing into action. Having obtained the precise location of the SatPhone inside Omar's residence, they have no trouble retrieving it. Just in case there are off-grid surveillance devices in the house and its vicinity, they do so very tactfully and pretend to comb through every room of the house, looking for stranded residents. Other teams do the same with every other house in the locality. After repeating the exercise for the houses immediately neighbouring Omar's, Mihir and Cyrus make their way down to the waiting fire engine.

They watch on anxiously, as Jose plugs the device and begins to type in obscure lines of code on his console. After twenty minutes or so, Jose unplugs the phone and hands it back to them. 'It's done,' he says, flashing a jubilant thumbs-up. Mihir and Cyrus run up to Omar's apartment, put the device back exactly where it was, and hurry back to the fire engine. With the siren wailing loud and clear, they drive off, even as the fire drill continues at full pace.

Back at the headquarters, everything is quickly put in place—a fully functional clone of Omar's satellite phone, a monitoring station tasked with tracing the location of the receiver, and a tray full of diabetic biscuits. The call is short and to-the-point. Omar is instructed by his handler to head to Mumbai the next day and stand outside a specific eatery in Dharavi at exactly 12.25 p.m. 'How will I recognize the receiver?' Omar asks. 'You don't have to. Just wait for a whistle and do what the man asks you to do. Your picture has been dispatched. And yes, do not wear the clothes of infidels. This is a divine mission, and you must dress appropriately.' Just as he is about to hang up, the unnamed man at the other end of the line adds, 'And never forget, nothing is purely accidental. When in trouble, follow the devout.'

* * *

Mihir, Cyrus and Jose are not exactly first-timers in Dharavi. The memory of their training simulation is fresh in their minds. Inside the dark confines of the telecom van—slightly larger and more well-equipped than the one Jose had used the last time—they keep a close watch on Omar, who stands outside the designated eatery, glancing at his watch from time to time. It is 12.23 p.m. They had left Delhi the previous evening with elaborate instructions from Ravi. He had told them that they needed to have Omar in their line of vision at all times. To be completely sure, he had also ensured that they mounted tracking devices on Omar's body as well as inside the briefcase. He had also told them that at the slightest hint of suspicion, they had to alight from the vehicle and pursue on foot. Finally, he had added, almost as a warning, 'If things go wrong, and they very well might, do not forget this. Whatever you do, do not endanger civilian lives. If we sincerely believe that we are different from them, then our actions must follow from that conviction.'

Exactly at 12.25 p.m., a man standing on the other side of the street whistles to Omar. He is clad in the exact same clothes as Omar, the traditional Indian Muslim attire of white kurta pyjama and a skull cap. With his head bowed down, Omar quickly goes across. They exchange no words, only signs and gestures. Inside the van, the trio struggles to interpret the exchange, which is evidently grounded in a private language that they are not privy to. They shuffle anxiously but stay put inside because the targets continue to remain within their sight. But after a minute or two of exchanging signs and gestures, they begin to walk away. At first, slowly, then briskly.

'Bastards,' Mihir curses out loud, as he hurries out of the van. With Cyrus in tow, he begins to follow at a safe distance. Omar turns around and catches sight of the two. He prods the other man. They freeze in their tracks and look around. All of a sudden, they start running and turn into a nearby street. Mihir and Cyrus continue to pursue them and have them in sight until a few bylanes further, where the two blend into a crowd of similarly dressed men all walking towards a nearby Masjid. Mihir and Cyrus follow earnestly but are unable to discern their targets from the others. Just as Omar and the other man are about to enter the Masjid, Mihir spots the briefcase. 'There,' he points out to Cyrus and begins to run after them.

Cyrus grabs Mihir and holds him back. 'Have you lost your mind? We can't barge in like that during prayer time.'

They call Ravi, who instructs them to wait outside.

'How long will they stay in there? They'll have to get out at some point. Besides, the tracker is still active, and I can still see their real time coordinates. Just stay alert, and don't expose yourselves.'

The prayer ends, and men begin to leave the mosque, but there is no sign of the targets. Even as the stream of men leaving the mosque thins down and eventually dries up, their coordinates on the tracking console remain unchanged. They are still inside the mosque. They call Ravi again, and tell him that everybody has come out except the two. They ask for his permission to enter. 'Not yet,' Ravi tells them, 'Wait for my clearance.' About five minutes later, Jose calls them with devastating news. The targets have disappeared off the map. It is almost as if they have vanished into thin air. Ravi asks them to abort the operation and return to Delhi immediately, despite their desperate pleas to continue scouting the area. 'You've failed. There's nothing else to be done. You'll only end up exposing yourself. Minimize the damage and return at once,' he tells them. There is a strange calmness to his voice, and it infuriates them.

With dejection and shame weighing heavily on their hearts, they return to the van. Jose, in particular, cannot believe what has just happened.

'It's not something you can take and throw away, just like that. It was firmly secured around his waist and the only way to turn it off would be to unlock it, or literally dismember the lower half of his body,' he vents in disbelief.

'What if they hacked into it. This Omar fellow is a computer guy too, after all,' Cyrus ponders aloud.

'That, I would understand. But this is not a digital lock. It is an actual physical lock that you open with a key. And this is a customized lock that you can't just break open with brute force. Like I said, you would have to literally cut him in half and then incinerate the device in a high-temperature furnace, both of which seem highly implausible. To the best of my knowledge, only two keys exist and both are at the headquarters,' Jose responds. There is nothing more to be said, and they begin to pack up.

The flight back to Delhi is a tense one. Although few words are exchanged, the look on their faces says it all. Demons from the past have returned to grip them in familiar patterns and try as hard as they may, they cannot free themselves. They desperately want to conceive alternative explanations, but only one theory makes sense, the theory they had arrived at only a few months ago. In their minds, that alone could explain everything—the ease with which Ravi had got Omar to spill the beans, how the fire drill had proceeded, the way the targets had disappeared off the radar. Finally, of course, the unsettlingly calm tone in which he had asked them to abort. Mihir could swear that he sensed a tinge of satisfaction in Ravi's voice during that final call. On these matters, he was never wrong.

* * *

Back at the headquarters, Mihir sends Ravi a text message informing him that they are back. He texts back, rather cryptically, 'Come meet me on our side of the two-sided mirror.' It isn't hard for them to figure out that he wants them to go to the interrogation room, although they can't fathom why. 'Two-sided mirror, two-sided traitor,' Cyrus mutters under his breath. On any other day, Mihir would have glared at him with fury for saying something like that, but today he merely sighs.

At the door, they collectively take a deep breath trying to calm their racing hearts and minds before entering. Awaiting them inside the room, along with Ravi, is another familiar face, although they cannot exactly place him. They look to their left, across the mirror into the interrogation room, and find both Omar and the other target in handcuffs. Before they can begin to piece everything together, Ravi launches into a familiar refrain, 'Well, well, if it isn't my favourite three musketeers, after yet another failed mission. Thankfully for us, and for the country, somebody else stepped in to save the day. Gentlemen, please meet one of our finest talents, Qasim Khan. You can call him by his codename, the Examiner. Or as you once knew him, Saifullah.'

Their jaws quite literally drop to the ground. The Examiner was a near-mythical figure at the academy. He often figured in case studies of exemplary deep undercover work and had featured prominently even in the case studies Madan Singh had run them through. And not so long ago, they had been misled into believing that he was the man responsible for the Mumbai train blasts. Whatever amazement they felt at having finally seen him in flesh and blood was buried deep under the overwhelming sense of guilt they felt at having suspected Ravi of treason, for the second time in as many months.

The silence is a little too awkward, and Mihir takes several moments to break it, 'I–if I may ask sir . . . how?'

Ravi chuckles before proceeding to explain, 'The Examiner wasn't in Dharavi just to test you. He'd been there for several months already, keeping a close watch on the man we apprehended, Basharat. Although we had nothing concrete, there were many leads suggesting his close involvement with the Lashkar-e-Hind. So anyway, when Omar was instructed to go to Dharavi, I was convinced that this was the man who would come to receive the money. Going by the cryptic message at the end, I also began to suspect that they had realized somehow that Omar is in our custody. The Examiner will tell you the rest of the story, and I want you to pay very careful attention. It's going to be nothing short of a masterclass.'

The Examiner picks up the narrative, 'When Ravi sir shared the contents of the call, I knew exactly what their plan was. The precise timing, 12.25 p.m. was a giveaway. In Islam, one is required to offer namaz six times a day. The third, what we call Zuhr, is the mid-day offering. It is usually performed at 12.35 p.m. So, it would give them ten minutes to . . . what was it he said, yes, follow the devout . . . basically disappear into the mosque. Now in the last year or so that I've spent undercover in Dharavi, I wasn't just keeping track of Basharat. I was also cultivating sources and taking important people into confidence. One among them was the mullah of the mosque, who I knew for a fact was being wooed by Basharat, under the hope that he would assist him in radicalizing Muslim youth in Dharavi. You've been there, you know how terrible the living conditions are. I knew it wouldn't be that hard to mislead already disillusioned youngsters. If it came from a position of religious authority, then it could turn into a potentially disastrous scenario.

'And so, it was very important to prevent the mullah from joining hands with them. But as I was to find out, the mullah had been averse to the idea from the very beginning and had openly threatened Basharat that he would report him to the police. But that wasn't such a good idea either, and so I gradually cultivated the mullah and tutored him. Over time, he reached out on his own to Basharat and pledged allegiance, winning his loyalty in the process. That is what gave them the confidence, even while being aware that we had their man in our custody, that they could find a way to have him escape. When Basharat and Omar disappeared into the mosque, and went to the mullah for help, he asked them to sit inside his chamber, while he figured out a way to get them out. But that, of course, was only a ruse. I was already inside the mosque. The mullah gave me the green signal, and I quietly whisked them away through a back alley into a waiting car that took us straight to the airport.'

'But sir, the whole disappearing act, when they vanished off the radar . . . what was the point of all of that?' Jose asks.

Ravi laughs. There is a mischievous glint in his eyes.

'I hoped you would ask, young man. That was just to freak you out, while also teaching you a useful lesson. My little way of showing you that no matter how sophisticated technology gets, the work we do rests entirely on human ingenuity and perseverance. But now we have an investigation to return to. Jose, you may head back to Insomnia. Mihir and Cyrus, I suggest that you remain here and observe while the Examiner goes over to the other side of the mirror. You might learn a thing or two.'

Crossfire

Unlike Omar, Basharat proves to be a tough nut. It has been seventy-two hours, but he hasn't disclosed any information. Nothing seems to work. 'They aren't all carved out of the same stone,' Ravi tells Cyrus and Jose in his office, 'and you have to always remember that. They might be broadly united by ideology, but they all come from very different backgrounds. They have their own different reasons for joining the ranks. Omar was easy to crack because he comes from a fairly well-to-do background and is a software engineer. He joined because of some vague romanticism about jihad, and not out of any real conviction. All it took to get him to spill the beans was to put him out of his comfort zone. But Basharat, from what our intelligence tells us, grew up in extremely miserable conditions. His father was an alcoholic who would beat him black and blue every single evening as if the perennial starvation wasn't bad enough. That's all we know of his background so far, but it's enough to suggest that none of those methods will work. Withstanding hardship is almost built into his muscle memory, to put it one way.'

Mihir nods, while Cyrus struggles to stifle a yawn. The bags under their eyes suggest most obviously that they haven't slept in days. Ravi is in no mood for pity, for he himself has barely slept recently. The phone rings. It is Subramanyam.

'Give me five minutes, Subramanyam. I will call you back.'

'No, sir. You have to hear this right now.'

'Okay, give me two minutes then.'

Ravi hangs up, despite Subramanyam's protests. Turning to Mihir and Cyrus, he continues, 'Anyway, it's a good thing that confessional testimony is not the only way of obtaining intelligence. The Examiner has returned to Mumbai, and even as we speak, a raid at Basharat's residence is underway. If we can obtain access to his email, then we might have some useful leads in hand. In the meantime, I want you to continue applying as much pressure as you can on Omar. Extract every little piece of information that he may be hiding from us. And watch out for his right palm. I've noticed that when he's bluffing, it quivers.'

A knock on the door interrupts them.

It is Subramanyam who walks in with a look of great anxiety. Without uttering a word, he walks up to Ravi's desk, picks up the remote and turns the TV on. The ominous words, 'Breaking News', are plastered all over the screen. A reporter is frantically shouting into the camera, ' . . . many facts are yet to emerge, but what we can confirm at this point is that ten minutes ago, a bomb blast was reported in Pune's affluent Koregaon Park area, about two kilometres from where I stand right now. An email was sent to our newsroom only a few minutes ago, and from what I've been hearing, to all newsrooms in the country. An unnamed spokesperson for the Lashkar-e-Hind has claimed responsibility for the attacks. We are yet to hear anything from the officials who are now beginning to arrive at the scene and have sealed off the area. I just saw scores of ambulances pass by, so it is possible that there have been casualties, but we will have to wait for official confirmation.' Ravi asks Subramanyam to turn off the TV, before banging his fist on the table. He begins pacing the room with his hands behind his back.

Addressing Subramanyam, he asks, 'Does Kale still head our Pune unit?'

Subramanyam replies in the affirmative.

'Get in touch with him and ask him to coordinate with the police commissioner immediately.'

'Any specific instructions, sir?'

'Yes, explosives. I need access to the initial analysis, ASAP . . . any forensic overlaps with the explosives used in the Mumbai blasts? Put our forensic unit in the loop, and ask them to . . . Actually, you know what, I'll speak to them myself. You speak to Kale.'

Ravi's mobile phone rings. He asks Subramanyam to see who it is. 'The big boss herself, sir,' he responds with a deep sigh. Ravi quickly returns to his desk and takes the phone from Subramanyam. Before he picks up, he asks the others to wait outside. 'You too, Subramanyam,' he adds.

The chief wastes no time exchanging pleasantries.

'I'm not calling to talk to you about the blasts, Ravi. There is something else, something that isn't all over the news channels, fortunately. Earlier this morning, four Israeli tourists were kidnapped in Kerala while they were vacationing on a houseboat. The Lashkar-e-Hind has claimed responsibility and has even sent a list of demands. One among them is the release of an individual who is in your custody, a certain Basharat Mir. We're trying all possible channels to secure the release of the hostages but prepare for the possibility of letting go of this man. This is not merely a matter of internal security but a diplomatic disaster in the making. The prime minister is absolutely furious. I know what you're thinking . . . How did they even know that he's been detained? That's the least worrying aspect of it. Going by the email they've sent, which I will forward to you immediately, they not only seem to know that he has been detained, but they also seem to know that he was arrested by an agent named Qasim Khan.'

Ravi is stunned. For once, he is lost for words.

The chief continues, 'How they know all of this is for you to find out, but it is a matter for grave concern with extraordinary repercussions. This, coupled with the blasts . . . I don't know how much longer I can shield you. I know that you are doing your best, and I continue to believe that you are the best man for the job. But things are close to reaching a point where what I believe and who I trust will cease to matter altogether. In fact, it's not just a change of leadership that we're heading towards. There are loud rumours going around . . . the government intends to completely take away the mandate of fighting terrorism from our hands, and create a separate agency altogether. Just like they took away external intelligence from us after the alleged failures of 1962.'

There is not much else to be said, and the call ends. Immediately after, the phone rings again. It is the Examiner.

* * *

As soon as they walk back into his office, Jose, Cyrus, and Mihir know that something has gone terribly wrong. There is no jovial welcome, no sarcasm, none of what they have come to associate with Ravi. It appears as if all the blood has been drained out from his face.

'Subramanyam . . .'

'Yes sir, I'm sorry. I will leave right away.'

'Bolt the door. I want you to stay.'

Subramanyam promptly bolts the door and returns to find Ravi lighting up a cigarette. He is taken aback. Ever since Ravi had heard of Subramanyam's aversion to cigarette smoke, he had always made it a point to refrain from smoking in the latter's presence. But the train of thoughts relentlessly crashing into one another inside Ravi's mind appear to have left no room for such consideration.

'Gentlemen, you have been summoned because at this moment you are only four people in C3 I can trust unconditionally. I no longer know who else is to be trusted, and in my position it is a very dangerous place to be in. What I'm about to tell you is a secret of the highest magnitude, and I expect it to stay within these four walls. Earlier this morning, a few hours before the blasts in Pune, four Israeli tourists were kidnapped in Kerala. The Lashkar-e-Hind, which has claimed responsibility for the bomb blasts as well, has sent in a list of ransom demands. Among them is the release of Basharat Mir, currently locked up in this very building. Before I go ahead, you're welcome to put forth your initial impressions. I want to know if you're seeing what I'm seeing.'

'Sir, if I may . . .' Cyrus asks. Ravi tells him to go ahead.

'It's quite clear that the target in both cases is not exactly India. Keeping aside the kidnapping, even if we just look at the bomb blast, prima facie it appears to have been an attack specifically directed at Israelis. I'm from Pune, and I know Koregaon Park. It's an area that's mostly thronged by foreigners. The specific cafe that was attacked is run by an Israeli man and his Indian wife. Even the police have now confirmed this. Adding that to the kidnappings, it's quite clear that Indians weren't the target this time around. These attacks might have been a way of expressing solidarity with the Palestinian Muslims, by sending a message to Israel.'

'You are correct, Cyrus. Our country, in this case, was merely the battleground and not the target of battle. When something like this happens, when distant conflicts spill over onto our land, one is indeed confronted with the more frustrating complexities of our work. And somewhere down the line, you can see that it lies at the root of many of the threats we face. Take the rise of militancy in Kashmir, for instance. It was the Afghan mujahideens, themselves a product of the machinations and intrigues of the Cold War, who triggered it all. But to think of this merely from a geopolitical perspective, as I too did as soon as I heard, would be a terrible mistake. There is more to it. Let me tell you why. The demands placed by the kidnappers are mostly absurd and completely impractical. They want Israel to completely withdraw from the Gaza strip, Israel to hand over Jerusalem, and so on. You would have to kidnap the prime minister of Israel to even begin to be taken seriously with such demands. I think it is only a smokescreen.

The only realistic demand, which I'm sure is what they really want, is the release of Basharat Mir.'

'But how did they even know?' Mihir interrupts.

'Well, they don't hear from their man for three days in a row, they assume that he's been detained. It's not the most implausible scenario. But that's not why I've called you here. We may perhaps have to release the man. What is truly frightening, and the real reason why I cannot trust anyone else, is that the email directly names the Examiner as the agent who apprehended Basharat. To put it in plain terms, we have a mole in our midst. This time, for real.'

A discomfiting silence engulfs the room.

'B–but it could very well have been the mullah, or a third individual who we know nothing about . . .' Jose speculates aloud.

'The mullah or any other third-party would not have known the Examiner under his real name, Qasim Khan. It would have been some fake identity.'

'Y–you don't think . . . it's the Examiner himself?' Cyrus asks.

Mihir looks at Cyrus and nods in agreement. He attempts to justify their speculation, 'I–it's not exactly implausible. A lot of things might then make sense. The ease with which the arrest happened, and then Basharat being silent because he perhaps knows he will be released soon.'

Ravi stubs his cigarette with an unseemly vengeance, almost knocking the ashtray over. 'That's enough,' he bellows, 'it seems to come almost naturally to the three of you, but I will not tolerate such strong accusations against a man who has served the nation with great integrity and honour for decades, constantly putting his life at grave danger. And for your information, just a little while ago the Examiner called. He has recovered crucial evidence from Basharat's residence, including his laptop. It will be for the people at Insomnia to dig deeper, but he has identified key correspondences in the inbox, including one with a black-market arms dealer in Ahmedabad.'

Mihir appears to be unconvinced. Gathering all his courage, he decides to speak up again, 'B-but sir, with all due respect, and please don't take this the wrong way. I am just speculating, it's purely hypothetical . . . but the Examiner's insistence on going back to Mumbai to conduct the raid himself. Maybe it's a way to tie up all loose ends and destroy any possible evidence. Perhaps the thing about the arms dealer is just a lie, just a fabrication to cover up his tracks. And most importantly, the fact that they named him in the email, wouldn't that be the easiest way to divert attention from the fact that he himself is the mole . . . I mean, which mole would willingly implicate himself? And so, we would never suspect him.'

Ravi freezes in his tracks, giving the others the impression that he is indeed considering the possibility that he had dismissed outright only a few moments ago.

'Brilliant,' he erupts, 'brilliant. That explains the one bit I couldn't figure out, which is the question of why they would specifically name the Examiner . . .'

His voice trails off, and he freezes again. The trio exchange looks of utter befuddlement, not for the first—and certainly not the last—time in their career. Even Subramanyam appears not to have the slightest clue where Ravi is going with all this.

After some moments of thought, Ravi resumes, 'It is an incredibly clever ploy, you see. By directly naming the

Examiner in the email, and not by using his codename, but his actual name . . . Qasim Khan . . . they've killed many birds with one stone. Let me explain. To begin with, they expect us to follow the exact same strand of deduction that you just came up with and conclude that the Examiner himself is the mole.'

Ravi pauses to light another cigarette. Looking at Mihir pointedly, he continues, 'The fact that he is a Muslim might only strengthen that conclusion for most people. It's an extremely convenient tale. And if we indeed end up doing what they expect us to do, which is to suspend and possibly imprison the Examiner, it will feed right into their narrative. Imagine a propaganda pamphlet, with the headline, "Honest Indian Officer Imprisoned for Being Muslim". Can you see what a powerful recruitment strategy it would make for? But there's nothing new here. These are the sorts of half-baked lies that the enemy uses to convince gullible people not just here but across the world that India is committed to persecuting Muslims. What is of immediate concern to us is that we do not follow this false trail and allow the real mole to get away. In fact, now that I come to think of it, it's probably not a mole that we're dealing with.'

'What then, sir?' Mihir asks.

'A complex game of counterintelligence kicked off by an unwitting touch of Stockholm syndrome, I'd suspect,' Ravi responds casually.

'Sorry sir, what?'

'Never mind. I'll tell you when I've figured it out. Thank you for your time, gentlemen. This meeting is over.'

* * *

A few hours pass by before Mihir and Cyrus are summoned back to Ravi's office. Jose and the Examiner are already there. The laptop that the Examiner returns with turns out to be a treasure trove. Perhaps owing to Basharat's carelessness, or the misguided confidence that he would never be apprehended, the services of Jose and his colleagues at Insomnia are hardly required. There is no security to be bypassed, and the information is all stored in plain text files requiring no decryption. In a matter of mere minutes, Basharat's plans are laid bare. The money shipped through the hawala route was to be used to procure arms and explosives from a black-market dealer in Ahmedabad. There is however no address available, only a name—Htes Radomad.

'Very simple crack. Just reverse the letters and you get Damodar Seth,' Jose announces.

'There you go, case closed. Basharat doesn't have to tell us anything,' Ravi adds.

'With all due respect, sir, I don't see how that's the end of it. I'm certain there are over a thousand Damodars in Ahmedabad alone. We can't possibly raid each of them. I suggest that we resort to the third-degree with Basharat. There is no other way,' Mihir says, playing devil's advocate.

'Patience, young man. You really do have a penchant for violent solutions, don't you? Intelligence is not a game of snakes-and-ladders where one thing leads to another, and you rely on the brute roll of the dice each time. This is more like chess, where you plan your moves well in advance and take the opponent by surprise when the time is right. Here, this is where we can find him,' Ravi responds nonchalantly, pointing to an address scribbled on his desk pad.

Before Mihir can ask further questions, Ravi continues, 'For quite some time, we've been sitting on intelligence about suspicious shipments going in and out of a seemingly abandoned warehouse on the Surat–Ahmedabad highway. Shipments come in from and go out to the Surat port, where well-greased customs officers let it bypass security screening. But as I hope you've learnt by now we don't just act on every piece of intelligence we receive. We let it accumulate in the same way that a skilled chess player would line up his bishops and knights in specific positions without necessarily attacking with each move. And so, we haven't acted yet, but now the time is right.'

Mihir is unconvinced, as is Cyrus, who speaks up this time, 'That's all well and good, sir. But you don't actually know what's in the shipments. Besides, it is perhaps safe to assume that in a large mercantile city like Ahmedabad, there are bound to be thousands of black marketeers dealing with all kinds of contraband, getting things passed through customs on the sly. How do we link it all to this Damodar Seth, whoever he is?'

'Ahmedabad municipal records indicate that the warehouse in question is registered in the name of Kantaben Patel whose husband, further inquiries revealed, is a certain Damodar Seth. Now, before you waste our time further by insisting that there could be a hundred different Damodar Seths involved in black-marketing, which is not a bad doubt to persist with, I'll let Jose answer. It is thanks to him that we can be convinced of our hunch,' Ravi responds, before looking at Jose.

'Um, so I and my colleagues at Insomnia have been going over transcripts of call intercepts of ISI functionaries, focusing on the days preceding the Mumbai bomb blasts, and now the Pune bomb blasts . . .'

'Now don't ask how we have access to call intercepts of ISI functionaries. Just listen to what he has to say,' Ravi interrupts.

Jose is evidently embarrassed by the prospect of coming across as being condescending to his friends, but continues in a polite tone, pretending not to have heard Ravi, 'We've been trying to look for patterns, to see if there is a way to predict when the next one is likely to happen. We found nothing out of the ordinary, or so we assumed, until quite literally twenty minutes ago. A few days before the Mumbai blasts, as well as before the Pune blasts, they can be heard talking to each other about whether the new recruits have visited the HR department to complete formalities. It does sound odd, but nothing out of the ordinary. But then, when I looked at what was on Basharat's laptop, it struck me immediately. HR are the initials for Htes Radomad, or Damodar Seth. Completing formalities stands for collecting explosives.'

Patting Jose on his back, Ravi turns to Cyrus and Mihir, 'So, what do you think is to be done now?'

'We go to Ahmedabad,' Mihir responds, 'and raid this warehouse.'

'Not at all,' the Examiner says, speaking up for the first time. 'You boys want to have all the fun, don't you? Now we take a backseat and let the police do their job. There's a saying we have around here, I'd be surprised if you haven't heard it at the academy—caught police, bowled intelligence. We're shadow people, and it's in our best interest that we remain out of the spotlight.'

After the others have cleared out, Ravi personally briefs the police commissioner of Ahmedabad and the home minister of Gujarat. He requests them to merely intensify surveillance for the time being and hold off a full-fledged raid until further instructions. The hostage crisis is far from being resolved, and he is worried that news of the arms seizure might only strengthen the kidnappers' resolve and lead them to take drastic measures.

It is well past midnight when the telephone in Ravi's bedroom goes off. It is the chief.

'Ravi, we've considered all options. A rescue mission is off the table, and it has been from the very start. They're holding them in a very thickly forested region of north-east Kerala, and that puts us at a massive tactical disadvantage. One misstep and they might kill the hostages. Israel is a very close ally, and the prime minister does not want to risk any diplomatic displeasure at this stage. I'm terribly sorry, and I wish there was another way, but it appears that the only option is to let go of the man in your custody.'

'But ma'am, we are talking about a man who has the blood of hundreds of innocent Indian civilians on his hands. I don't mean to compare, and I say this with all due respect, but by letting go of him, aren't we sending a message to the enemy that we care more about diplomatic displeasure than our own citizens? And if we give in this time, we'll have to give in every time. And there's nothing that we can do to prevent something like this from happening again. We can't possibly assign armed protection to every foreign tourist in the country.'

'I understand, Ravi. This is exactly what I told the prime minister. But these are his orders, and I am merely the messenger. You will have to make arrangements immediately.'

'Can't we buy more time, ma'am?'

'I'm afraid not, Ravi. We're lucky that news of this hasn't leaked out to the media yet. And we have to put an end to this before it does. I wish there was another way, and I fully share your outrage, but I hope you understand that my hands are tied.'

'I understand, ma'am. Where?'

'Baramulla, Kashmir. Just ensure that he is securely transported to the Hindon airbase by 7 a.m. I'll take it from there.'

After the chief hangs up, the fury with which Ravi bangs the receiver onto the bedside table is loud enough to wake up Rita, who is otherwise quite accustomed to sleeping like a rock through her husband's late-night phone calls.

'What happened, Ravi?' she asks.

'Politics, what else?' Ravi responds angrily before storming out into the balcony.

He spends the entire night there, repeatedly glancing at his watch as he runs through an entire pack of cigarettes. He is otherwise a rather disciplined smoker, but it is at moments like these that he can't help himself. Hours go by like this, and at the break of dawn, he finally gets up. He texts Cyrus and Mihir, asking them to assemble at the headquarters in thirty minutes. Rita insists that he eats breakfast before leaving, but he turns her down. As he picks out clothes from his wardrobe, the phone rings. It is the chief again.

'Ravi . . .'

'I am on my way to the headquarters, ma'am. Everything is on track, as instructed.'

'No, listen to me. You don't have to. The most extraordinary thing has happened. The hostages have escaped, all four of them. They overpowered their captors late last evening, and just ten minutes ago I received a phone call from the DGP of Kerala.'

'Are you being serious, ma'am? But how?'

'In all the scenarios we drew up, there's one thing we overlooked, the possibility of the hostages escaping. Now, it's standard operating procedure to omit the possibility, especially when we're talking about armed captors, but we didn't take into account the fact that these are Israeli hostages we're talking about. Do you get it?'

'No ma'am, sorry I don't understand what the connection is.'

'Israel has conscription. All adults above the age of eighteen are mandatorily drafted into the army for a few years. They're trained for all sorts of combat scenarios, including . . .'

'. . . escaping enemy captivity,' Ravi chips in.

'Exactly. And they didn't just run away. They also managed to snatch two AK-47s from their captors. You're a man with great imagination, Ravi, you know what this means don't you?'

'Not only do we not have to let go of Basharat Mir, forensics can look at the guns and compare them with what we're going to seize from Ahmedabad. We connect the trail. This is huge.'

The chief chuckles and compliments Ravi on the good work before hanging up.

'Rita!' Ravi yells out in jubilation. 'How about that breakfast you were talking about?'

* * *

At Ravi's residence in the evening, the entire team—Ravi, the Examiner, Mihir, Jose and Cyrus—watches the news on TV with eagerness. The DGP of Gujarat is speaking to the media, with the home minister and the police commissioner of Ahmedabad by his side.

'I am proud to announce that the Gujarat Police has seized a record haul of explosives, arms, and ammunition from a warehouse in Ahmedabad. Acting on a tip off, we have pursued this rigorously for several months now, and under the able leadership of the honourable home minister, who personally supervised today's raid, we believe we have neutralized a major . . .'

'Enough work for today,' Ravi announces, turning off the TV.

'Please, sir. The pride on their faces is such a treat to watch. Let's just finish watching,' Cyrus protests.

'Oh, you'll get used to it. It's the same story every time,' Ravi dismisses him. 'I have something more exciting for all of you. Some months ago, when you were here for the first time, when you were discreetly eyeing my liquor cabinet, I told you that you'd have to earn the privilege of even catching a whiff of the fine stuff. Well, I believe you have done so today. All of you. And not just a whiff . . .'

Ravi instructs Shabbir to fetch some glasses. Picking out a bottle of expensive Scotch from his cabinet, Ravi insists on personally pouring out the drinks.

'I propose a toast,' the Examiner says, holding out his glass. 'To the shadow people!'

'To the shadow people,' they all exclaim in unison.

'And to Octopus, lest we forget,' Ravi adds, 'If not for him, none of this would have happened and we'd still be stumbling in the dark.'

'Who is this person? And what's the story behind how he became Octopus?' Cyrus asks.

'That's a story I will carry with me to my grave. And the same should be the case with you. Never, ever, speak of your deep-cover agents unless absolutely necessary. And even then, withhold as many details as possible. It takes very little to put their lives in grave danger. I try to withhold details from myself as well.'

'I'm sorry, sir. I don't exactly follow. How can you withhold details from yourself?'

'To give you an example, I myself no longer remember Octopus' real name, even though it was I who recruited him. From the very beginning, I referred to him even in my thoughts, by his nom de guerre. So, even if I were to be badly tortured by the enemy, I won't be in a position to reveal his identity or of any of my deep agents. Not even if I wanted to. But Octopus will always hold a special place . . .'

Ravi is interrupted by Ranger who dashes into the living room. He runs around excitedly and leaps at each of them, his way of welcome. Jose who is afraid of dogs, recoils slightly, but is put at ease by Rita who walks in with Ranger's leash. 'Don't worry. He's the friendliest creature alive. Wouldn't harm a fly. In fact, we're worried that he'll wag his tail and do nothing even when an actual burglar breaks in.'

Ravi smiles and introduces her to his officers, 'Gentlemen, this is my wife, Rita. Rita, these are my musketeers. Cyrus, Mihir, and Jose. Qasim, you have met. I would have introduced you all to my sons as well, but they're both away. My older one, Saurav, lives in Bangalore. He is finishing his MBA at IIM–B. And Abhinav, the younger fellow, lives with us but is at a friend's place right now. They grow up fast, I tell you.'

Rita quips in light-hearted jest, 'Especially when you aren't around most of the time. But of course, he'd always come home to tuck them into bed and read out stories from the *Panchatantra*. He is an expert on exotic animals, after all, with friends called Octopus, Anaconda, Takshak, etc.'

They all burst out laughing except Mihir.

'Does ma'am know about your agents, sir,' queries Mihir.

'I admire your sharp observation, kid. And that is why you are here in C3. We need emergency communication channels with our agents apart from the regular ones. Panditji is our regular channel with Octopus. Both the channels have a number of cut-outs with the last interface like Panditji. These emergency nodes have my secure mobile number. The number of the final node is saved as agents' nom de plume so that I do not have to tax my brain. Rita would have seen these names flashing on my mobile sometimes. Beyond that, she does not know anything. At least I have been able to keep few things hidden from my wife.' Ravi finishes with a wink.

Rita smiles. 'Anyway, I will leave you all to your little celebration. Sorry about Ranger. It was very nice meeting all of you,' she tells them, before turning towards her husband, 'And Ravi, please don't bore them with more shop talk. They're young boys. I'm sure they have other interests.'

'She's right,' Ravi tells them, after she leads a reluctant Ranger out of the living room into the garden, 'Enough work-talk for today. Since we were talking about toasts and proposals, you have to tell me about your personal lives. By personal lives, I don't mean your families. What I mean is, your love lives.'

His eyes acquire an all too familiar glint of mischief. The three of them grin nervously.

'Oh, come on. Don't pretend like you've never been in love. We might be shadow people, but we're people at the end of the day. So, you don't have to feel embarrassed about it. It's the most natural thing in the world. Bring it out. Girlfriends, love affairs, crushes, I'm all ears,' Ravi prods them.

Cyrus downs his drink in one go, and volunteers, 'Um, so I have a girlfriend. We've been together for a long time. Since high school, actually. And on my next trip to Pune, whenever that is, I intend on asking her to marry me.'

Ravi smiles approvingly.

'And what is her name, this girlfriend of yours?'

'Gehna, sir. She's a journalist.'

'Well, that's good news. If we ever get into trouble with the press, we know who to contact.

'And you two, fall in love. For that is the only way to handle tension.'

Mihir and Jose look awkward and wonder how Ravi knew they weren't seeing anyone.

'Talking of love and romance, sir', adds the Examiner, 'I recall that moonless night when we were sitting by the sewer canal waiting for an Al-Qaeda suspect who never came. To beat the boredom, you recited a romantic poem.'

'Oh! that was an attempt to divert attention from the bites of elephant-sized mosquitoes. But such is the power of love that even its imagination can take you away from all kinds of pain, physical or mental. I think the poem was an extract from *Urvashi*, a magnum opus of Ramdhari Singh Dinkar.'

They continue talking well into the night until Ravi says, 'It is already 3 a.m., shall we call it a day, guys? 'See you tomorrow at 9.30 a.m. sharp in my office.'

'Thank you, sir.'

As they exit along the driveway, Jose remarks, 'How does boss know about our personal lives?'

His query is heard by Examiner. 'You are foolish to think that you are in C3 only on account of your professional skills. Boss has done a 360-degree evaluation of you all, including me. He has all the facts about us. So do not try to fool him.'

Falcon

From his drawer Ravi pulls out a box of chalk and walks to a blackboard that sits inconspicuously wedged between two large filing cabinets in a corner of the room. 'Can somebody draw a map of India for me, and mark out Thrikkaipatta, Mumbai and Baramulla?' he asks.

Cyrus walks up to the board and charts out a rough map and marks three dots. 'It's not accurate . . . actually it's wide off the mark,' Mihir immediately observes. 'How does it matter? A rough sketch should do. We'll get the idea, I'm sure,' Cyrus responds. Mihir is irked, 'How does it matter? Really? It's not just the locations that you've gotten wrong, even the outline. Going by the map you drew, I'd be a Pakistani citizen, because you only included Jammu and not Kashmir. And Arunachal Pradesh would belong to China. Tens of thousands, including my own father, have given up their lives to maintain these borders. I think it bloody well matters.'

'Just relax, man. We're just trying to connect the dots here. For God's sake, I'm not actually modifying the borders by drawing them incorrectly,' Cyrus tries to reassure him. Mihir will have none of it, and snaps back immediately, 'Let me connect the dots for you, mister third-generation spy. There is a task most fundamental, something that lies right at the heart of everything that we do. It's the only thing that truly matters. Preserving the territorial integrity of our country.'

Ravi intervenes, 'Seriously, the two of you, cut it out. Mihir, I fully respect your sentiments and I stand by it wholeheartedly, but you're not doing yourself or the country any favours by tearing into Cyrus like that. If you're so offended, and I'm not saying you shouldn't be, then why don't you just go up to the board and draw an accurate map of India, and then we'll all be happy.' Although Ravi says this light-heartedly, it is perhaps only to ease the tension. Something in his eyes conveys a secret admiration for Mihir's forthrightness.

Mihir snatches the chalk from Cyrus, and in less than two minutes draws a precise map of India.

'Well, well . . . would you look at that? Where on earth did you learn to draw such an accurate map?' Ravi chuckles, evidently impressed.

'Srinagar. The place that Cyrus had decided a few moments ago to hand over to Pakistan. My father never believed in lip service, and certainly didn't believe in hypocrisy. He believed sincerely that Kashmir was, is, and will always be an integral part of India. Even before I joined school, while other kids my age were busy drawing fruits and animals, he taught me to draw the Indian map. I practised every day for years and . . .'

'I'm sure it's a very fascinating story, but could we get to work?' Cyrus interrupts snappily, eager to get back at Mihir.

'Okay, that's enough. After we're done here, you'll both apologize to each other, and that'll be the end of it. Instead of this pointless infighting, let's turn our energies to fighting the enemy,' Ravi admonishes sternly.

'Sorry, sir,' Mihir and Cyrus mumble in unison.

Ravi pays them no heed and turns to Jose. 'Jose, would you care to brief us?'

Jose, equally eager to put an end to the unexpected hostility amongst his friends, walks up to the board and begins briefing them, 'So, we have Thrikkaipatta in Kerala, Mumbai in Maharashtra, and Baramulla in Kashmir. Thrikkaipatta is where the kidnapped tourists were held, and where the demand for Basharat's release originated. Not just that, we have tracked down the satellite phone that Omar had contacted, and that too appears to have been located in Thrikkaipatta. Mumbai is where the emails claiming credit on behalf of the Lashkar-e-Hind have been originating. It is also the site of the first bomb blasts, as well as the place where we apprehended Basharat. And Baramulla is where they wanted Basharat to be sent in exchange for the release of the abducted tourists.'

Ravi takes over, 'Thank you, Jose. That was a sufficiently elaborate account of where we stand with regard to the Lashakar-e-Hind. So, gentlemen, any thoughts on how we must proceed?'

'This place in Kerala, Thirik . . . Thirikipatna' Mihir ventures forth.

'Thrikkaipatta,' Jose immediately corrects him.

'Right. So, if we have very accurate coordinates, why don't we involve the police or the NSG and stage a raid? They don't know that we know.'

Ravi dismisses the suggestion, 'They don't know that we tracked down satellite phone records, but they do very well know that four hostages escaped from captivity and would have revealed their whereabouts to the police. It's been well over two days. That's more than enough time for them to have shifted location. Besides, the place we're talking about is several square kilometres of dense forest. The local police did their scouting and found nothing.'

'What about Mumbai?' Cyrus asks.

'All we know is that the emails, prima facie, are originating from Mumbai. We don't yet have an exact IP address. As you might imagine, it's very cleverly routed and rerouted. We need more time to work our way through the trail,' Jose responds.

Ravi continues, 'And that leaves us with Baramulla. Mihir, of course, needs no lessons on this, but the two of you . . . if you paid any attention to lectures in history and geopolitics at the academy, or if you've been reading the newspapers, you would know that it is a city that carries enormous historical and strategic baggage. It's precariously close to the border and is an extremely important point of entry for infiltrators from across. My hunch is that when they wanted Basharat to be released in Baramullah, they wanted him to cross over into Pakistani territory. And what does that tell us?'

Mihir takes a shot, 'That the Lashkar-e-Hind has been propped up by the ISI?'

Ravi takes a few moments to think. Lighting up a cigarette, he begins, 'Yes and no. It is an indisputable fact that all Islamic fundamentalist organizations working against India are in some way or the other backed by the ISI. The money, the arms, it all comes from across the border. But what is distinct about the LeH is that it seems to be operating out of India at a fundamental level. I'll tell you what I mean by that.

Other Islamic terrorist organizations we've tackled in the past have had little units, what in our parlance are called sleeper cells, strewn across India. But the higher rungs have always been located either in Pakistan, or at the fringes of Kashmir, from where they can quickly escape into Pakistan at the slightest hint of trouble. Naive and vulnerable young men are brainwashed into entering the actual line of fire, but the leaders will never expose themselves to such risks, preferring to control things from a safe distance.'

'That's why Bin Laden's still at large, despite billions of dollars being spent on attempts to capture him,' Cyrus interrupts.

'Correct. You see, the only way to fully neutralize a terrorist organization is by taking down the leadership. Everything quickly disintegrates if you bring down those at the top. Like chess, again. You don't win or lose based on how many pawns you've conquered, but on whether or not you've managed to capture the king. And that's precisely why the war on terror is turning out to be such a prolonged one. We can capture and kill all the pawns, but it's very difficult to capture the king. There are very complex political and diplomatic reasons that underlie all of this. If the leaders of a terrorist organization are based in a foreign state, and that foreign state is hand-in-glove with the organization, as is the case with Pakistan, it's safe to assume that they'll never cooperate. And to actually go into a foreign state to capture or kill somebody without the state's consent would constitute an act of war. Nobody wants that. Two of the most populous countries in the world, both nuclear armed, it would be an absolute disaster. Which is why we're often helpless, even when we know exactly where a wanted militant leader is hiding.

'I have a strong feeling going by what we know so far, that the leadership of the LeH has been based out of India all along. Kerala, to be specific. It's an altogether new modus operandi. We can't wait until we have more clarity about the Mumbai connection. One of you needs to go to Baramulla, figure out what's happening and cultivate fresh sources of intelligence. We already have plenty of them in that region, but the old ones are obviously either in the dark or have been compromised. Otherwise, it wouldn't have taken us so long to figure this out.'

'I'll go,' Mihir volunteers straightaway. 'I know the language, I know the geography.'

Ravi shoots him down immediately, 'That is precisely why you will not go. Unless you have some sort of a suicidal wish. Your father was a fairly well-known man in those parts, and somebody or the other is bound to recognize you. You will stay right here and continue interrogating the two men in custody until something concrete comes up on the Mumbai front. Cyrus, you will have to go. And we don't have time to waste.'

Ravi senses some hesitation on Cyrus's face. 'What is it?' he asks.

'Nothing sir. I'm good to go,' Cyrus responds.

'No, tell me. You seem hesitant. What is it?'

'I-I was hoping to fly down to Pune over the weekend, propose to my girlfriend. I didn't tell her that, but we'd made some pretty big plans. But honestly, I'll cancel. It's no big deal. Nothing compared to this, anyway.'

'Excellent, that's what I was hoping to hear. Meet Madan Singh straightaway. He will groom you, train you, bring you up to speed . . . basically, whatever's necessary. Shouldn't take more than a day or two since this isn't exactly your first mission. And if I remember correctly, you did spend a couple of years in Kashmir as a kid, didn't you? When your father was posted there?'

'That is correct, sir.'

'Great. As for . . .'

There is a knock on the door.

'Sir . . .'

It is Subramanyam.

'Come in,' Ravi yells out.

'Sir, the chief just called. There's a meeting in an hour's time,' Subramanyam announces as he walks in.

'Just give me a minute,' Ravi replies, before returning to face the trio, 'This meeting is over. I will get in touch if there's anything. Thank you for your time, gentlemen.'

'Yes, Subramanyam. Meeting in an hour's time. What's on the agenda?' Ravi asks, after the others have left.

'No specified agenda, sir.'

'And who else will be at the meeting?'

'No one else, sir. But the chief's secretary offered me a helpful hint. Just before her meeting with you, she has one scheduled with "him".'

Ravi sighs.

'Him. I see. What does my horoscope indicate, Subramanyam?'

* * *

Ravi walks into the chief's office only to find that Anil is still inside.

'Good to see you, Ravi. It has been a long time,' Anil says, stretching his hand out.

'Good to see you too, sir,' Ravi responds, shaking his hand.

'Oh, enough with the formalities and the sir business. Just call me Anil. I'm senior to you only in rank, but you pretty much run the show around here,' Anil exclaims with a smirk, continuing to shake Ravi's hand with great vigour. Ravi flashes a wide grin and gently eases himself out of the handshake. He chooses not to say anything in response.

'Anyway, madam, I will take your leave now. Thank you for your time. And Ravi, it was a pleasure seeing you, as always,' Anil says, as he proceeds to walk out the door.

Ravi waits for Anil to leave, and then responds in a soft, mocking tone, 'Oh, pleasure's entirely mine.'

Sarita watches on with a hint of amusement. As she looks at him, her expression turns serious.

'So, Ravi. Let me get to it straightaway. Many months ago, in this very office, I assigned you full charge of getting to the bottom of the Mumbai train blasts. More importantly, as it went without saying then, as it goes without saying now, you were tasked with preventing a repeat. It is no secret that you haven't exactly been up to the mark on both counts. Now I understand that this is not something that can be accomplished overnight, and indeed, I personally believe that you have done a fairly good job so far, and we are well on track. But as I would expect you to understand, not all of it is up to me. I might be your boss, but I have bosses, and they have bosses and so on. The general sentiment at the home ministry and the PMO is that we aren't doing enough. You're not going to lose your position as the head of C3, nor are you going to be taken off the mission, although that was very much on the cards, especially after the events of the last seventy-two hours. I put my foot down and insisted, as I had at the beginning, that you were and continue to be our best bet.'

'Thank you, ma'am.'

'But having done that, I also had to come up with an alternative, just to be seen as doing more if nothing else. And so, I have also decided to bring Anil on board. Before you can protest, let me assure you that you will continue to run your show independently. You will still be reporting directly to me. Anil will lead a parallel operation, also reporting directly to me. All I expect from you is cooperation and sharing of intelligence. I have spoken to Anil as well, and the expectation of cooperation and sharing of intelligence will be mutual. Can I count on you to do the needful, Ravi?'

'Of course, ma'am. Whatever you think is best.'

'Great. Now that this is out of the way, tell me, where do we stand? Is this a homegrown organization that we're dealing with?'

'Well, it's not exactly homegrown or indigenous, ma'am. Over the last month we've intercepted the money, we've intercepted the arms, all coming from across the border. It's something in between homegrown and foreign, something unprecedented. Whatever we choose to call it, it is a terrifying reality that we must face up to. If the higher rungs of the LeH have indeed been based out of India all this while, as I suspect, it signifies something ominous. It's not just provocation they're after this time around, but full-blown conflict. But I'm confident that we're very close to achieving major success.'

* * *

Cyrus takes a taxi from Srinagar to Baramulla. It is a rather short journey, lasting a little over an hour during which he rehearses the lies that will provide him cover. Although it was a long time ago, Cyrus still remembers a little of what Kashmir was like in his childhood. His family had stayed in Anantnag for three years, where his father had been under cover as a PWD inspector. This was when militant separatism was in its infancy, and Kashmir was still a vibrant hub teeming with multicultural richness. The Kashmir that Cyrus now visits is only a pale shadow of what it was like all those years ago. People still go about their routine as always, but the ominous presence of barbed wire and army checkposts, scattered all across the valley, serve as a stark reminder that normalcy is a fragile construct.

At Kanispora village, only a few kilometres away from Baramulla district headquarters, a barricade forces his vehicle to stop. An armed soldier walks up to the taxi. After inspecting the driver's documents, he knocks at the rear and asks for the window to be rolled down.

'ID, please,' the soldier demands.

Cyrus retrieves his wallet and pulls out a Pune University ID that identifies him as Shaakib Khan, a doctoral student in Sociology.

'Purpose of visit?' the soldier asks.

'I'm doing research on public perception of Indian governance in the border-regions of Kashmir. I'm here as part of my field work,' Cyrus replies.

The soldier looks at him suspiciously, a response that Cyrus was expecting. While conceiving his cover, Madan Singh had warned Cyrus that the army would be sceptical of such a project, for it was often the case that such projects served as a cover for separatist activists and intellectuals to move freely even in the most heavily militarized parts of Kashmir. It was a clever gamble, for although the army would be sceptical, this cover would make it easier for Cyrus to win over locals, particularly those with separatist leanings. In any case, he had come prepared to allay the army's suspicions.

'Please get out of the car and follow me. Kindly carry all relevant documents with you,' the soldier tells him, and Cyrus promptly does as instructed. The soldier leads him to a makeshift camp a few metres away from the check post and asks him to wait outside.

He returns with a tall, turbaned man with a large pair of binoculars around his neck. He introduces himself as Major Balvinder Singh and asks Cyrus about the NGO he works for.

'Not an NGO, sir. I'm affiliated to the University of Pune as a PhD student,' Cyrus responds.

'Are you aware that this is a high-security zone, and such studies are not permitted?' Maj. Singh asks him.

'Yes, Major, I understand. I have obtained special clearance from the home ministry,' Cyrus replies, handing him his permission letter. Maj. Singh is surprised and takes a few moments to inspect it.

'Such permissions are not usually given, especially with a project that so explicitly appears to be of an anti–India nature. I hope you will pardon me for having my doubts, and please do not take it the wrong way, but I would like to verify the authenticity of this letter before letting you pass. As you know very well, this region is a powder keg waiting to explode, and we cannot take any chances,' Maj. Singh tells Cyrus.

'Of course, Major. You have to do your job,' Cyrus replies.

'This will take some time, so I think it would be best for you to clear your dues with the taxi driver and send him on his way,' Maj. Singh tells him, before instructing a subordinate to go over and fax the letter to Delhi.

Cyrus pays the taxi driver, takes his luggage, and returns to the camp, where Maj. Singh is waiting for him. 'Don't worry, once this is all over, we'll drop you at your location. In any case, if it turns out that the letter is fake, you'll have to come with us,' Maj. Singh jokes. 'But on a serious note, do not worry at all. This is just procedure that we have to follow. Please take a seat and be relaxed until then.'

Cyrus is touched by the officer's gentlemanly etiquette. 'Are you fond of birds, Mr Khan?' the Major asks, peering at the sky through his binoculars.

'Not particularly, Major,' Cyrus replies.

'Well, too bad for you. Kashmir's a real heaven on earth if you're into birdwatching like I am . . . common, rare, endangered, you'll find all sorts here,' Maj. Singh adds, his eyes still fixated on the binoculars. 'There, you see that,' he points to a white bird flying at a considerable distance from where they are, 'that's a Siberian crane. Extremely rare bird, there are probably only five thousand of them left in the entire world.'

Without the use of binoculars, Cyrus can only see a white nondescript flying object. 'Ahh, there's no use. You're not interested anyway,' Maj. Singh sighs, as he takes a seat next to Cyrus, 'So tell me more about this project of yours. What exactly do you intend to uncover?'

'It may have come across wrongly when I explained it in brief earlier. Basically, I'm trying to look at how approachable and how honest government officials serving in the border areas of Kashmir are in the eyes of the public. By governance, I don't mean governance in the broader sense of being under Indian rule, but about the efficacy of local officials. To achieve this, I'm hoping to speak to as many locals as possible. Just to be very clear, I am as pro-India as one can get, and I think that listening to the people and what they have to say is the most important step towards doing what's best for them,' Cyrus tells him, merely parroting a well-rehearsed explanation.

'Interesting. Do let me know what you uncover. I've been in this area for almost six years now, and when you stay in one place for so long, you develop a certain attachment to the place. I'm particularly interested in this one official at the revenue department. He's the most corrupt man you'll ever find. Not a single file moves unless you grease his palms, doesn't matter how poor you are or how badly you need something. He's a heartless son of a bitch, to put it simply. He does it all very smoothly, through some sort of a letterbox arrangement, so there's never any evidence.

'He's like a falcon, that man. Deadly birds of prey they are, in case you don't know. They can see better than most

birds, fly faster than most birds, and so you just can't catch
hold of them. Nobody has bothered to complain about him
either, because everybody just assumes that this is how things
generally are. But that's not the only reason why I'm interested
in him. I've often spotted him at the wrong places with the
wrong people, and something tells me he is up to no good,'
Maj. Singh tells Cyrus.

'You mean to say he is associated with anti-India groups?'
Cyrus asks, his interest fully piqued.

'Well, that's the thing. I've noticed that there are two
kinds of anti-India people around here. The first kind is
those who wear their separatism on their sleeve and are
unapologetically open about it. They're even prepared
to die for their cause. I prefer them because you at least
know who they are and can accordingly take action. And
then there are those who nurture these sentiments in the
shadows. They're spineless creatures who have absolutely
no integrity. Like this man I was telling you about. He
works for the Indian government, draws his salary from the
Indian treasury, and cares deeply about being seen in public
as pro-India. He would never want to be openly associated
with any separatist figure because his extended family is
dispersed across India and he would never want them to
know. The shame and disgrace alone would kill him. And
yet, I suspect that he is channelling funds for organizations
across the border, and might even be recruiting for them,'
Maj. Singh replies.

Cyrus is all ears, thrilled at having unexpectedly stumbled
on an ideal candidate for infiltration. 'Why won't you take
action?' he asks.

'There is no evidence whatsoever, and on these matters you have to tread lightly. If we apprehend the man, a government employee no less, without any solid evidence, it can easily feed into the separatist propaganda and further alienate the locals who might not exactly have an opinion on these things,' Maj. Singh replies.

'Major, would you mind telling me who this man is, so I can specifically seek information on him when I do my surveys?' Cyrus pushes his luck.

Maj. Singh erupts into laughter. 'Nice try, young man,' he says. 'But there is no way I would do that. I don't even know at this point if you are who you claim to be. I might have said too much already, and I better get going. I will come back after we've heard from Delhi. Please remain here until then.' Left to himself, Cyrus toys with the idea of revealing his real identity and the purpose of his visit to the officer. After all, his cooperation and assistance would save him precious time. Cyrus decides to give it some more time and thought.

After over an hour, the subordinate finally returns with a faxed confirmation from the home ministry affirming that the letter is indeed authentic. The Major returns and pats Cyrus on his back, 'My apologies, Mr Khan, but procedure is procedure. The undersecretary responded with not just a confirmation of the letter's authenticity, but also a request to extend all possible cooperation. Clearly, your work is of some importance. To make up for the inconvenience caused to you, and also to take our conversation forward, I'd like to invite you to join me for lunch. It is already way past lunchtime anyway.' Cyrus hasn't eaten in several hours and gladly accepts the invitation.

The officers' mess is almost deserted by the time they reach. Cyrus broaches the topic again, as soon as they have settled down, 'I'm sorry to go off-topic, Major Singh, but I'm really intrigued by this revenue department official you were talking about, the man you compared to a falcon. He is exactly the sort of person that I'm interested in studying public perceptions of. It would be really useful to me if you could give me his name. You can count on me to keep your disclosure fully confidential.'

'You're a researcher, aren't you? You should be able to figure it out if you spend enough time talking to people. I've given you enough clues already, and you have all the time in the world. It's not like national security depends on your study, with all due respect,' Maj. Singh replies.

Cyrus lets out a deep sigh. 'Fair enough, Major. I will not press you any further.'

Cold Start

'Right here in Delhi, beneath our noses, the men we seek so desperately have come to hide. It's astonishing how something like that could escape anyone's attention. But now that we know, there is no time to waste. Before this too leaks out and they get away, I suggest that we act, and act now,' Anil rages as he concludes his briefing. The accusatory look in his eyes as he stares at Ravi is unmistakable.

Sarita listens keenly, while Ravi looks completely unconvinced. 'If this is correct, then it really is worrisome. But to be very honest, I have my doubts, sir. Would you mind telling me exactly where you're getting this information from?' Ravi chimes in, exercising great restraint.

'Come on Ravi, I cannot give you my exact source, if that's what you're asking. All I can tell you is that it is somebody very close to the LeH leadership,' Anil responds with a triumphant flair.

'With all due respect, sir, if this is somebody who's infiltrated LeH, why have we been completely in the dark in the past? Why didn't this source alert you about the blasts? Can we be completely certain that this is credible information?' Ravi is in no mood to yield without putting up a challenge.

'I suppose my source didn't know either, but now he does. It has taken him time to earn their trust, you can't expect that to happen overnight,' Anil stands his ground.

Having made their positions clear, both Anil and Ravi look towards Sarita for arbitration. 'What is it that makes you doubt this information, Ravi?' she asks, before adding 'and don't mince any words. Whatever it is that's making you hesitate, lay it out as plainly as possible.'

'Well, ma'am, it may very well be the case that Anil sir is right, but perhaps we shouldn't act so hastily. Perhaps we should investigate further. I'm not suggesting that we don't act at all. Since Anil sir has definite information about their coordinates, we can maintain intensive surveillance so that they don't get away. But at the same time, to swoop in immediately may be too premature, especially considering that this is Chandni Chowk we're talking about. I don't have to point out that it is among the most densely populated areas in the country, if not the world. One misstep and we run the risk of civilian casualties. And it could all be a trap, especially considering that this is a source that has . . .'

Anil does not take kindly to Ravi's words. 'Premature? These are dreaded terrorists we're talking about, not some small-time hawala operators or arms dealers. Every moment we let them remain out there, we run the risk of another bomb blast. And if you do not recall what I said in my briefing, it's the Parliament that they're looking to target this time. You're welcome to have your doubts Ravi, but you'll have to keep them to yourself. I'm not going to let another bomb blast happen, not on my watch.'

Sarita raises her palm, as if to ask Anil to watch his temper.

'Gentlemen, please. Let's not allow our emotions to take over. Anil, keep up the excellent work. We have a one-on-one meeting scheduled for the afternoon anyway. Let's take this forward then. You may get back to work now. I would like to spend a little more time speaking to Ravi.'

On his way out, Anil bids goodbye only to the chief. He refuses even to make eye contact with Ravi. Sarita waits for a few moments and begins chuckling. 'I'll never understand what it is with the two of you. I sometimes feel like I'm the headmistress of a school. God knows how the two of you will manage being in the same organization after I retire.'

Ravi smiles awkwardly. 'I hope you understand that there's nothing personal underlying my hesitation, ma'am. It's coming from a purely professional place.'

'I know Ravi, don't worry. And so does Anil, let me assure you. Anyway, coming back to the matter at hand . . . while your objections are perfectly valid, I must admit that I think there is some merit to Anil's plan. We cannot afford to be indecisive, not when the stakes are this high. Yes, there is the risk of civilian casualties, but let me put it very bluntly, a few civilian casualties versus the very embodiment of this nation's sovereignty, the Parliament. At this stage, it is not a risk we can afford to take at all.'

'But, ma'am, it's quite absurd to think that anybody could even pull off an attack on the Parliament. I mean, not after 2001. It's impossible to carry even a small blade inside without being frisked and questioned.'

'Ravi, you've made your point, and I've heard it. When I told you after Anil came on board that you would continue to enjoy complete autonomy, I think I also made it very clear that I expected it to be mutual. You pursue your leads, Anil pursues his, and that's the end of it. Now tell me about your own leads. Where do we stand?'

'I'm terribly sorry, ma'am, I didn't mean to trespass. As for where my team stands, we've been closely pursuing the digital trail. Every bomb blast has been followed immediately by an email claiming responsibility. As you would expect, it is very carefully routed and rerouted, but we can now say with certainty that the emails have been originating in Mumbai. We are very close to obtaining very precise coordinates, and once that happens, it will be the most concrete lead thus far. And this individual, or group of individuals, sending these emails clearly must be very intimately enmeshed in the leadership tiers of the LeH. This we can be very confident of because all the emails have been sent at the exact same time as the blasts themselves. If we get to this individual, or group of individuals, it's our most realistic chance of getting to the masterminds behind all of this.'

'That's excellent, Ravi. And what about the physical trail . . . what about Baramulla?'

* * *

Cyrus waits outside the large stone arch that marks the entrance to the Baramulla deputy commissioner's office, a large complex that houses much of the district's administrative apparatus, including the revenue department. While Maj. Singh hadn't divulged specific details, he was still very thankful to have received such a valuable lead during his first conversation in Baramulla.

He had been coming to the deputy commissioner's office for several days, had spoken to many locals entering and exiting the building, but they were all too caught up with their own problems to pay any heed to his vague questions about corruption and efficiency. One man, who had enthusiastically responded to his questions at first, had merely laughed at the more pointed queries. 'Everybody is corrupt, saab. Why are you wasting my time and yours?' he had responded, putting his palm against his forehead.

As he stands outside for the umpteenth day in a row, he realizes that it is a foolish plan. He decides that he has been a little too sincere to his cover and must explore alternative options. He is deeply engrossed in his thoughts, his eyes almost shut, when an armed constable comes up to him and shakes him by his shoulders.

'I've seen you loitering around here for many days, trying to talk to people. You clearly do not seem to be from here. What is all this nonsense?'

'I'm a researcher, sir. I have permission from the home ministry.'

'Researcher? Home ministry? Do you take me for a fool? Save your explanations for the SHO. Get on my bike right now.'

'Here we go again,' Cyrus thinks to himself as he is forced to get on the constable's old, rusted motorcycle.

A long wait lies in store at the police station, as the SHO has been summoned to Srinagar for a meeting. Cyrus is asked to sit on the ground, right next to the entrance. The worn-out flooring is extremely cold, but it barely bothers Cyrus who has been trained to deal with much worse conditions. Restless as always, Cyrus decides to strike a conversation with the man seated next to him. As it turns out, he, too, is awaiting the SHO's arrival. But he is unwilling to say anything more than that, despite Cyrus's many attempts. The constable who has brought Cyrus to the station notices this. Picking up his lathi, he begins to walk towards Cyrus, muttering curses under his breath. After admonishing the sentry for turning a blind eye, he wields his lathi and lands a heavy-handed blow on Cyrus's knees. Cyrus barely flinches, which infuriates the constable even more, leading him to wield the lathi a few more times.

'Sopori . . .'

Halfway into another heavy-handed swinging of his lathi, the constable freezes in his position. He quickly puts aside the lathi, stiffens his body and launches into a full-blown saluting position. It is the SHO who has just returned from Srinagar.

'Who are these two?'

'S-sir, this man here was loitering suspiciously outside the DC office. For many days he has been stopping people going in or coming out and asking them weird questions. And the other is Owais, you might remember him, sir.'

'Owais?'

'The charas dealer, sir. He got out on bail only last month and has started dealing again. I caught him red-handed, sir, outside the Government Medical College.'

'Oh, him. Lock him up, for now. I'll deal with him later. Bring this other man in for now. There better be a good reason for why you were hitting him so badly.'

An almost ditto repeat of the encounter with Maj. Singh follows. Preliminary questioning, doubts over the veracity of his permission letter, fax to New Delhi. The SHO, a

handsome young man named Matteen Abdullah, is overcome
with embarrassment when the reply arrives. It is a facsimile
copy of the previous reply, asking for special assistance to be
meted out to Shaakib Khan in his research.

'My sincerest apologies, sir, for what happened earlier.
Constable Sopori certainly overreacted. He will, of course,
issue a personal apology, but I will also make sure that he is
suitably reprimanded for his actions.'

'That won't be necessary, sir. And please, call me Shaakib.
Constable Sopori was only doing his duty. Of course, the lathi
was uncalled for, but that's only because I violated station
decorum by speaking to the man next to me, Owais. I guess
my research instincts got the better of me. I mean, I knew I
had done nothing wrong, but Sopori didn't know. So, it's all
good. Please don't worry.'

'You did nothing wrong, Shaakib. And please call me
Matteen. We're both young, perhaps of the same age, and
there's no point hiding behind formalities. You committed
no crime in trying to speak to that man. You see, I joined
the police force precisely because I wanted to reform it, in
whatever little way. I love my country very dearly, and I
want my fellow Kashmiris to recognize that any alternative
is horrendous. Your research work is very important because
how officials such as I behave with the public directly shapes
their perception of the Indian government. And from that
point of view, what Sopori did was unpardonable. There must
be something I can do to make up for the treatment meted
out to you.'

'Well, if you insist, there actually is something I'd like your
help with. The permission letter you read offers only a brief

summary of my PhD dissertation, which is at large concerned with the public perception of Indian government officials in the border regions of Kashmir. But the specific department that I'm interested in studying here in Baramulla is the revenue department. Would you happen to know anything about the officials in that department? Who the good ones are, who the rotten ones are . . . that sort of thing?'

The SHO laughs. 'What a strange thing fate is. As it so happens, my father just retired from the revenue department a couple of months ago. If there is anybody who can tell you about what goes on in there, it's him. And I'm certain that he'd be more than happy to talk to you.'

Cyrus smiles. Lady luck is clearly on his side.

* * *

When news of another blast claimed by the LeH emerges, this time in Varanasi, Ravi doesn't quite know how to react. On the one hand, he stands vindicated. Anil's operation, which had culminated in the death of four alleged terrorists, had evidently been a miscalculation. But at the same time, Ravi isn't the sort to play the blame game, not when it concerns the lives of civilians. These blasts had happened under his watch, the second in just a month. Unless he can get to the bottom of it all soon, there was no telling how much more damage the enemy might inflict. He is pacing around his office, contemplating these things, when the phone rings. He is certain it is the chief, calling to berate him. With a heavy heart, he puts the receiver against his ear. But it isn't the chief. It is Jose who asks Ravi to hurry to Insomnia as fast as he can.

'Sir, we've finally made a breakthrough,' Jose tells Ravi as soon as he enters the dimly lit confines of Insomnia. They are in the server room, assured of complete privacy.

'You traced the email?'

'Yes sir, in less than ten minutes after the blast.'

'How? What's the connection?'

'I will explain, sir. They were using an ingenious strategy that had confounded all our attempts until now. Basically, it wasn't a fixed route of IP addresses that they were using to mask their actual coordinates. Rather, it was something that kept evolving and shifting with every minute that passed after the receipt of each mail. The last couple of times, it had been several hours before we actually got our hands on the emails they'd sent claiming responsibility, and by then the trail had sort of wound up in very convoluted ways. This time, we had befriended some of the journalists who've been receiving these emails, so that any email from the IDs we've been tracking would immediately be forwarded to us. We ran a trace and got what we needed before the trail closed in on itself again.'

'I think I understood only twenty per cent of what you just said, but that doesn't matter. Where are the mails coming from?'

'It's coming from an unsecured Wi-Fi network at Grand Meridien Mumbai, sir.'

'A room number, guest name, anything else that can help?'

'No, sir. It could have been any of the guests or staff, or anybody else physically located within the hotel, and using the Wi-Fi.'

'Fine. We should be able to take it from here. Have you told anybody else about this?'

'No, sir. Like you asked me to, I've kept this completely confidential. Only Jyotirmoy Sir knows, but only the broad details.'

'Good. I need a timestamped list of all the emails originating from the LeH. How soon can you put it together?'

'It's already done, sir. I'll mail it to you straightaway.'

'Great. Were you able to find out any correlations between their guest register and these dates?'

'I will try, sir, but from the little snooping I could manage to do before you came, it seemed like they don't maintain a digital registry.'

'I see. Mail me the list. And let me know if you manage to find anything. Keep up the excellent work.'

'I will sir, thank you.'

Ravi walks out of Insomnia with his head held high. Finally, there appears to be real progress. As he goes through the hallways, he texts Mihir, 'My office. ASAP.' It is a rather long walk, even for someone as brisk as Ravi. It takes him over ten minutes, by which time Mihir has already arrived and is waiting outside the office. Ravi ushers him in and bolts the door from the inside.

'As it turns out, dark clouds sometimes do have a silver lining. Thanks to the attack in Varanasi, you get to stay at a fancy hotel in Mumbai at taxpayer's expense,' Ravi tells Mihir, as he opens his inbox.

'I don't exactly follow, sir,' Mihir responds, clearly taken aback. He had come in expecting Ravi to be in damage control mode, not the sarcastic casualness that he otherwise reserved for less stressful situations.

Ravi points to his monitor. 'What you're looking at is a list of the exact time and date at which each of the emails claiming credit for the attacks over the last few months, including today's blast in Varanasi, have been sent. They've all been traced to Grand Meridien Mumbai. I want you to go down there and get your hands on their guest register. Find out who's been staying there on these dates.'

'Yes, sir.'

'You will have to be extremely delicate with this. Use your charms, use your brain, do whatever, but don't just go and directly ask to see the register. We can't trust anybody until we know more. Not the staff, not the guests. One misstep and all our efforts over the last several months will have been for nothing. This is our most important breakthrough so far, and if we blow this, it's back to square one.'

'Understood, sir.'

* * *

Thanks to the SHO's father, Cyrus believes he has zeroed in on the man he has christened Falcon as an appreciation of Maj. Singh who was the first to provide the information. After he uncovered Falcon's real identity, finding out more is hardly a challenge. The man is quite notorious, and many in Baramulla have suffered on account of his corruption. Once Cyrus begins to specifically name him, the local people are more than willing to share anecdotes. Some of the stories they share sicken Cyrus.

One villager used to own some acres of land that had gradually come to be encroached upon by some wealthier relatives. The property was lawfully registered in his father's name, but the man hadn't bothered to have it transferred to his name after his father's death. The lawyers he had approached had told him that he would have to obtain a clear title deed if he had to legally fend off the encroachers. The man had repeatedly visited the revenue department for help with obtaining the deed, which unambiguously belonged to him, but he was turned away under some pretext or the other.

The naive villager had realized only after many such visits that the officials weren't going to do anything unless he bribed them. Falcon, the revenue inspector for the area which the man's property came under, had demanded a large sum of money to help with the transfer, money that the man simply did not have. Frustrated, he had complained to higher-level officials in Srinagar. They had then enlisted an ombudsman to look into the matter and investigate the allegations of corruption. But Falcon was a smart operator who never did anything that would implicate him directly. His brother-in-law served as a middleman of sorts, but he, too, never took any money directly. They had set up an elaborate system of proxies that could never be traced back to Falcon.

Without any evidence, the allegations were dismissed, and Falcon remained in his job. Incensed by the villager's attempt to bring him down, Falcon had connived with the man's wealthy relatives to have him booked under the much-dreaded Public Safety Act, usually reserved for terrorists and treasonous elements. They had stealthily planted arms in his house and tipped off the police who refused to believe the man when he insisted he didn't know where the arms had come from or who they belonged to. He was sent off to jail for a few years, and on his return had found that his entire property had been encroached upon, leaving only his house. That incident had only cemented Falcon's fearsome reputation, and nobody dared to go after him. Cyrus had asked the villager how Falcon had managed to obtain arms.

'It's an open secret, saab. He is in cahoots with the enemy. Everybody knows that he uses some of that bribe money to fund terrorist groups.'

'Why don't you go to the police?'

'For just complaining about his corruption that man took away everything I had. If I complain about something like this to the police, God knows what will happen to me. And even if I wanted to complain, who will believe me? I myself am a terrorist, according to them. And he's a senior government official. There is no evidence.'

Although he has collected many such anecdotes, and has concrete information about Falcon's family, Cyrus is unsure of the right approach to take. He has all the information he needs, but he remains undecided on what exactly he will do with it. If he errs even slightly in his approach, it will not only take him back to square one but much further below into the negative. So many things could go wrong. Under the pretext of buying time, Falcon could tip off the militants and even have him executed. The thought itself has robbed him of a good night's sleep for weeks at end.

After poring through what he can recall from his training and all the case studies they had carefully gone through, Cyrus is still unable to arrive at a concrete plan. As his thoughts drift to fragments of Ravi's cryptic musings on the craft of espionage, Cyrus is reminded of his gambling analogy. The only way to win, in this case, would be to go all-in at the very beginning.

It is a high-risk strategy, but the stakes are inordinately high. He continues to examine other ways.

Finally, it is news of the Varanasi blast that shakes him out of his indecisive state. He realizes that he has to act and act urgently. Madan Singh's words ring out loud in his mind as he confronts the reality of his current situation, 'If you hit a roadblock, make a frontal assault. We call it, in our parlance, a cold start. But remember, a cold start should be a last resort. Be prepared for failure.'

Cyrus decides that if a cold start is what it will take, that is exactly what he will do. It is close to end of office hours when he walks into the revenue department. It wears a deserted look. One of the clerks, who is on her way out, tells Cyrus that the office is closed. She asks him to come back the following day. But he tells her that he has an appointment and walks into Falcon's tiny cabin in a corner of the cramped office.

'Who are you? What do you want? Office hours are over. Whatever it is, come back tomorrow.'

Cyrus smiles and takes a seat without invitation.

'What is this? Don't you know how to behave in front of a government official?'

'If you behaved like a government official, then I would too . . .'

Falcon looks up, perplexed by Cyrus's cheeky response.

'I think I know who you are. You're the snoopy little bastard that's been going around asking people about me, aren't you? Yes, I know. This is my territory, and I have my ways of finding out.'

Cyrus laughs. 'Excellent. That saves me the trouble of introducing myself. Now, if we can get to business . . .'

Falcon springs out of his chair and grabs Cyrus by the collar.

'Who the hell do you think you are? Get out of my office, or I'll call the police.'

'Please call them. I was hoping to talk to you in private about all the shady things you've been up to. But if you want the police to find out as well, be my guest.'

Falcon lets go of the collar, finding that he can barely move Cyrus's well-toned muscular frame.

'What do you mean? Are you trying to threaten me? Do you know who I am?'

'Yes, a little too well, in fact. I know that you are the most corrupt man in all of Baramulla.'

'Do you think you're the first man to throw these allegations against me? There has been a thorough inquiry already, and I have been given a clean chit.'

'Yes, but that was because there was no evidence. What if I told you that I have solid evidence?'

'Do what you have to with your evidence. But if you've spoken to the locals, I'm sure you found out what happened to the last person who tried to mess with me.'

'Yes, every little detail, including how you planted arms in that poor man's house and got him framed.'

'Don't bark nonsense. You can get into serious trouble for making such serious allegations against a senior government official.'

'Then you should also know very well about the serious trouble that a senior government official with links to terrorist organizations can get into.'

'What is the meaning of all this? Are you trying to blackmail me?'

'Yes, please sit down so I can tell you my demands.'

'I will not negotiate with you because what you are saying is rubbish. There is no evidence. And who will believe you? You're a lowly researcher, and I am a senior government official.'

'Please, stop saying "senior government official" again and again. I know you're very proud of it, but if you truly respected your position, you wouldn't be conspiring against your own government. I cannot tell you exactly who I am, such is the nature of my profile, but I can assure you that I am not some lowly researcher. We have substantial evidence of your links to terrorist groups. Your phones have been tapped for a long time, and we've been following your movements. And we don't even need so much evidence. You sent that poor man behind bars under the Public Safety Act. You should know all about it.'

Cyrus is bluffing, of course. He has learnt more than a few tricks from Ravi and is at the moment thoroughly enjoying himself.

'I don't believe you. And in any case, I have nothing to hide. I'm a proud Indian. I would never dream of doing such a thing.'

'Fine, don't believe me. Perhaps you will when tomorrow morning the IT department will raid your son-in-law's residence in Lucknow and confiscate your daughter's jewellery for having acquired it through ill-gotten money. Your son-in-law belongs to a very illustrious family, doesn't he? You bent over backwards to make the match happen. Imagine what he will do to your daughter after being subject to so much embarrassment. At the very least, he's going to say the dreaded word thrice, and your daughter will be back home. And then, imagine at the same time, your son in Dubai will see images of you in handcuffs plastered all over the news. And the next day, a few journalists will be tipped off that the ill-gotten money was also used to fund anti-India terrorism. Imagine what a field day they'll have.'

'What do you want from me?'

'Continue doing exactly the same thing that you've been doing all along. With a few alterations.'

'What do you mean?'

'I want you to continue working with the militant groups you've been funding all along. But you will take on a more active role. In fact, a full-time role. You will resign from your job with immediate effect. And you will pass on information to me. Every little thing, however unimportant it might be. Movements of arms, movements of terrorists, plans, strategies.'

'But I can't just resign like that. I have almost ten years of service left. What will I tell my family?'

'You should have thought of all that before conspiring against your own country. I'm amazed that you still have the guts to call what you do service. I'd like to think of it as ten years of treachery left. I don't care what excuse you come up with. In fact, for the information you provide, we will continue paying you the salary you draw. You're not going to get bribe money, of course, but it's a small price to pay for your sins. Just be grateful that you'll continue to be a free man. But let me warn you, if you feed me incorrect information, or if I have grounds to believe that you've withheld something from me . . . in fact, if you even think about deceiving me, I will make sure that your loved ones cannot even dream of walking around with their heads held up. You have a day to consider this. We will meet again tomorrow to work out the specifics of our arrangements. And I'm sure you're thinking you can get me killed. Let me be very clear about this. I'm not the only one who knows all this, we're not fools. If any harm comes to me, you and your family will meet a fate a hundred times worse than what I described. There is no escaping this. Is that understood?'

Falcon is a shaken man.

Spin Master

'I very well understand that the plan was to capture and not kill them, ma'am. I came up with it, after all. But my men overreacted and went for the kill. Of course, they erred in their judgement, but I implore you to look at the bright side. Political pressure was mounting on the agency, on you personally, and we had to do something. One thing you cannot deny, ma'am: that encounter made us look good. Not only did it take the pressure off briefly, but public morale also went up. It fits right into the strong-arm image of the government. Everybody is pleased when terrorists are killed,' Anil defends himself vigorously, although his confidence is quite evidently diminished.

Ravi can't help but find it all very amusing. Only a few weeks ago, Anil had stood in this very room, triumphant and disdainful. He had scoffed at every word of Ravi's, with little regard for professional decorum and the chief's presence. And today, in the same room, in front of the same people, he cuts a sorry figure. He is in no position to disregard Ravi today, not after having embarrassed himself and the agency so openly. Nevertheless, whatever Anil might lack in operational competency, he more than makes up for it with his ability to cover his tracks by persuading others to look at the bright side.

But Sarita is not one to be fooled by Anil's patronizingly clever talk. She is a straight shooter, a thorough professional who executes her duties with unquestionable integrity and impartiality.

'Since when did the work we do become all about warding off political pressure? Governments come and go, and we are not here to pander to their political agendas. We directly serve the people of this country, and ensuring their safety is above all political considerations. I do not deny that there is a political dimension to everything we do, but that is just an occupational hazard. A hazard that I must negotiate, not you. You had clear orders, and by extension, your men had clear orders. To capture, not kill. And from your own report, it appears that they were unarmed. It is a disgraceful violation of the foundational ethics of our work.

'I would have forgiven you if the encounter had actually accomplished anything. And that is why I remained silent. I did not berate you. I did not say anything to you. But now I have to. Your source had led us to believe that the targets were, in fact, high-level functionaries of the LeH, and yet only a week later, we've had a bomb blast in Varanasi, again claimed by the very same organization. Clearly, the information you had was dubious. We all make mistakes, that's not why I'm angry. The fact that you are so averse to admitting that you were wrong and that you are still intent on spinning it off as a success story is what annoys me so much. We are not a PR agency, for heaven's sake. We're not supposed to look good or look bad or look like anything. We're not supposed to be

seen at all. That's the very essence of our work. You are a very
senior officer, and it pains me deeply to be speaking to you
like this, but I have to.'

'Ma'am, I can wait outside,' Ravi gently interrupts.
Although there is no doubt in his mind that Anil deserves the
chief's wrath, Ravi is acutely sensitive to his own place within
the hierarchy and does not believe that he deserves to be privy
to this conversation.

Sarita shakes her head.

'No, Ravi. Please. I understand I'm putting you in an
awkward position, but you deserve to be here. You had the
gall to speak truth to power, as we all ideally should seek to do,
and stood your ground against two superiors. I should have
trusted your judgement, but it's too late for that now. But I
would like to hear what you have to say.'

Ravi hesitates for a few moments. He has always been a firm
believer in there being a time and place for everything. Now
certainly is not the time or place to be settling personal scores.

'Like you said, ma'am, it's too late now. What's done is
done. What I'd like to talk to you about is the way forward.
There are some very crucial leads we've obtained. Some are
rather urgent, in fact. I, um . . .'

Ravi casts a quick glance at Anil, who sits with his head
bowed down, unmistakably fuming at being humiliated in
Ravi's presence.

Ravi hopes that the chief picks up on his hint, which
she does. She looks at her watch and pretends to be late for
another meeting.

'Well, I didn't realize that we'd overshot our time here.
I'm sorry, gentlemen, I'm scheduled to meet the National

Security Advisor in thirty minutes. I better get going right now if I want to beat the traffic and get there on time. And if I'm not mistaken, Ravi, you're supposed to be part of that meeting too, correct? Why don't you come with me in my car, and we'll talk on the way?'

Ravi nods, silently admiring the chief for her quick thinking.

'You're a good actor, Ravi,' she mockingly compliments him as they walk towards her car.

'Not nearly as good as you, ma'am,' Ravi responds in jest as they get in.

'Pratap, just drive till the NSA's office and then drive back,' the chief instructs her driver, before turning to Ravi, 'Just tell me one thing, before anything else, why didn't you say anything to Anil? You had your chance. Don't tell me that you've suddenly buried the hatchet?'

Ravi chuckles. 'I certainly do have my problems with him, ma'am. I will speak my mind unabashedly if it is a plan or a strategy that we're discussing. And it has nothing to do with him in particular. With all due respect, I would do it if even it were you who had to be challenged. But after something's already been done, I sincerely believe it is none of my business to be castigating somebody senior to me, whatever problems I might have with him or her. If it were someone junior to me, I wouldn't have been nearly as kind as you were to him. In any case, I see no point kicking a man when he's already down.'

Sarita laughs. 'You're of a dying breed, Ravi. Not many gentlemen left these days. Anyway, what is it that you want to discuss? And why couldn't you do it in Anil's presence?'

Ravi appears uncertain. 'Here, ma'am? Are you sure?'

She waves off his concerns. 'Don't worry, Pratap is like a wall. He absorbs nothing, gives out nothing. Once you get to my position, you'll be spending half your time in your car moving from this building to that building, one meeting after the other. If you don't have a driver you can trust unconditionally, you'll never be able to get any work done.'

Ravi nods. 'Fair enough, ma'am. As I've already briefed you, we've finally uncovered the exact location from where the emails claiming credit for each of the attacks have been originating. My man is down there as we speak and is working on determining the identity of the sender. But there's something else that has come up in the last twenty-four hours. The reason I didn't want to discuss it in Anil sir's presence is that it is something . . . how do I put it . . . political. I don't think the irony would have been lost on him if I brought up something with very immediate political implications just after you'd chastised him for being concerned about politics.'

She looks at Ravi with concern. 'What do you mean?'

'Our people at Insomnia, while trying to look into the email trail, decided to take another look at Basharat's laptop. To be honest, I don't exactly understand the technical aspects of it, but they needed to crosscheck and verify some details. But while they were at it, they stumbled upon something they had missed during the initial combing . . . an online bulletin board, a discussion forum of sorts that the LeH had somehow failed to block Basharat's access to. Maybe they didn't expect us to find it, or they just forgot . . . doesn't matter . . .'

'What if it's a trap, Ravi? What if they are deliberately trying to mislead us?'

'That's what I thought as well, ma'am. But the contents led me to reconsider my initial suspicion. The bulletin board contained well laid out plans for each of the attacks that have happened so far. It accurately matches up to what actually happened, and they're all accurately timestamped. I'm told by our experts that it's impossible to fabricate timestamping. Mumbai, Pune, the Kerala abduction, even Varanasi, it's all in there. If we'd found this earlier, maybe we could have prevented them. But we can prevent what they have in store . . .'

'And what's that?'

'A kidnapping. And not some foreign tourists this time. What they have planned is perhaps the most high-profile kidnapping in the history of independent India, of a much higher magnitude than the ones we encountered at the peak of Kashmiri insurgency in the 1990s. They're planning to abduct Kishan Jadhav.'

'The leader of the Prajaprabhutva Party?'

'Yes, ma'am. The same man, who in every pundit's opinion is our next prime minister.'

'I will immediately put in a request for Z-plus security. Do you have any information about their modus operandi?'

'It's a rather elaborate plan, as you might expect, and we're in the process of putting it all together ma'am. The execution of the plan is still a month or two away from what we've gathered so far. But from what we know at this point, they have highly trained hitmen coming in from across the border. Exactly where, how and when, we do not know at this point.'

'That's not a very good place to be in. Can't you trace the people posting on this bulletin board?'

'I'm afraid not, ma'am. Unlike emails, these bulletin board messages carry no trail whatsoever. It's just like the platform that our IT people are now trying to build for seamless and anonymous communication between our field agents and the headquarters. The digital trail ends at the messages. From there on, we have to do it the old school way.'

'And I have no doubt that you will be able to uncover the trail. What else could you find on this bulletin board? Surely this can't be their only plan?'

'As of now, it is their most concrete plan, ma'am. But we could pick up some chatter about other targets. All are tentative plans for kidnappings. I have sufficient reason to believe that the blast in Varanasi was the last of its kind for the time being. With the raid in Ahmedabad, we shut off their primary channel for procuring explosives. Before they can figure out an alternative, I am optimistic that we can completely neutralize them.'

* * *

The Grand Meridien is almost obscene in its opulence. It is not the sort of place that Mihir is used to. Nevertheless, as Rajinder Talreja, heir to a multimillion-dollar fortune, he must pretend as if it is the sort of lifestyle he is accustomed to. At the lobby, as a friendly receptionist runs him through the check-in formalities, he pays careful attention to the subtle details. She takes down his name, address and phone number, and enters them into her computer. He smiles at her as he takes his key, but in his mind, a thousand wheels run amok. The reason he is at the hotel in the first place is that José had claimed that the guest registry was not computerized.

A bell boy whose brass badge identifies him as Sunny Kapoor helps Mihir carry his luggage up to his eighth-floor room, with windows that open up to a breathtaking view of the Juhu shoreline. Mihir fishes out a thousand rupee note and hands it over to Sunny, who doffs his hat and flashes an all-knowing smile, immediately throwing up red flags in Mihir's mind. After bolting the door, he reaches into a hidden compartment in his suitcase and pulls out a little black device that could pass for a mobile phone. It is a radio frequency scanner that can detect hidden bugs and cameras within a ten-metre radius. After a minute or so, it gives out a flat, almost inaudible beep, indicating that the area is clear of surveillance equipment. Putting it back in, he pulls out his mobile phone and calls Jose.

'You were wrong. The registry's computerized,' Mihir tells Jose in a soft tone.

'Could very well be. All I said was that it's not online,' Jose responds, hardly surprised by the discovery.

'So, is there a way to get access to it from within here?'

'Theoretically, yes. But it's a multi-step process. First, I'll need to know what software they're using, so I can write up a script accordingly. I'll then mail you the script, which you'll have to load into a USB drive and find a way to physically plug into their servers.'

'And where on earth will I find their servers?'

'Since it isn't online, it's definitely located within the premises of the hotel. Most five-stars display their floor plans on all floors, just next to the fire exit. It won't be all that difficult to locate.'

'How do you know so much about five-star hotels?'

'It's what you get from having parents who confuse quality family time with lavish vacations.'

'I'm sorry I asked. Anyway, even if I did find out where it is and managed to get in, how do I know where to plug it in?'

'If you can get more than two to three minutes inside their server room, it will be easy to find. It's just an ordinary USB port, just like the one on normal computers.'

'Fine. I'll figure out a way.'

'I think you should get to it right away. It's going to take me at least a couple of days to put together that script.'

Mihir hangs up, goes to the bathroom, and quickly washes his face. After changing his attire into something more casual, he leaves his room and takes the elevator to the ground floor. He walks to the lobby and approaches the friendly receptionist from earlier. She rises from her seat and smiles, 'Is everything all right, sir? I hope you're well settled into your room.' Mihir nods, 'Yes, everything's all right. But I just realized that I left my laptop charger back home, and I urgently need to send an email. Do you think I could use your computer?' Before she can respond, Mihir tries to hurry over onto the other side of the reception desk, but she turns off the monitor before he can look at anything.

Again, red flags go up in Mihir's mind. Perhaps he is overthinking. It was a strangely desperate move on his part anyway, and he had in his sudden dash come dangerously close to making physical contact with the receptionist. Anyone in her position would have felt uncomfortable. He raises his hands in apology and moves back to the other side. 'I'm sorry, I didn't mean to. It was just a very urgent email. Not easy running a multimillion-dollar company, you see,' he explains. She smiles and waves away his apology, 'I completely understand, sir. You don't have to apologize. I'm sorry I can't allow you to use this computer, it's strictly meant for internal use, but you are most welcome to use the ones at our business centre. I will have someone escort you.' She rings the bell on her desk, and Sunny Kapoor immediately arrives, having been watching everything from a distance. He flashes that unsettling, all-knowing smile from earlier. As he escorts Mihir to the business centre, he clears his throat several times in succession.

When Mihir pays no heed, Sunny speaks up in a soft voice, 'If it's that urgent, why don't you ask me, sir? You've paid me for it, after all.'

Mihir snaps back, 'What do you mean?'

'Don't worry, sir. After ten years working in this hotel, I can recognize desperation when I see it. And I understand why you tried what you tried. She is a pretty one, isn't she? But sadly, she has a boyfriend already. He comes every once in a while from Pune. Tall and handsome, almost like a Pathan from Afghanistan. But don't worry, I can arrange for someone prettier.'

'What rubbish?'

'Relax, sir. Nobody will find out. It's quite commonplace. Tell me your preference, and I'll arrange for it. Indian, Russian, American, Italian, you name it.'

'Who do you take me for? It was a genuine accident, what happened at the reception. I'm not that sort of guy.'

'Is it drugs then? What do you want, cocaine, ecstasy, hashish . . .'

'What is wrong with you? I'm not interested in women or drugs. I'm here on business.'

Sunny's expression changes to one of panic.

'Please forgive me, sir. It's just a misunderstanding. You see when somebody gives you a thousand-rupee tip for just bringing up their bags, it's common sense that they're after something like that. I guess I have met a genuinely generous man for the first time in my life.'

Mihir chuckles and thinks for a few moments.

'Well, you're right. Nobody is generous without a good reason. I am after something, and I need your help. But I can't tell you here. Come up to my room.'

Sunny smiles again and follows Mihir back to his room.

'Just to be very clear again, before you can throw any more disgusting offers, I am not interested in women, drugs, or any of that nonsense. Like I told you, I am here on business. You see, my father and I are looking to enter the hospitality business. We tried to buy this hotel, but the owners refused our offer. My father's a stubborn man, and when he likes something, he really wants it. If we can't have this hotel, we've decided we're going to build one that looks exactly like this. So, I'm here to take down every little detail. What you saw me doing at the reception was just that. I was just trying to look into the software backbone of the hotel's operations. I will need many favours from you, but for now, I need you to find out the exact name of the software that they use to manage guest registrations. Can you do that for me?'

Sunny nods vigorously.

'I can help you, not just with getting the name of that software, but with getting many other things. But before that, I need to know what is in it for me. You're asking me to steal information from my own employers. A thousand rupees won't do.'

'Of course. Like I said, I am a businessman, and I have a deal for you. Two things I need you to do, think of it as a test to see if you can be trusted. First, I'll need the name of that software immediately. And after a couple of days, I will need you to take me to the server room and make sure that I get at least a few minutes of uninterrupted access, so I can take down the details I need. For this, I will pay you five thousand rupees, straightaway. But if you blabber a single word of this to anyone, I'll make sure that you not only lose the job you already have but also that you will never work again for anybody. I am a very powerful man, and you don't want to mess with me. But if you do what is asked and do it discreetly, there is a lot more money to be made. In fact, I will guarantee you a job at our new hotel. Double the salary, and a better position. How does that sound?'

Sunny extends his hand. Mihir shakes it before pulling out five crisp thousand-rupee notes and stuffing it into Sunny's front pocket.

'How soon can you get me that name?'

'I have it already, sir. It's the same software that we're required to use to make a note of room-service orders. It's called Hotelisys. I can even get you the name of the company that maintains it for us. They come every month for service visits, and it's all recorded in the entry log. That tall, handsome Pathan I mentioned, he works for that company. But of course, he comes for other kinds of service visits too, if you know what I mean.'

* * *

Cyrus visits Falcon in his office at the same time the next day. The hostility of the previous evening has given way to servility. Falcon gets up from his seat as soon as Cyrus arrives and asks if he'd like some refreshments. Cyrus shakes his head, making it clear that he is there to talk business. 'Have you decided?' Cyrus asks. 'Yes, I'll help you,' Falcon responds feebly, his pride appearing to have been completely ravaged.

'That's good,' Cyrus tells him plainly, 'I assume this is your last day at work.'

Falcon nods and shows Cyrus his resignation letter.

'That's settled, then,' Cyrus remarks, 'It's now time to start making arrangements to cross the border.'

Falcon's jaw drops.

'Cross the border? What do you mean? It wasn't part of what we agreed upon yesterday?'

'We didn't agree on anything yesterday. I told you explicitly that I would work out the specific details of our arrangement and come back today.'

'B–but . . . how can I possibly leave my family?'

Cyrus pays Falcon's hesitation no heed as he pulls out a sheet of paper from his bag and places it on the desk.

'This is a charge sheet that details each of the crimes you have been complicit in. Corruption, abetment of terrorism, treason, it's all in there. Now, if you want this to be dropped, you'll do exactly as you're told. In fact, crossing the border is your best chance to escape all of this. Your family will be taken care of, you have my word. In any case, you're not going to have to cross over immediately, not until you've proved your worth to me. Something's come up in the last twenty-four hours, and I need information. Think of it as a test. If you fail, you know exactly what I will do. And if you pass, you get to cross the border and continue giving me information.'

'B-but . . . that's like having to choose between a rock and a hard place.'

'You can think of it using whatever metaphors that help you understand, but this is the situation you have created for yourself. We have little time to waste, and I need you to get to work immediately.'

Disentangling

Mihir looks at the diagram in his possession, hand-drawn by Jose. He needs to go into the server room and plug the USB drive into a particular slot. It appears to be a simple enough task, but in Mihir's line of work, there is no such thing. The simplest unrelated error could potentially cost innocent lives somewhere down the line. After going through the plan several times in his head, he calls room service. In five minutes, Sunny arrives promptly with a cup of tea. Mihir wastes little time, 'I need to get to that server room today. As soon as you possibly can.' Sunny smiles. A man of few words, he gestures that he will be back in five minutes.

While he's gone, Mihir calls up Jose and tells him to be ready to attempt logging on in ten minutes. Sunny returns and asks Mihir to follow him. The server room is located in the basement, next to the parking lot, alongside a large diesel generator. Sunny pulls out his master key and lets Mihir in. It's an in-and-out job that lasts less than a few minutes. On their way back, just as they make a turn into the hallway leading up to his room, Sunny tries probing, 'You were barely in the room? What did you want to do in there anyway?' Mihir pretends not to have heard him.

Back in his room, the tea has gone cold, but Mihir drinks it anyway. He turns on the TV and begins watching the news. All he can now do is wait. About an hour later, his phone rings. He expects it to be Jose, but it is the boss himself.

'Mihir, something's not adding up. There's no consistent overlap between the emails and the guest registry. I never ask, but I need to know this time, because I need to be able to absolutely rule out the possibility of sabotage. Who enabled all this access for you?'

'A guy who works at the hotel, sir. Completely a financial arrangement. I don't think its him.'

'Okay. But have you noticed anything odd? Do you think somebody else in the hotel might know? About you . . .'

'No.'

'Are you absolutely certain?'

Mihir thinks for a few moments.

'Well, nothing credible at least. I did feel a little suspicious. This lady who's a receptionist here. I was trying to look at her computer, and she quickly turned it off. But I thought that maybe she behaved like that because I tried to go over to her side to use her computer.'

'That's a highly irresponsible way to try to procure information, especially when we have no clue who the target is. It could be anyone, man or woman.'

'I am sorry, sir. I assure you I did nothing suspicious. I have a solid cover that explains everything.'

'Forget it. Tell me about this receptionist.'

'Nothing out of the ordinary, sir. I don't have reason to believe she has anything to do with all this.'

'Fine, then. As we speak, Jose is running some tests to see if the data has been tampered with in any way. At first glance, he doesn't think it has been, but we don't want to take any chances. Until then, I want you to continue snooping around. Get your hands on a complete list of all employees and fax it over, so we can run a background check on each of them. It's important, now more than ever for you to be very careful with how you proceed. Stay out of trouble. And keep me informed. For now, stick to the guy who's giving you access and information. Don't take anyone else into confidence without consulting me. Whatever it is, even the slightest thing, you speak to me directly. And use the radio–frequency scanner every day.'

As Ravi hangs up, Mihir feels a cold shiver run down his spine. If the data is not sabotaged, then it essentially means that he has been in the same building as a leading operative of the LeH for the last several days.

* * *

Cyrus had been something of a reluctant entrant to the world of espionage. His grandfather, Feroze Bandookwallah, had been a wealthy Parsi arms dealer in Burma who had built strong ties with the British military establishment during the Second World War, all the while acting as a high-level spy for Subhas Chandra Bose's INA. He had played a critical role in the INA's operations in Burma and had successfully evaded detection. Upon India's independence, he had returned triumphantly to Bombay and taken up the surname Kufiyawallah as a mark of pride, now that he no longer had to worry about detection.

But Cyrus hated the surname. It made him the butt of all jokes at his school. Frustrated by the persistent bullying, he had persuaded his parents to shift him to a different school and also change his surname. When he was twelve years old, he became Cyrus Bandookwallah, reverting to the family's original surname. But while he could change his surname, there was no escaping the heavy burden of his family's legacy that had been foisted upon his shoulders right from the moment of birth. He found it amusing at times.

Within the Parsi community, it was something of a norm for children to carry on with their family occupation. The straightforward surnames they all bore, was evidence of it. But it was usually law or business or medicine, or something more ordinary. It wasn't exactly the case that he had been forced into it, but by the time he was finishing college and had to make a choice, he realized that there was nothing he was really passionate about. It made sense to take a leap of faith and follow in his father and grandfather's footsteps. He hadn't particularly found it all very appealing at first, and even regretted his decision some months into his time at the academy.

But whatever doubts he might have had then had all evaporated over the last many months. He now appreciated the profound significance of the work he did and even enjoyed it.

But it had come at a cost, he thinks to himself, fiddling with a diamond-studded ring as he sits by himself in the tiny guesthouse in Baramulla that has been his home for the last several weeks. It is the ring he intends to propose to his girlfriend with, although at this point he is not sure if and when that might happen. Ever since he had been pulled out of the academy by Ravi, he hasn't had a single day's break. He hasn't even had an opportunity to meet his girlfriend. It is something he has been thinking about recently, for it is the first time in his life that he has been entirely alone for weeks on end.

His thoughts are interrupted by a knock on his door. He puts the ring back in its place and asks who it is. There is no response. His sleuth instincts kick in immediately and he cautiously opens the door, only to find that there is no one there. As he steps out to look around, he nearly stumbles on a heavy brick placed right outside his door. He picks it up to find a tiny note attached. It is a message from Falcon, carrying the information he has been waiting for for several days now. He heaves a sigh of relief. The decision to go in with a cold start appears to have paid off.

* * *

'I can try, but I can't guarantee it. As far as I know, only the GM has a list of all employees. And his office is the one room in the entire building that I cannot access with my key. I could still figure out a way, but it's risky. I have an alternative solution. I have been working here for so long now that I can just give you everybody's names,' Sunny tells Mihir.

'That won't work. I need their full names and addresses,' Mihir replies.

'It is none of my business, sir, but why exactly do you need that?' Sunny probes.

Mihir has been on his guard, ever since that phone call with Ravi, and has a ready response to all possible questions.

'Headhunting. We want to make this hotel pay for not accepting our takeover offer. We're going to lure away every employee with better pay and perks. For that to happen, our HR department needs to plan elaborately, and that cannot happen without a complete list.'

Sunny nods, visibly impressed.

'I see,' he says, before turning silent. It is clear that he is waiting for Mihir to propose a deal.

'I know it's going to be risky, which is why I'm going to make an offer that you simply won't be able to resist. You will get another five thousand rupees straightaway, but that's just loose change compared to what you stand to earn if you do this for me. Here's the deal. If you get me that list and help us with reaching out to individual employees, we will pay you a ten per cent commission on the one month's salary for every employee that joins us. There are almost a hundred people working in this hotel, and some of them already draw close to a lakh. Put together, the expenditure on staff salary must easily be close to thirty-forty lakhs a month. Ten per cent of that figure, you do the math.'

Sunny's eyes light up. He agrees straightaway and promises to procure the list by the end of the day. As he turns to leave the room, Mihir stops him.

'There's something else I want to ask you about. That receptionist, what do you know about her?'

'Ambitious woman, sir. She's from a small town in Madhya Pradesh and has had to work very hard to get to where she is now. It's not exactly a dream job, but given how hard she has to fight her family at every stage, it is impressive that she's even got this far. But I feel sorry for her, sometimes. That boyfriend of hers, I don't know what promises he has made to her, but I just don't see why she is still with him.'

'What do you mean?'

'I mean, on the surface, it appears as if he goes out of his way to meet her regularly. She'll make up some excuse and complain about an issue with the software, and he'll promptly come over on a service visit. Everybody knows, but they keep quiet. They find it cute and romantic, and all that. Anyway, it's not their father's money that goes into paying for those visits. But I'm not so sure of his motives. He always seems a little distracted, and he doesn't spend so much time with her, even when he comes. Even she seems a little uncomfortable in his presence. Like I said, I don't know what promises he has made to her that keeps her still interested in the relationship, but it all seems a little phoney to me.'

In Mihir's mind, a thousand wheels are set into motion, but he pretends not to care.

'I'm not really interested in all these personal details, but speaking of service visits, we also need to lure away all service providers as well. You had mentioned last time that you have access to the service visit registry. Can you get me printouts of every day's logs for the last one year?'

'That would be a little difficult, sir. I'll have to enter each date separately and print it out one by one. One year's logs might take me an entire day to generate, and if I spend so much time at the computer and print out so many sheets, someone is bound to get suspicious. But I'm sure there's some shortcut to getting it all at once. Computers are not really something I'm very good at. But if you want, I can speak to a friend of mine who works in the accounts department. His job requires him to sit in front of a computer all day, and so nobody will suspect anything. He can be trusted because he hates this hotel and has been looking to leave for long. I suppose you'd be interested in hiring him too?'

Mihir shakes his head.

'No, don't bother. We can't have anybody else know at this point. I'm not saying I don't trust your friend, I'm sure he's very reliable, but I don't want to take any chances at this point. You understand, right? There's definitely a job waiting for him, but I don't want you talking to him or anybody else just as yet. Can I count on you to follow my orders?'

Sunny nods. Tucking five thousand rupees into his cummerbund, he salutes and leaves the room. Mihir locks the room from inside and pulls out the radio frequency scanner from his suitcase. It emits a flat beep, a confirmation that the space is still secure. He pulls out his phone and is about to dial Jose's number when he remembers Ravi's orders. He is to call him directly.

'Sir, something has come up. I think my initial instincts about the receptionist might have been right. There is something off . . .'

'What do you mean?'

'Well, may I please loop Jose into this call? I need him to look something up.'

'Give me ten minutes. I'm on my way to the headquarters. I'll head straight to Insomnia and call you back.'

Mihir hangs up. The more he thinks about it, the more plausible it all seems. After all, it was quite unlikely that a top operative of a dangerous terror outfit would take up a full-time job at a hotel just to gain access to its Wi-Fi network.

Besides, given how long it had taken for Jose to follow the trail to its end, only a software engineer would have the requisite know-how.

The phone rings.

'Mihir, I have Jose with me. What is it that you need him to look up?'

'Jose, that USB drive I inserted . . . Does it give you access to the service visit registry as well?'

'If it's digital and hosted on the same server, it should be there. Let me check. Anything in particular you want me to look up?'

'The overlaps you were looking for in the guest registry, run the same test on the service visit registry.'

'Okay, hold on.'

Mihir's heartbeat quickens as he waits for Jose to run the search.

'Mihir . . .'

It is Ravi on the line.

'Yes, sir.'

'Keep up the good work. I think we have our man.'

* * *

Cyrus waits with bated breath to see if the information Falcon has provided is correct. Falcon's message had informed him that three young men sporting skull caps and long beards had crossed over from Pakistan somewhere near the Mendhar sector of Poonch district and would board a bus to Srinagar the next day. From Srinagar, they were to go to Delhi, and then finally to Maharashtra where they were to undertake a special operation. It could all mean only one thing. These were the hitmen who were to kidnap Kishan Jadhav. In itself, it wasn't much to go by. For in all likelihood, any man headed from Poonch to Srinagar was likely to be dressed in that attire. What was really clinching and useful was another detail Falcon had mentioned. The men were also wearing brand new Nike sneakers, something that wasn't all that common. Cyrus had relayed the information to the headquarters, and they had, in turn, alerted the J&K Police.

Because of a recent spurt in militancy, bus connectivity had been restricted to only one bus operating every day. It wouldn't be that difficult to spot the men if Falcon's information was indeed accurate. A checkpoint had been set up a few kilometres outside Poonch, and the police flagged the bus down as soon as it passed them. They couldn't find anybody matching the description provided, and they'd allowed the bus to go through. Cyrus had been confident of the veracity of the information. He had too much leverage over Falcon for him to lie so early on. And so, he can't believe it when the headquarters informs him that the information was inaccurate.

He decides to speak directly to the policemen who had conducted the inspection. They tell him that they checked every bearded man with a skullcap. Nobody had been wearing Nike sneakers.

'But were there other men in the bus?'

'Yes sir, a few college students. They were clean-shaven and were dressed in T-shirts and jeans.'

'Did you check their shoes?'

They hadn't.

Alarm bells go off in Cyrus's mind. Fortunately for him, the bus ride from Poonch to Srinagar takes a good six hours, and it is unlikely that the bus would have already reached its destination. He immediately gets in touch with the J&K Police headquarters, and they set up another checkpoint twenty kilometres outside of Kashmir, along the route that the bus is to take. Falcon's information turns out to be correct, and the three men are nabbed. To evade detection, they had shaved off their beards and switched to jeans and T-shirts. But they hadn't bothered to change their footwear.

* * *

The service visit registry has identified the suspect as Abhinav Prakash. But because it is likely to be a fake identity, the only way to track him down is through the company that he purportedly works for, Hotelisys. In consultation with Ravi, Mihir arrives at a plan. It is decided that Mihir, continuing to pose as a budding hotelier, will contact the company about procuring their services. He sends them an email through an ID set up on a fake domain name procured just to make it seem as authentic as possible. They reply almost immediately, asking him for his number so that they can discuss it over the phone.

After exchanging brief introductions and going over their proposal, Mihir gently shifts the conversation towards what he really is seeking to know.

'I'm most concerned about maintenance. You see, our group already owns three hotels across North India, and the main reason we're not satisfied with our current software providers is that they can't be relied upon for regular maintenance. If something goes wrong, we expect somebody to fix it immediately. And so, what we really would want to know before taking this forward and enlisting your services for our new venture in Mumbai is whether you have a designated service person based in the city. And if so, we'd like to also meet him.'

'I understand, sir. It is a perfectly valid concern that you have. The reason why we're better than other companies in this space is that we outsource maintenance and services to smaller firms based out of every major city in India. And that's also the reason why every major hospitality group, including the international ones, trusts us. In Mumbai alone, we have fifteen firms that serve as our authorized software maintenance providers. They're on call at all times.'

Mihir is stumped.

'Fifteen companies, or fifteen individuals?'

'Companies, sir. Our software currently powers over eight hundred hotels. Whether it is a budget hotel or a five-star, we're everyone's preferred choice. To ensure that everyone has assured access to IT professionals whenever they need it, we work with many companies.'

Mihir realizes that it is a futile task and soon brings the call to an end. His only hope is to apprehend the man on his next visit to the hotel. But because these visits are not scheduled in advance, from what Sunny has told him, there appears to be only one way forward—to cultivate the receptionist.

He gets on a call with Ravi, discussing possible strategies.

'What else do you know about this woman, apart from the fact that she's the target's girlfriend?'

'That she's ambitious, sir. That might work to our advantage. If we make the right offer, we might be able to bring her on board.'

'It's all the more reason to tread carefully. Ambition is a dangerous trait. And I am absolutely certain that she knows what he is up to. We've carefully gone through the logs. I don't know if it is arrogance or stupidity, but he has hardly bothered to cover his tracks on that front. Every service visit he has made in the last year perfectly overlaps with the attacks. Even if she is not actively in on it, I'm sure she's not that blind. Every single time he's in the hotel, there is a bomb blast.'

'You're right, sir. My source in the hotel informed me that there appears to be little romance between them. He told me that she's always a little uncomfortable in his presence. I suspect there's some element of blackmail involved here.'

'Find out more and get back to me. Don't approach her just yet, but remember, we don't have much time.'

Spa Maid

Mihir waits for the receptionist to finish her night shift, and quietly follows her at a distance. Just as she is about to enter the Santa Cruz train station, he quickens his pace. It is still rather early in the morning. The first train is at least thirty minutes away, and the station is relatively empty. She settles down on a platform bench and is looking through her handbag for something when Mihir taps her shoulder. Taken completely by surprise, her body reacts with an involuntary jolt. She looks up to find Mihir smiling at her.

'Mr Talreja, what . . . what are you doing here?' she asks him, still startled by his unexpected interruption.

'I've always been fascinated by the Mumbai local. Every time I'm in town, I try and take a ride. It's best to do so around this time, when it's least crowded,' Mihir replies, 'Can I sit down?'

'Yes, yes, of course,' she says, after regaining her composure.

'So, you're headed home?' he asks her.

'Yes. You?'

'Well, I'm not even sure if I have to go anywhere. It's all up to you, really.'

She glares at him.

'Excuse me?'

'Yes, you heard me right. It's all up to you. If you cooperate with me right now, you'll save me the trouble of following you all the way, and I'll save you the embarrassment of what will happen if you don't cooperate. Your parents moved to Mumbai only a couple of months ago, right? I wonder how they'd feel if they found out exactly how you could afford to rent out a place of your own in a city like this, so early in your career.'

A look of alarm dawns on her face.

'What are you suggesting? How do you know about my parents?'

'All I'm suggesting is that your father already has a weak heart. The poor man had a bypass surgery only three years ago. Imagine what would happen to his heart if he were to find out that it is your boyfriend who has been paying for everything.'

'Go ahead and tell him. I don't know what you want, but you can't blackmail me like this. My father will understand if I were to tell him.'

'Fair enough. But what if he were to find out that your boyfriend is a Muslim? Would be a little too much to digest for an old conservative man from a small town, no?'

'He is not Muslim.'

Mihir smiles in an unsettlingly sinister way. He can tell from her body language that she doesn't quite believe what she is insisting on.

'Let's stop pretending, shall we? You and I both know very well that his name isn't really Abhinav Prakash. The real question is, do you also know that IT maintenance isn't really what he does?'

'Who the hell do you think you are? Do you have any idea what he will do to you if I tell him about all this?'

Mihir chuckles.

'I'd love to find out. By all means, go ahead and tell him. In the meantime, I will also speak to my friends who're standing right outside your housing colony to go ring the doorbell and speak to your parents. Do you really want to take the chance?'

She falls silent as she puts her face in her palms. Tears roll down her cheeks.

'I thought not. Now that we've gotten that out of the way, let me tell you what I want from you. And I want you to listen very carefully. Your boyfriend is no ordinary computer engineer. He is a dreaded terrorist with the blood of thousands of innocent lives on his hands, including those who died in the train blasts. Many were killed just a few hundred metres from this very station. Now before I can proceed any further, I want you to tell me, and I want you to be very honest. Have you known all along?'

'I did not know anything at the beginning, I promise. He was the sweetest man I'd ever met, and he was so nice to me. I had been seeing him for almost a year before I found out. And when I did, there was nothing I could do about it. Things had progressed very rapidly between us, if you understand what I mean. And he'd secretly recorded videos of me in very compromising positions. He said he would leak all of it unless I continue doing his bidding.'

'But why didn't you go to the police?'

'He told me that nobody would believe me and that if I even dared to do something like that, he would release the videos without sparing a thought. And if he did get caught, he said he would name me as well, and I would go to jail too. I was too scared. Every day, I dread going to sleep. People I've never met are in my dreams, pointing accusingly at me. I'm just as responsible for all those deaths. I can never forgive myself. If not for my parents, I would have gone to the police long ago. I just don't have it in me to bring them so much shame.'

She begins sobbing uncontrollably. Mihir gently pats her on her shoulder reassuringly.

'You don't have to be so hard on yourself. If not you, he would have found someone else. And if the guilt truly haunts you that much, I'm giving you a way to make amends. If you do as I say.'

'You don't know him, sir. He's a monster. There's no way anyone can do anything to him. This is all futile. I might as well just kill myself, which is what I've been planning on for so many months now.'

'You might know him, but you don't who I am, who I work for, and what we're capable of. By we, I'm referring here to the combined might of the Indian police and the armed forces. He's not even a close match. It's only because he's been operating in a cowardly manner that he's gotten away with it so far. Despite that, we've found him, haven't we? Soon, with or without your support, he's going to realize who he's been messing with. And if you don't help us, you'll meet a similar fate.

'We're not monsters, we'll destroy those videos regardless, but if you don't help us, we won't be able to save you from going behind bars. If you don't do as I say, I will ensure that the full force of the law of this land comes crashing on you. But if you help me and do what I ask you to, I can save you from it all. He will be locked away for the rest of his life, and you won't have to live in fear any longer. Think about it.'

'What do you want me to do, sir? I'm prepared to do anything if it means the end of him in my life.'

'You will lead us to him. That's all we ask of you.'

'But he'll get suspicious, sir. He knows I no longer have any feelings for him and that I do his bidding only out of sheer fear. I don't know where he lives, and if I ask to meet, he'll immediately know there's something fishy.'

'Well, in that case, you will wait. How many days in advance does he usually ask you to schedule these maintenance visits at the hotel?'

'It varies, sir. But it's usually a day or two in advance.'

'And never on the same day?'

'No, sir.'

'Okay. And then what happens?'

'I don't really know, sir. He comes, spends some time pretending to fix whatever issue I've raised. And then he gets a phone call from somewhere, and he'll quickly pull out his laptop and send some emails. In the meantime, if there are others around, he'll pretend to flirt with me. Usually, by this time, everybody's attention is geared towards the breaking news on the TV. But the last time he came over, because I knew what to expect, I decided to keep an eye on him instead of the TV. He logs in to the hotel's desktop and clears out all Wi-Fi access tokens for the last half-hour. What that does is also log all guests out of the network briefly. We explain it away as routine maintenance work, but I think he does it to erase all traces of his laptop having been connected to the hotel's network.'

'No wonder we had such a difficult time tracking him down.'

'I'm telling you he is extraordinarily intelligent. If only he wasn't blinded by hate.'

Before she can launch into another bout of remorse, Mihir stops her,

'Whatever it is, I'm not interested. This is what I want you to do. You will alert me the moment he contacts you and requests you to schedule a service visit. That's all. We'll do the rest. And don't forget, not for a single moment, that we have you under full surveillance. If you try to betray us, we will know immediately. And then there's no saying what my bosses might decide to do. Is that understood?'

'Yes, sir.'

'That's good,' Mihir says as he hands her a small cell phone. 'There's only one number saved on this, and that's the one you will call. I have a hunch that you won't have to wait too long before he contacts you.'

As he gets up and leaves, she calls out to him, 'Sir . . .'

'Yes?'

'What's your name?'

There is something unsettling about the manner in which she poses that question. Despite her heartfelt confession, Mihir doesn't entirely trust her. But he shrugs it off and smiles, 'You already know. It's Rajinder Talreja.'

* * *

At the C3 headquarters, Cyrus waits for Ravi to arrive along with the captured terrorists. The plan initially had been for them to be handed over directly to the state police, but Ravi had decided against it at the last minute. A special team, led by Ravi himself, had travelled to Srinagar to bring the captured men back to Delhi. Cyrus had been completely kept out of the loop and had only been asked to return to Delhi by a separate flight. Cyrus understands that it was necessary because, as a field operative, it is essential for his cover to remain in place at all costs. But as to why Ravi had altered the plan, he remains completely in the dark.

'Bandookwallah, up! To my office, right now.'

It is almost evening, and Cyrus has unwittingly fallen asleep. But Ravi's voice, even at the gentlest of volume, can stir him awake from the deepest of slumbers. It is not just on account of his training. Such is the authority and respect Ravi commands. Cyrus slaps himself a few times to fully wake up before following Ravi into his office.

'Well done, Cyrus. The men are safely in our custody,' Ravi congratulates him.

'Thank you, sir. But why did you change the plan at the last minute? And why did you go yourself?'

'I'll answer the second question first. I went myself because my best men were all out on the field. And at this point, even the slightest mistake could mean the end of our careers, if not the end of this organization itself. I will say only that for now. Apart from the fact that it's too early in your career for you to be concerned about politics, it is the answer to the first question that is more . . .'

A knock on the door interrupts them. It is Jose. Cyrus rises from his chair, happy to see his friend after what has been their longest time apart since the beginning of their training at the academy. Unmindful of Ravi's presence for a brief moment, Cyrus hugs him warmly. Jose, who has a professed distaste for physical contact of all sorts, awkwardly frees himself.

Ravi clears his throat. 'As much as I'm touched by your sentimental reunion, we have business to attend to.'

Some months ago, Cyrus would have felt embarrassed, even ashamed perhaps, but today he feels completely sure of himself and doesn't feel the need even to apologize. He merely smiles in acknowledgement.

'So, while you were away in Baramulla, a lot else has happened. We've zeroed in on our target in Mumbai. The only way for us to actually nab him, and also retrieve the evidence we're looking for, is to have him believe that the men we now have in our custody have succeeded in their attempt to kidnap their target. What we now have to do is to get the kidnappers to confirm to their handlers in Pakistan that they have everything in place. Then, if the past attacks are anything to go by, our media-savvy terrorist, the one who's been sending all these emails, will be notified and he will promptly walk into the trap we will set.'

Cyrus nods.

'So, we begin interrogating them?' he asks Ravi.

'That won't be necessary. I did that already, on the long drive from Srinagar to Delhi. Before your jaws drop in awe, let me tell you that it just so happens that luck really has been on our side. These men in our custody are professionals, notorious kidnappers who went on a deadly spree in the nineties, targeting the most elite figures of Karachi and Islamabad, extracting hefty ransoms in exchange. Their luck finally ran out when they tried to kidnap the ISI chief's daughter, no less! They were caught and sent to jail. They still had a lot of money stashed away with friends and relatives, and they used a major chunk of it to hire the best criminal lawyers in Pakistan who filed one bail application after the other. But because you simply don't get away in Pakistan with something as outrageous as attempting to kidnap the ISI chief's daughter, their money meant nothing at all.

'Judges who would have otherwise gladly accepted the hefty bribes they were offering not only turned them down but also booked them separately for attempting to corrupt the judiciary. They'd resigned themselves to life in jail when an unexpected reprieve arrived some months ago. They were just released, no reasons given, and whisked away to a training camp in Pakistan-occupied Kashmir. That's where they were given this assignment. If they succeeded, it would be a life of freedom in Pakistan. All charges dropped, just like that. Do you realize what this means?'

Cyrus, who is trying to process all this information, hazards a guess, 'That we can now directly link the LeH to the ISI?'

Ravi chuckles. 'I knew you'd say that. But that's something we've always known. But they'll just deny it, make up a story about them having escaped from jail, or even worse, that we staged the whole thing. Trust the ISI to come up with the most creative explanations. But you are right. This is a goldmine as far as evidence goes. Yet that is quite obvious. And in any case, what is to be done with the ISI angle is a diplomatic and political decision that lies way outside my pay scale, forget yours. I was asking you if you realize what this means from a perspective that's more immediately relevant to our operation.'

Cyrus thinks for a few moments. But before he can answer, Ravi resumes, 'It's fairly simple, and it all comes down to just one word . . . motive. What distinguishes terrorists from ordinary criminals is what drives them. Men like the ones we now have in our custody are not driven by some higher calling that renders them blind to material considerations. That's why you can't, except in outlier cases, bribe or corrupt a terrorist into giving up information. They'd rather die than spill the beans, which is why you often have to resort to extreme measures. But ordinary criminals, especially of the sort we're dealing with, are driven entirely by material considerations and are completely unsympathetic to any ideology. I offer them money to kidnap you, they'll do it. And tomorrow, if you offer them money, they'll be ready to kidnap me. They know very well that Pakistan is going to disown them the moment they find out they've been captured. Which is why I've offered them a solid deal. I told them that they were very valuable to us because they could testify against the ISI. In exchange for that and for doing as instructed, I've promised them asylum in India, and well-paying jobs in government departments of their choice. You should have seen the way their eyes lit up.'

'Don't you think that's being too generous, sir?' Cyrus wonders aloud.

Ravi laughs. 'You don't actually think we're going to honour any of those commitments, do you? I mean, they'll be lucky to get away with life imprisonment. If I had to put my money on it, I'd say they're getting the death sentence. To infiltrate the country with the intention of carrying out a conspiracy to kidnap a member of Parliament, the leader of the Opposition no less, amounts to an act of war and a hundred different things. Right now, we need to focus on what's ahead of us. Mihir is still in Mumbai, and I want you to join him there. Jose will go with you as well.'

Jose is taken by surprise. 'Sir, me? On the field?'

'Yes, since we already know that it's digital evidence that we should be expecting to recover. And because you, among all of us, know exactly how smart that bastard is, we can't afford any let up at the eleventh hour. At the slightest hint of suspicion, he might try to erase all data. And we then might not have enough evidence even to have him convicted, let alone find our way to his bosses. If you're there, even if he does try to erase data, you'll be able to salvage something. Weren't you saying something to me the other day . . . something about there being a critical window of mere minutes for recovering data that has been deliberately deleted?'

Jose nods. 'That's right, sir. And even if he doesn't manage to erase the data, he might have set up some sort of a script that would delete everything after a pre-defined interval. A digital version of a time bomb, to put it crudely. And if that happens to be the case, it might all be gone by the time they bring him and the laptop to Delhi, even if we catch him completely off guard. You're correct, I have to be there. I wouldn't have thought of it myself.'

'That's why I'm the boss here, and you're not. I will leave it to the two of you, along with Mihir, to chalk out a plan. Just keep me in the know at all times. Mihir tells me everything is in place. He has ensnared the suspect's girlfriend, who also happens to be the receptionist who's been giving the suspect access to the hotel's networks. For our purposes, we shall refer to her as Spa Maid. It's a rather quaint and, I must admit, funny nom de guerre, but it's what Mihir came up with. Being her point of contact, he gets to decide. Anyway, this is what's going to happen. In about twenty minutes from now, the men in our custody will place a call to their handlers in Pakistan and confirm safe passage to Delhi. They will then confirm that the plan is on track, and their orders will be executed in exactly two days. Somebody will then contact our Mumbai target, who will in turn contact Spa Maid, requesting her to schedule a service visit. Spa Maid will notify Mihir, who will then notify the rest of us.

'It's really a long chain of communication. Even if one link breaks or goes against what we think we know about their modus operandi, then everything that we have worked towards in the last few months will perhaps have been for nothing. Would you gentlemen like to accompany me?'

'Where, sir?' Jose asks, even as Cyrus remains lost in thought.

'All the way down to hell,' Ravi replies with a smirk. Jose gets the hint. It takes Cyrus a split second longer, but he gets it too. They follow Ravi, through the maze of hallways, elevators, and staircases that leads to the detention cells.

The three men in custody have been allowed to retain their clothes and left unshackled. When Ravi and Cyrus enter, they are gleefully feasting on a grand meal ordered from a nearby hotel. Jose, who is setting up network masking on the other side of the two-way mirror, is baffled to see the men get up to greet Ravi like an old friend. One of them speaks up, 'Supremo, I must tell you, you're a man of your word. Your hospitality is unmatched. You have won over our hearts.'

'And our stomachs,' a second adds. They all burst out laughing. Ravi joins in the laughter.

'I was telling them,' Ravi says loudly, turning to Cyrus, 'that here in India, we treat guests as gods. As I have briefed you already, these wonderful gentlemen here are particularly precious to us. We are united by a common enemy, the ISI, and they will help India expose Pakistan on the international stage. Therefore, they are not to be treated as criminals. We'd like to think of them as refugees. Which is why, anything they need, anything they ask for, it is our duty to provide.'

'Understood, sir,' Cyrus replies, trying very hard not to laugh.

'Now, before we can have desserts brought in for you, could I count on you to hold up your end of the bargain?'

The men nod as they gobble up the rest of the food.

'Good, so as discussed, you will now call your handlers using the phone you've been given. And you will say exactly what you would have said had you actually landed up in Delhi on your own. Like I said earlier, you honour your end of the deal, and we honour ours. We have our ways of knowing if you try to fool us by issuing some sort of a coded warning or using any other channel. And if that happens, the deal is off, and you don't want to know what will happen to you.'

'Why would we let you down, Supremo? We are businessmen, and we have a clear deal. We will do exactly as instructed. You need not fear any betrayal from us.'

Ravi smiles.

'I know, I completely trust you. But as businessmen, you might agree that it's best to be very clear about the terms of any deal, just in case . . .'

A buzzer goes off at one end of the room, a signal from Jose that they are good to go. Cyrus goes over to the other side and returns with the cell phone. The men take a few moments to compose themselves and assume a serious demeanour. Although only one of them will speak, it appears as if they operate as one unit.

'*As-Salaam-Alaikum*, saab. We are in Delhi, headed to Nagpur. Please make arrangements for the handover of oranges. We're very busy, now is the season. So, two days. That's as long as it can wait.'

'*Wa-Alaikum-Salaam*. Everything will be ready in two days. Call me once you are ready to deliver the oranges,' comes the curt response from the other end before the line goes dead.

'Excellent,' Ravi says to them. 'Now you can relax. Order whatever food you want, anything to drink, smoke, be my guest. I won't disturb you for two days. You'll just have to make another phone call, telling them that you are ready to deliver the oranges.'

'Of course,' the men reply in unison. Ravi and Cyrus are almost out the door when one of the men calls out, 'Supremo, there's just one more thing.' Ravi turns back inquiringly. 'You mentioned many things . . . food, drinks, cigarettes, but you left out something very important. Do you reckon you might be able to arrange for, you know, some women? Imagine our plight. We've spent so many years in jail starved for it, if you know what I mean.'

Ravi laughs.

'I completely understand. But I must, unfortunately, ask you to wait for a couple of more days. You see, this is the headquarters, and a lot of eyebrows will be raised. Unnecessary attention that we don't want to be drawing at this critical phase. If all goes well in two days from now, you'll be free men,' he says, before turning to Cyrus with a sly grin. 'And my colleague here is a bit of a veteran when it comes to these matters.'

Cyrus is flabbergasted, but he merely nods in confirmation. By now, he knows exactly what Ravi is up to. As soon as they leave, Jose jumps out of the monitoring room and accosts them just outside the door.

'What on earth was that all about?'

Ravi chuckles, louder and longer than usual, and is about to explain when Cyrus chips in, 'It's called killing many birds with one stone. By saying and doing all that, Ravi sir managed to completely win over their confidence and left them with no room for doubt or hesitation. More importantly, perhaps for Ravi sir, was the amusement value of it all. And in the end, as the crowning glory of sorts, he saw an opportunity to have a final laugh at my expense. Am I correct, sir?'

'You're a quick learner, Bandookwallah. And because you are, I have decided to reward you. If, and only if everything goes well in Mumbai, you can head to Pune, and propose to your girlfriend and do whatever else you have to. I won't bother you while you're there, no matter what happens. Absolutely no work for three days.'

Cyrus is touched by Ravi's gesture and thanks him profusely.

'What about me, sir? Don't I get a break?' Jose tries his luck.

'You will get a break too. But there's an if here. If and only if you find a girlfriend or a boyfriend or whatever it is that you fancy and are ready to propose to that person, I will give you time off.'

Breakthrough

Cyrus, Mihir, and Jose eat a hearty breakfast and take up their respective positions within the Grand Meridien hotel in Juhu. The plans have already been laid out, ironed over, and finalized. It is now only a matter of execution. As they had been expecting, the call to the Pakistan handler had in a matter of mere hours triggered off a chain of communications culminating in Mihir confirming to Ravi that he had received a notification from Spa Maid. By then, Jose and Cyrus had already landed in Mumbai. Jose was introduced to Sunny as an expert on digital security who was there to inspect the hotel's security infrastructure. As part of his inspection, he would require private, uninterrupted access to the hotel's CCTV monitoring room for half a day. Sunny had demanded a hefty sum, as it would involve bribing the hotel's chief of security as well, and Mihir had readily agreed.

As the clock inches closer to the target's expected time of arrival, they confirm to each other over the phone that they are in position. Sharp at twelve noon, a tall, muscular, and fair man with sharp features walks through the entrance into the lobby with a laptop bag slung around his shoulder. He walks up to the reception and smiles cordially at Spa Maid. Mihir, sitting in the lobby and with a direct view of the reception desk, pretends to be working on a spreadsheet.

Sunny, who is completely oblivious to their plans, walks up and whispers to Mihir, 'That's the man I was telling you about. What did I tell you? He looks like a Pathan, doesn't he? And also, just watch out for how uncomfortable she gets around him.'

'I'm busy, Sunny. Do you mind?' Mihir replies, before pulling his phone out of his pocket.

Sunny apologizes and walks away. Mihir types out a message to Ravi, informing him of the target's arrival. He then sends a message to Jose, who confirms that he has clear visuals. Mihir returns to the fake spreadsheet.

In the CCTV room in the basement, Jose has his eyes fixed on the feed from a camera positioned right behind the receptionist's desk. From that angle, Jose can clearly see the contents on the man's laptop screen. He is watching intently for a sign when his phone beeps. It is a message from Ravi, signalling that the call to Pakistan has been placed, and that they are to prepare to swing into action. He types out a message to Mihir and Cyrus, 'Be ready. Any time now.' Jose watches as the man receives a call on his phone. It lasts only a few seconds, after which he opens his laptop and keys in his password. He then begins copying from an already-typed document into his browser client. Jose hits the dial button on his phone and exits the CCTV room. He gets into a waiting van parked right outside, and the driver heads to the main road and parks right in front of the main entrance to the hotel.

In the lobby, Mihir's phone rings. He picks up and starts moving towards the reception, announcing loudly over the phone that he is trying to get better network coverage. Cyrus, who has been standing outside all this while, walks in and surreptitiously moves towards the reception. As has been decided already, at the sight of Mihir walking towards the reception, Spa Maid excuses herself to go to the restroom, leaving the target all by himself behind the reception desk.

'Excuse me, can you tell me where I can get good signal in here?' Mihir asks the man.

'I don't know,' the man replies curtly.

'What do you mean you don't know? Isn't it your job to know?'

'No, it isn't. Now, if you'll please stop bothering me, I have work to do.'

'What is the meaning of all this? Do you know who you are talking to? I will get you fired, you arrogant son of a bitch . . .'

The man is genuinely annoyed but maintains his calm and continues fiddling with his laptop. 'I don't care who you are, sir. But it is not my job to know. I'm an IT engineer here to fix the network. I understand you're anxious, but please mind your tone.'

Mihir flies off into a rage and grabs the man by his collar. 'You'll tell me what tone I should speak in?' Caught completely off guard, the man's jaw drops as Cyrus swoops in and picks up the laptop, which is still open. He makes a mad dash towards the entrance, and the man follows behind pushing Mihir away. Mihir picks himself up quickly and follows the man, who is hot on Cyrus's trail.

Cyrus runs towards the waiting van and hands over the laptop to Jose. The van speeds away, leaving the man stunned. He is yet to register what has just transpired when another similarly unmarked van comes through the traffic and pulls up beside him. He decides to flee, but before he can get going, Mihir gives him a hard shove from behind. As he falls against the van, the doors swivel open, and the Examiner pulls him inside. Cyrus and Mihir get in as well. Both vans are headed to a nearby air force base, where a special aircraft is on standby.

From the first van, Jose calls Ravi, who has already been notified by Mihir of their success.

'What's the verdict on the data?' Ravi asks.

'It's all in here, sir, from what I can tell. And I have already commenced the process of cloning the entire drive before any self-destruct scripts kick in,' Jose replies.

* * *

The three men in custody at the headquarters are fast asleep in their well-appointed cell when Ravi walks in.

'Time to go,' Ravi tells them.

'Now, Supremo? We were beginning to get used to all this comfort, and it's quite late, isn't it?' one of them says as he yawns widely, while the others try to shake off their sleep.

'We're not yet letting you go. Just moving you elsewhere for the time being until we can be sure that you are going to be absolutely safe outside. Also, as per protocol, we're going to get in touch with Pakistan and inform them that you are in our custody. All this takes some time, I'm sure you understand,' Ravi tells them.

The men are quietly herded into a van stationed right outside the sub-basement entrance to the detention centre. As nobody else at the bureau except the chief has been informed yet of the circumstances surrounding their capture or of the subsequent events in Mumbai, it is all being done very discreetly and rather late at night. Ravi himself is in the driver's seat, while Mihir sits with the men in the back. At the sound of the back door thudding to a close, Ravi puts his feet on the throttle and speeds away through a back road. Their destination is less than a kilometre away—the dilapidated hunting lodge next to the headquarters, what locals refer to as Bhoot Mahal.

At the sound of the approaching van, a pack of hounds begin howling and barking unrelentingly. The sole resident of the lodge, a frail man, dressed in unusually grand clothing, steps out to inspect the cause of the commotion. He is about to set his restless dogs free when he hears a familiar voice call out to him, 'Prince Saab, it's me, Ravi.'

Somewhat reassured at hearing Ravi's voice, the man keeps the dogs tied and walks towards the van.

'I'm sorry to wake you up, Prince Saab. But you know how it is,' Ravi tells him, extending his hand.

'It's fine. I don't sleep much anyway. Do what you need to do.'

'Thank you, Prince Saab. Same as usual. Unless I specifically tell you otherwise, there is nobody here.'

'Of course. When has anybody dared to even set foot in here, except you? They call it Bhoot Mahal, after all. And you come once in a year if I'm lucky.'

Only Ravi knows that the man's claims of being a descendant of the Nawab of Awadh are all part of an elaborate fraud that had been orchestrated by his deceased mother. The man is notoriously hostile to visitors, and nobody dares set foot on the premises. Ravi had threatened him with the prospect of spilling his secrets unless he complied with his requests from time to time.

Ravi signals to Mihir to escort the men out of the van. Although it is now many centuries past its prime, the lodge is still a massive structure, large enough to accommodate a small army. Inconspicuously nestled at the far end is a room that stands in stark contrast with the rest of the crumbling complex. While everything is built out of stone and marble, this room is made of concrete and is evidently a recent construction.

Ravi pulls out a bunch of keys from his pocket and unlocks a series of heavy locks that guard the door. Inside, the room doesn't look all that different from the detention centres at the headquarters. Mattresses with bedsheets appear to have already been laid out on three of the bunker beds that stand neatly arranged along the widest wall. Ravi uncuffs the men and instructs them to stay put until the next day. Before they can ask any further questions, Ravi swiftly shuts the door and locks them in.

Mihir waits until they're back in the van before attempting to unleash the flood of questions that has been building up inside him. But Ravi pre-empts all of it and explains without waiting for Mihir to articulate as much as a single word, 'After the drubbing they received in Kargil, it was clear to us that it was unlikely that Pakistan would attempt any sort of conventional warfare for quite some time. The attack on Parliament not long after only strengthened our hunch. Terrorism was going to be the new normal. And so, in anticipation of a possible scenario where there was the sudden infiltration of more terrorists than our existing detention facilities could handle, we set up several such safe houses turned detention centres across parts of the country, particularly Delhi and the border regions. These places are completely off the books, and very few people even know of their existence. It was my idea to have one such centre in the immediate vicinity of the headquarters. It's perfectly suited for a number of scenarios. In this case, for instance, it makes it very easy for us to keep them in custody until we take them to a more well-known safe house from where they can be handed over, without making it seem that way.'

'I'm sorry, sir, I don't understand. What exactly do you mean by that?'

'If the state police pick them up from the headquarters, then the official records will have to indicate that they were in our custody before being handed over. We don't really want that to be happening. For all practical purposes, these men were arrested by the J&K Police in collaboration with the state police concerned. Don't forget that it is a rather long chain of deception that has led us up to this point. It is essential that it remains that way at all times, and our involvement appears vague to all external observers. We're shadow people, remember?'

* * *

Sarita and Ravi find themselves in slightly unfamiliar, although not entirely unknown territory. Given the political sensitivity of the matter, not to mention its inextricable entanglement in a larger conspiracy, they are yet to fully unearth, field intelligence alone will not suffice. They need more concrete evidence. As they meet in Sarita's office, it is this delicate matter that dominates the agenda.

'What do you think, Ravi?' Sarita asks.

'For a state to conspire to kidnap a foreign member of Parliament is an act of war, whichever way you look at it. And I'm certain that if we dig deeper, we're going to obtain more than just their confessions as evidence. These men had been in prison, after a much-publicized trial and conviction, and then they were mysteriously set free. All off the books, mind you, no court order, nothing of that sort. For all official purposes, they're supposed to be in prison. Next thing anybody knows, they're found in India. It's too thick a trail for even the ISI to cover up.'

Sarita smiles.

'So, it is a costly mistake they've made. Either they're getting lax or we're getting better.'

She thinks for a few moments before continuing, 'Unless we provide more concrete evidence, it will not be easy to convince the world that these men are Pakistani citizens. And if that doesn't happen, Pakistan could paint the whole thing as a conspiracy on our part. If we're going to get any leverage out of this, it is essential that there is some tangible acknowledgement from the terrorists themselves. And again, it can't just be a custodial confession. It can easily be dismissed. What do you think we should do?'

'Diplomacy at this formal level isn't really within the ambit of my duties, technically speaking.'

'It isn't now, but it could be soon enough if you keep saving the day like you have been. I see big things in store for you, Ravi, much bigger than I could have ever aspired for in my own career. Who knows? Maybe even NSA, if you play your cards right.'

'I sincerely appreciate your faith in me, ma'am, but I prefer to focus on what's in front of me.'

The chief chuckles.

'Ever the humble soldier. Anyway, that is exactly what I'm asking you to do, to focus on what's in front of us. How do we deal with this?'

'I think we should go with the time-honoured strategy of involving a reputed journalist, someone who can visit and confirm that the men are indeed Pakistani and were on a mission to kidnap a politician. We can record the whole thing, for proof. It can then be used as propaganda.'

The chief nods in agreement.

'That's not such a bad idea. In ordinary circumstances, they might not have agreed, but the chips are stacked against them here. And in any case, we have nothing to fear. They've been taken good care of. I'm sure I can trust you to arrange for a journalist and for the audio of the interview to be recorded,'

'Video, ma'am. The era of audio is long gone. Radio has long given way to primetime television, and our practices must be in line with the changing times. We currently don't have the required means at our safe houses, but I can have my people set it up.'

'As you deem fit, Ravi. You're the one surrounded by young people. I trust you to do what is necessary. Thank you for this. You can get back now. I will let you know if anything comes up.'

'There is one more thing, ma'am. We need to arrange for the men to be handed over to the state police at the earliest. A day or two in transit is an understandable justification, but we can't explain away several days at a stretch. It's been five days since they were arrested by the J&K Police. We can't keep them in our custody any longer without drawing unnecessary attention. If we can get them off our hands, we can then fully turn our attention towards the man we nabbed in Mumbai.'

'Yes, I understand. You can notify them immediately.'

* * *

Jagriti Saha, one of the country's most eminent journalists with a fierce reputation for objective and non-partisan reporting, is chosen for the task. In order to protect the secrecy of the detention chamber nestled within Bhoot Mahal, the suspects are moved yet again, this time to a safe house that is in the official books—a dilapidated bungalow on the industrial fringes of Delhi. The plan is for the men to be interviewed by Jagriti, after which they are to be taken into custody by a team from the state police. As per the terms agreed upon, Jagriti is to speak to the men alone. To ensure her safety, the suspects have been handcuffed, and the room in which they are held has been left unlocked so as to allow her to leave at any moment she senses a threat. It is merely precautionary, for the men have little desire to escape, lost as they are in their fantasies about a new life of prosperity in India. Mihir waits right outside. His eyes are fixed on the door, straining to hear the conversation going on inside.

Ravi and Jose are in a separate room on the second floor of the safe house, monitoring the feed from cameras that have been specially set up to record the proceedings. The interview moves in line with their expectations, and the men repeat what they have told Ravi. Because they do not have to lie, the men are able to confidently respond to Jagriti's questions without batting an eyelid. They speak in glowing terms about the treatment meted out by the Indian authorities. State police personnel enter the scene as planned but to Ravi's horror they start firing without giving any warning. It is followed by a blood-curdling shriek—a woman's voice. Ravi sprints down the stairs. He fears the worst. Outside the room downstairs, he finds Mihir on the floor with his hands held up, two uniformed policemen holding him at gunpoint. Mihir is shouting at them, insisting that he is an intelligence officer, but they seem to pay no heed to his protests.

'What on earth do you think you're bloody doing?' Ravi shouts, his voice louder than anyone has ever heard.

One of the policemen turns and points his gun in Ravi's direction, but is stopped immediately by a colleague who comes out through the door along with three others. 'Put your gun down unless you want to lose your job,' the pot-bellied policeman, presumably the most senior officer on the team, barks at his subordinate before slapping him vigorously on the back of his head. He then immediately assumes a saluting position—'*Jai Hind*, sir. Myself, Inspector Jairam, in-charge officer.' The others follow suit, but Ravi brushes past them and walks into the room. The three suspects lie motionless, still handcuffed in their chairs. There is blood splattered all around. But it is the sight that greets him next that sends a shiver down his spine—Jagriti Saha, lying in a pool of her own blood. Ravi turns her around to find three bullet wounds on her forehead. He checks her pulse. Nothing.

'Your orders were to take them into custody. Is it that bloody hard to do? And where is your DCP? Isn't he supposed to be leading this operation?' Ravi shouts at the inspector, holding him by the collar.

'S-sir, DCP sir had to stay back in headquarters for personal reasons. He delegated it to me. But why are you getting so angry, sir, they were terrorists anyway.'

Ravi lets go of the man's collar and shakes his head in disbelief.

'And the woman? Do you know who she is?'

'Of course, sir. Who wouldn't know Jagriti Madam? The entire department is scared of her. If we knew she was in there, we wouldn't have dared to even enter.'

'And still you did. What about my man here telling you not to go in? Wasn't that clear enough?'

'Sir, actually, we weren't informed that there would be somebody from your agency . . . we were told it would be an unmanned handover. We would have to come here and then contact you.'

'I see. And yet you didn't feel the need to contact me. And my man telling you clearly that he is a C3 officer did nothing to alter your impression?'

'No sir, actually, like I said, we weren't informed that there would be somebody. I have been here before, you might remember me from a handover that was done two years ago. So, I knew where to go and what to do. I would have listened to him, but because the room was unlocked, I thought something had gone wrong. I didn't want to take any chances or waste any time in trying to contact you, and so we just went ahead.'

'I see. And so you storm in, and you find three men handcuffed to their chairs. On what grounds exactly did you feel the need to open fire?'

'S–sir . . .'

'That alone is inexcusable, but I know exactly why you did it. Medals, newspaper mentions, interviews, the usual. It's a guaranteed shortcut to glory. But what about Jagriti Saha? Don't bloody tell me now that she got shot accidentally. Three bullets through her forehead. I looked at the wounds. That's about as deliberate as it gets.'

'S–sir . . . Only after firing at the three men and moving in closer did we realize that it was her. I–I mean, she has been the most vocal critic of our department and of encounter killings. If we'd let her leave that room, it would have meant the end of all our careers.'

'And so, you thought it would be best to just finish her off?'

'I–I didn't think, sir. I just panicked at seeing her and fired. B–but, think of it this way, sir. What's done is done, but at least now we can justify the encounter. We can say that they shot at her, which is why we had to . . . if you can corroborate this story, I don't mind sharing credit with your team also, sir. This is going to be breaking news, all over the world anyway.'

Ravi lets out a hollow laugh, sickened at the absurdity of the situation. He still cannot believe what has happened, let alone the outrageous propositions the inspector is putting forth.

'You don't mind? How generous of you. Unfortunately, I'll have to decline. The credit will belong solely to you, perhaps to your DCP too, although he'll only get credit for dereliction of duty. You, on the other hand, will get credit for the cold-blooded murder of one of India's most prominent journalists. Get out of my sight right now.'

Yin Yang

An elaborately attired steward refills Anil's glass as he settles into a plush leather chair in a private lounge within the Delhi Gymkhana, one of the most elite clubs in the capital. Sitting opposite Anil is Gopinath Pawar, the home minister of the state whose police officers were involved in the shootout. He is in Delhi to defuse the crisis that looms in the wake of the encounter gone awry from earlier in the day. Unlike Ravi, who has a professed distaste for socializing, particularly with politicians, Anil takes particular interest in nurturing such connections. He and Pawar go back a long time, having been inducted into the elite Indian Police Service at around the same time. While Anil had stayed on, Pawar had quit only a decade into his service to enter politics. He had steadily risen through the ranks and had become home minister of the state.

The mood is somewhat grim. Pawar tells his former colleague, 'Anil, I don't know why you wanted to meet me. Whatever plan you might have in mind, things aren't looking good. Jagriti's family has been notified. And it is only a matter of time before every news channel in the country is going to be talking about it. And when that happens, my resignation is going to be inevitable.'

'Not necessarily, Gopi. This isn't the first time you're stuck in something like this. We can spin the narrative.'

'The problem is, Anil, that this is the death of a leading journalist we're talking about. Heads will have to roll. There's nothing that can be done.'

'Yes, Gopi. That is right, heads will roll, but what I'm saying is, it doesn't have to be yours . . . The way I see it, it is not even your fault to begin with.'

Pawar shuffles nervously in his seat. His fingers scratch at his bushy beard.

'Whose is it then? Let's not forget that my men fired those shots. At least that much is irrefutable, no matter how we spin it.'

'Jagriti Saha's death is clouding your thinking, minister saab. Don't forget how and why the whole thing started in the first place.'

Pawar appears to be irritated.

'Look Anil, I have no time right now for your cryptic suggestions. I have a meeting with the CM and PM in an hour. Whatever it is that you have to say, get to the point.'

Anil chuckles.

'Okay. Let me state this as clearly as I can. This saga began with the arrest of those three men in Kashmir. The J&K Police picked them up, acting on a tip-off. Now, under established protocol, the men were supposed to be handed over to your department directly. If that had happened, you wouldn't have found yourself in this situation. But what happened instead? C3 took them into custody and kept them for close to a week before notifying you. The question is, why?'

'Yes, it is not exactly as per protocol, but then again, they could easily justify it. C3 is the premier counterterrorism agency of our country, and these men were terrorists.'

'I'm not very convinced of that, Gopi. I don't mean to sound like a human rights activist, but we have to be very careful about how we use the word terrorist. These men were allegedly embarking on a mission to kidnap Kishan Jadhav. You always did better than me on legal subjects at the academy. You should know better. Under what section of the law, or under what generally accepted convention is a political kidnapping an act of terrorism? C3 might have stumbled upon the information, but it was none of their business to be taking the suspects into custody. It all seems a little too fishy to me.'

Pawar smiles for the first time all evening.

'So, you're suggesting that the whole thing was a set-up?'

'I wouldn't say it out loud myself, but it could very well be the case. Look, I know Ravi very well. He has always had outsized ambitions. The chief is set to retire soon, and I wouldn't be surprised at all if he is plotting to replace her.'

'But that makes no sense, Anil. You're next in line, and he's almost three years junior to you. And even if you are right, I don't see the connection.'

'The connection is very clear. Whether you like it or not, the hard truth is that your party is going to be voted out at the Centre in the next general election. Kishan Jadhav is our next PM, any kid on the street will tell you that. What better way to get in his good books than by appearing to have saved his life? Ravi might pretend to be this saint who is above politics and partisanship, but that's just a smokescreen. As for protocol and hierarchy, Ravi has no regard for any of that. The men that he surrounds himself with these days haven't even completed their training. He pulled them out of the academy, and it's like a small cult of minions he's built for himself. They have higher clearance on some operations than I do. Can you believe it? He might be three years my junior, but he still got picked over me to head C3, didn't he?'

Pawar smiles, appearing to have finally connected the dots Anil has been laying out for him.

'Now I see it. Jadhav's charismatic appeal owes a lot to the fact that he is very young. If and when he assumes office, he might want to surround himself with young faces. That sort of thing appeals to voters these days. They somehow seem to think of youth as a virtue. And in any case, if it is an appointment ordered directly by the PM, who gives a damn about protocol? Ravi's quite the player, isn't he? He's playing for the biggest prize. He should be in politics, really. It's a brilliant plan, now that I think about it. Not only would he have gotten the chance to come across as Jadhav's saviour, but news of the plot would have heightened public sympathy and pushed Jadhav's poll numbers up.'

Anil nods with a wicked grin.

'I'm glad you're beginning to recognize this for what it is. In fact, it gets even better. Of all the journalists in this country, tell me who has been the most sceptical of Jadhav's charms?'

'If what you're suggesting is that this was a deliberate attempt to eliminate Jagriti, it might be pushing it too far, Anil. She has been a scathing critic of every politician . . . me, my CM, the PM himself. It's not like she has gone after only Jadhav.'

Anil begins to laugh.

'I'm disappointed in you, Gopi. You're the politician here, you should know better. You're right, she has gone after you, she has gone after the PM, but so have many other journalists. But when it comes to Jadhav, only Jagriti has raised serious questions about his credibility and the image of honesty he wears so proudly on his sleeve. Besides, this isn't about facts, but about perceptions. You just put it all out there . . . an alleged kidnapping plot, the death of a journalist who was critical of the alleged target of kidnapping, violation of protocols pertaining to custody, no solid evidence, inadequately trained agents . . . and see how it all plays out. If you spin it right, you'll be the one playing for the biggest prize. Forget having to resign, you might be up for a massive promotion. I hear that the PM and the HM haven't exactly been on very good terms recently. If you wean yourself out of this and also tarnish Jadhav's image in the process, the position might be handed to you on a platter. And then . . .'

Pawar's phone rings. He picks it up, says to the caller that he is on his way and hangs up.

'Anil, I have to go. But before that, I need to be absolutely sure. Once this plan is in motion, there will be no going back. The PM's not the sort to play dirty. He's a man of integrity. Especially with elections around the corner, he will want to play it safe. He will approve only if we can be absolutely certain that this is indeed a conspiracy. I'd rather resign gracefully than have my career finished once and for all.'

'Look, you don't need to accuse Jadhav of anything. The media will inadvertently do the dirty work for you. In any case, as far as the legal side of things go, it's a low-risk gamble. It is Ravi you will be targeting, not Jadhav.'

'Yes, but what if Ravi does have evidence? What if there really was a plot to kidnap Jadhav?'

'Even if there really was a plot to kidnap Jadhav, the only substantial evidence would have been a confession from the arrested men, and whatever else that might have emerged from interrogation. But they're dead, and nothing will hold in court. I've been in intelligence long enough to know how it works and how this is going to unfold. Whatever tip-off led to their arrest would have come from an undercover source who cannot be exposed at any cost. And because kidnapping isn't exactly an act of terror or a threat to national security, he can't get away by simply saying it was classified information. He might then try to justify it by saying that the suspects were working at the behest of a terrorist outfit or the ISI or something like that, but that too would be very hard to establish concretely, especially now that they are dead. As for the interview that was happening before the police team barged in, there is only going to be an audio recording of it. That's standard practice. Nothing conclusive as to who did it and how will be apparent. It'll be ambiguous at best, leaving room for interpretation. And so, it'll come down to one singularly important fact, which is that the men who fired those bullets are your men. Give them the words, and they'll sing it. There'll then be no ambiguity, no room for interpretation. I've given you the bricks, it's now up to you to decide what to build from it.'

'Well, if it's my grave, then you can be sure that I'll make extra room for you.'

Anil laughs, as Pawar gets up to leave.

'I'll be watching the news, minister saab. First thing tomorrow morning is when you'll want to strike. If you need more juice, you know how to reach me.'

* * *

First Jose had called, and now Mihir is calling. Perhaps they want to congratulate him. But this early in the morning? One couldn't fault them though. He was up too, after all, despite having no work to attend to. Whatever it was, it would have to wait. Ravi had promised Cyrus an undisturbed vacation, and he was going to make the most of it. He puts his ringer on silent and wonders if he has ever been as happy as he is now. He was supposed to have been graduating from the academy in a month's time, but instead, here he is, having played a crucial role in neutralizing an extremely serious threat to the nation's internal security. If that wasn't enough, Gehna had agreed to marry him. He couldn't have possibly wished for more. These thoughts run through his mind as he lies in a hotel room, tucked in cozily with the love of his life, one last time before he returns to Delhi. But it would only be a momentary parting, for plans were already afoot. They would get married in two months, and then they wouldn't have to live apart from one other. As a journalist her work would entail some travel, but his job required that too. What was important, they told themselves, was that they would return to the same home.

Gehna's phone now begins to ring. Annoyed at being woken up this early, she puts it under the pillow. But it rings incessantly, forcing her to wake up. As she goes to the balcony to take the call, Cyrus looks at his phone. Twenty missed calls, all from Jose and Mihir, in just three minutes. It rings again. This time, it is Ravi.

'Sir.'

'Turn on the TV.'

'Sir, which channel? What happened?'

'Any news channel. But no matter what they're saying, and they are going to be saying awful things in just a short while, don't panic. I promise you I'll get you out of this, all of you.'

Before Cyrus can respond, Ravi hangs up. By then, Gehna comes back into the room, looking distraught.

'They killed her, she's dead,' she tells him, fighting back tears.

'Who?'

'Jagriti Saha. The only person I've ever looked up to . . . the reason why I'm a journalist,' she gasps, before collapsing into his arms.

Alarm bells go off in Cyrus's head. Even as he tries to comfort Gehna, he wonders if the LeH was responsible. Only that would explain the flurry of calls that early in the morning. Surely, nothing else would be playing on the news. But what was Ravi talking about? What was it that he promised to get all of them out of? What had he gotten into?

With great trepidation, he reaches for the remote. The first channel that comes on is broadcasting an interview with Inspector Jairam.

'So, inspector, could you please walk us through what happened yesterday?'

'As a matter of professional ethics and legal procedure, I am not supposed to be commenting on an ongoing investigation. But today is a dark day in the history of our country, and the people deserve to know. I have nothing to fear, for this is the truth. Yesterday, I and five others travelled to Delhi to take into custody three alleged terrorists who had been arrested by the J&K Police and were being held in a safe house. Our orders were simple. We just had to take them into our custody.'

'Inspector, would you mind telling us exactly what they were suspected of being involved in?'

'I cannot comment on that. Details will be revealed in due time. I can only tell you what happened in front of my own eyes. We went there at the designated time of handover. And as I was saying, our orders were straightforward. But when we went there, a very senior officer, who again I cannot name at this point, told us that the men inside were armed and that we had to tread carefully. Coming from such a senior officer, who were we to ask any questions? What he did not tell us was that Jagriti Madam was also in the room. It was only after we barged in and opened fire that we realized, but by then, it was too late. The men weren't even armed. We had made a costly mistake.'

The inspector breaks into tears, and the reporter tries to console him.

'Inspector, it takes a lot of courage and determination to speak the truth and admit to one's mistakes. I urge you to stay strong in this time of mourning. Specific details will, of course, emerge in due time, but there are questions that I am sure are on everybody's mind. What were the charges against the men who were killed in the encounter? Who was the senior officer in question, and why did he deliberately mislead Jairam and his team? Most importantly, what was Jagriti Saha doing there? Today, as the nation stands united in grief, we demand answers.'

* * *

Janaki Kaul offers her obeisance to a tiny Shivalinga on her bedside table, as soon as she wakes up. The linga had been hand-carved by her grandfather, a renowned artisan. Ever since she was a young girl growing up in Srinagar, praying to it was the first thing she did every morning. Even when she had lost her husband tragically, even when her family had been violently shunted out of their homes into a lifetime of exile, her faith had remained unshaken. Indeed, it was this faith that had kept her going throughout. She was convinced that the Lord himself was responsible for the stable and respectable marketing job that Mihir had bagged soon after graduating. So, what if she didn't get to see him as often as she would have hoped? At least she didn't have to worry about his safety, a worry every Kashmiri mother from those troubled decades was most intimately acquainted with.

As she walks out of her room into the hall and unlatches the front door, the landline begins to ring. She is surprised. Nobody ever calls, except Mihir and the occasional telemarketer. But Mihir calls only on Sundays, and it is too early in the day for telemarketing.

'Hello . . . *Mauji?*'

'Mihir?' Janaki responds with a marked hint of exhilaration in her voice.

'*Mauji*, before you find out from someone else, I thought I should tell you myself . . .'

'Tell me what, Nechu? Have you eloped with some girl and gotten married?'

'No, it's not that. Something's gone wrong, and some people are spreading false rumours about me. It's all over the news. But don't believe a word of what you hear. In fact, don't watch the news. I'm on my way home. I'll be there in five minutes and explain everything. You don't have to worry about anything.'

'What are you talking about? What rumours . . .?'

The line goes dead.

Never the sort to watch the news first thing in the morning, Janaki decides to turn on the TV. Her pulse quickens as she switches to a news channel.

'. . . we await further confirmation, but sensational details have emerged in the last hour in connection with the tragic demise of Jagriti Saha. Initial reports indicated that she had been caught in the crossfire during a tense standoff between armed terrorists and the police, during a routine handover in New Delhi. Late last night, the Central government had announced that the CBI would be immediately commencing an investigation into the matter. Fresh information now coming in paints a very sinister picture. It now appears that the men killed in this shootout had been arrested for allegedly conspiring to kidnap Kishan Jadhav, the leader of the Prajaprabhuthva Party. Highly placed sources tell us that the investigation is now firmly focused on senior

IPS officer, Ravi Kumar, head of the Central Counterterrorism Command. Ravi Kumar allegedly misled the police with false information, culminating eventually in the tragic encounter that silenced Jagriti Saha once and for all. Exactly what motivated officer Ravi Kumar to provide false information is yet to be determined. We are being told that he, along with three officers, Cyrus Bandookwallah, Mihir Kaul and Jose Cherian, will be summoned by the CBI for questioning later today. We will share more details as soon as they emerge. But the question that remains unanswered is this: what was Jagriti Saha doing there in the first place? With no information forthcoming either from the government or from our sources, speculation is rife, and conspiracy theorists are having a field day, with many suggesting that the whole thing was staged to garner sympathy for Kishan Jadhav, widely seen as a strong contender to be the next prime minister of India. It is a rumour that is now gaining wider currency, with highly placed sources telling us that Ravi Kumar is a close associate of Kishan Jadhav.'

Mihir can hear the news blaring at full volume from several metres afar. He runs into the house hoping to turn it off, but stops in his tracks, dazed by the sight that greets him— his mother on the floor, convulsing violently.

* * *

Rita watches on helplessly as Ravi paces up and down their bedroom with unusual fury, even by his standards. He smokes frantically, one cigarette after the other—each lit by the dying embers of the previous one—but nothing can calm his nerves today. When the news had broken some hours ago, he had reacted somewhat calmly. 'It's just politics, as usual. I'm just a convenient scapegoat for now. Nothing will come out of this,' he had assured Rita.

But as the stories continue to compound and morph into bizarre abominations of the truth, his patience is growing increasingly thinner. The final straw was the sight of Inspector Jairam bursting into tears on live television. Ravi had flung his ashtray at the TV, and hurled such terrible curses that Rita had to rein him in with force, something she had never done before. 'For Abhinav's sake, please,' she had pleaded. After that, he had fallen completely silent and taken to pacing the room.

After stubbing out his umpteenth cigarette, he finally decides that it is time to speak to the chief.

She picks up at the first ring.

'Ravi, thank God! I tried calling so many times and you've never ignored my calls in all these years. I was so worried.'

'I'll be fine, ma'am. They can spout all the nonsense they want, but facts are facts. I have never met Jadhav, forget being a close associate of his. You have been in the know all along. You have been kept fully aware of the circumstances that led to the arrest of those men and also of what happened yesterday.'

'I know, Ravi. Not for a moment have I believed any of this nonsense. If I hadn't been kept in the dark, I would have never allowed things to get to this stage. I promise you that you will come out of this unscathed.'

'Thank you, ma'am. Speaking for myself, I really have nothing to worry about anyway. My family stands by me, and I will certainly come out of this unscathed. But I'm deeply concerned about my team being dragged into this and the devastation it has inflicted on their personal lives. Mihir's mother, who had no idea that her son had followed in his father's footsteps, suffered a severe paralytic stroke when she heard the news. As we speak, she is in the ICU at Safdarjung. Cyrus was on a well-deserved break. He'd gone back to propose to the love of his life, and she'd agreed. As it so happens, Jagriti Saha was her mentor and her biggest inspiration. When she listened to the filth that was being spewed on TV about her fiancé's involvement, it took her only a few moments to discard the ring he had given her and walk out. My men, who've served the country with great honour and integrity, are not going to escape unscathed ma'am.'

'I am so sorry to hear that, Ravi. This is terrible, terrible news. We must put an end to all this. I suggest that you put together whatever evidence you have and meet the CBI investigators right away.'

'I will, ma'am. But not right away.'

'What do you mean, Ravi? We have to limit the damage, before it spirals completely out of control.'

'The damage has already been done, ma'am. There's nothing left to be damaged. Now, it is only their vicious lies that can spiral out of control. Because at the end of the day, after everything's been said and done, facts will remain facts. It's the one thing whoever plotted all of this failed to take into account. I'm sure they were counting on it being, as it usually is, all based on intelligence coming in from sources who cannot be contacted as a rule of thumb. But this case is different. We have extremely strong evidence on all fronts. Thanks to our successful recovery of the laptop in Mumbai, and call recordings from that day, we have undeniably incriminating proof of the LeH plot to kidnap Kishan Jadhav and the role of the three deceased suspects. And more importantly, we have video and audio footage of the extra-judicial killing of the three suspects and of Jagriti Saha by uniformed officers of the police department.'

'Exactly my point, Ravi. Why do you want to wait?'

'We first need to tackle the damage that would be caused if the LeH leadership is allowed to remain free. Our officers have a clear lead on the group. All of this is an unnecessary distraction at this point, ma'am. To put it simply, a clear choice confronts me and my team. Either save ourselves, or save the country from the nefarious designs of our enemies. We are at a make or break juncture in our pursuit of the LeH leadership, and if we get sidetracked now, we might lose them completely, and it will be back to square one. From the laptop that we recovered in Mumbai, we have managed to retrieve important clues about the whereabouts of the top cadre of the organization. We are certain that they are in Bangalore. But there's a lot more that needs to be done. We need to track down their satellite phone numbers and obtain precise coordinates. In ordinary circumstances, our job would have been over at that, and the rest would have been handled by Bangalore Police. But in light of recent events, my gut feeling tells me not to risk it. I'd like to handle it myself. And on all of this, I speak not just for myself, but also for my team. Despite the personal tragedies they've endured in the past few hours, they have conveyed to me their desire to return to work immediately, and finish what we've all been working on tirelessly for months on end. For that to happen, I will need you to do whatever it takes to keep the CBI investigation at bay until this is all done. And at no point will my men be summoned for questioning, no matter what happens. They've been through enough already.'

Damage Control

Sarita is walking towards the office of the director of the CBI when her phone rings. It is the home secretary, who she has been waiting to hear from all morning.

'Sir.'

'Sarita, I have managed to get what you asked for. I had to pull some strings, but it's done. The plane will be ready to take off in an hour.'

'Thank you, sir. I really appreciate you doing this for me.'

'Oh, don't thank me, Sarita. I'm not doing this for you. I'm just doing my job. Under ordinary circumstances, you wouldn't have had to contact me for this. In fact, I don't think Ravi would have needed your approval. But you know how it is. We're surrounded by a pack of vultures. The smallest thing can be made to seem like we're abetting evasion from the law.'

'I understand, sir. Which is why I'm grateful.'

* * *

In Ravi's office, he, Jose and Mihir sit together, filling the room with nervous silence. On the one hand, they have to work hard to ignore the unyielding onslaught from the media and the prospect of a CBI interrogation. On the other, they are also trying to focus on the impending operation to nab the leaders of the LeH. They have vowed not to let the investigation bother them, but it almost increases their drive to succeed and be vindicated.

As far as the on-ground operation itself is concerned, there is little left to be decided. They have precise coordinates—a rented house in Nagarbhavi, not far away from the National Law School of India—and a clear plan of action. They even know who they are looking for, having found pictures and other identifying details on the laptop recovered in Mumbai.

What they are working on is the logistics of getting to Bangalore. Although the chief has ensured that they haven't been suspended, they cannot operate freely. With their names and faces having been broadcast on every television screen in the country, taking a passenger flight to Bangalore would surely attract attention and inadvertently alert their targets. But at the same time, it is to be a quick in-and-out operation, the sort that would not merit the time-consuming process of assuming fake identities and disguises. The only way out, it has been decided, is to take a special IAF aircraft. As he waits for the chief to confirm the arrangements, Ravi goes about the elaborate process of readying his pipe—a luxury he hasn't had the time for recently. The others sit around, simply waiting. Sensing the young recruits' frayed nerves, Ravi had decided that it would be a good idea to have the Examiner on board.

After much fidgeting, Cyrus gets up and walks around the room. Pulling out a pack of cigarettes from his pocket, he asks, 'Sir, would you mind if I smoked as well?'

Ravi looks at him with a mix of amusement and surprise.

'I didn't know you smoked.'

'Not until yesterday, sir. Last night I was tossing and turning in bed and thinking to myself how is it that you manage to deal with all the stress that you're constantly dealing with. And then it struck me . . . cigarettes. And so, I went out and bought a pack and smoked my first cigarette. Not exactly a magic wand, but it helped me feel a little lighter.'

Ravi laughs.

'Well, if you want to dig your own grave, be my guest.'

The Examiner chips in, 'But let me warn you, that feeling of lightness, you might want to enjoy it while it lasts. Some years from now, if you're still a smoker, and I hope you won't be, you'll look back and wonder why you started smoking in the first place. Because by then, you'll just be smoking for the sake of smoking, no lightness, no nothing. It's a lot like power, you know.'

The phone rings. Arrangements are in place.

* * *

Saranjit Singh, the director of the CBI, rises to greet Sarita with genuine warmth as she walks into his office. Sarita has known him all through her career. He is only three years her senior.

'Sarita, it has been such a long time. It's always comforting to see a familiar face. Please, sit down.'

Sarita shakes his hand and takes her seat.

'I'm sorry to have kept you waiting so long, Sarita. You know how it is, you overshoot one meeting, and it's like a house of cards.'

'I understand, sir. It's completely fine.'

'What brings you here?'

'You know exactly why I'm here, sir. It is about Ravi Kumar. You know him better than most. If I'm not mistaken, you are both from the same state cadre and you were one of his earliest bosses. If there ever was a man of integrity and commitment, it's him.'

'Well, if I were to speak for myself personally, I have no doubt whatsoever that he isn't guilty of anything. But when I speak here, I do not speak for myself, but on behalf of this office. As far as the CBI probe into the killing of Jagriti Saha goes, nothing can be presumed on the basis of what I personally think. We have officers from the police department going on record against your man. Their claims have to be thoroughly looked into, at the very least.'

Sarita sighs. 'Fair enough, sir. But I do not see why all of this had to be announced to the public before you'd thoroughly looked into it. At the very least, the sensitive nature of the work C3 does should have been taken into account.'

Saranjit smiles.

'Sarita, Sarita. Relax. I know you're angry, but you need to understand that we never announced anything. You know how it is, information gets leaked, and then the media runs its own trial. And you can't be naïve enough to not know what is motivating all of this . . . not at this stage of your career.'

'I know exactly what they're trying to achieve, sir. A smear campaign to distract focus from the real perpetrators is one thing, but for that to translate into a demand for custodial interrogation? Let us not forget that this is a decorated officer with an outstanding track record we are talking about.'

'It's not all up to me, Sarita. You know that just as well as I do. I told the powers that be that custodial interrogation at this point would be too premature. Trust me, I argued on Ravi's behalf. But you know how it is. In politics, nothing is premature.'

Sarita takes a deep breath.

'I do know, sir, unfortunately. I don't expect you to call off the investigation, or anything of that sort, because a fair probe will exonerate him of all charges. Of that, I am certain. I'm here with a rather simple request. I would tell you more if it weren't classified, but this case is directly intertwined with a long-running investigation with massive ramifications for national security. To take Ravi into custody at this point would undo months of progress and could prove extremely costly. Neither the PM nor the HM would want that to happen. As a fellow officer of the Indian Police Service, I implore you to hold off on taking him into custody. Do what you have to, but please buy more time.'

Saranjit sighs.

'All right, I will send over a questionnaire or something like that. But I can't defer for longer than a week unless you can be specific as to exactly why. If not custodial interrogation, he'll have to at least come in for questioning.'

'Thank you.'

They are interrupted by a phone call. It is the home minister who is calling on the restricted line in Saranjit's office.

'It never ceases to amaze me, sir, how officers at the IB, even IPS officers, seem to believe that they are exempt from the rules that apply to us mortals,' Saranjit quips, somewhat awkwardly given Sarita's presence in the office.

The home minister begins to laugh raucously. Even though she is a few feet away from the receiver, Sarita can hear him say loud and clear, 'Well, the law will take its course.'

* * *

The suspects are thought to be living on the second floor of a two-storey building, atop a coaching centre for UPSC aspirants in Nagarbhavi. Ravi can't help but laugh at the irony of it all as he and the Examiner drive back and forth along the road. They are in an old car that has a large board affixed on its roof, with the name and address of a driving school. The Examiner is a driving instructor, while Ravi is an over-enthusiastic middle-aged man learning to drive after finally buying a car of his own. They leave nothing to chance, playing out their roles while still keeping an eye out for activity.

They are operating in teams of two, with Mihir and Cyrus comprising the other.

After Jose confirms over the phone that the location they are at conforms precisely to the coordinates of the SatPhones, they begin to set their plan into motion. To obtain physical confirmation of the suspects' presence in the building, Cyrus and Mihir resort to an old ploy, one they had employed on their very first mission.

Dressed as telecom workmen, they carry a long ladder and rest it against a concrete wire pole that stands right outside the building. While Mihir holds the ladder in place, Cyrus carefully climbs up until he is at the same level as the second floor. Much to his dismay, all the windows are shut. But the pole is so precariously close to the building that one can easily hear conversations inside. Carefully craning his ears but doing so in a way that wouldn't draw attention even if someone were to see him, Cyrus begins to pick up bits and pieces of conversation. It is all in Malayalam, a language he doesn't understand. From the shabby old satchel he wears around his shoulders, he pulls out something that looks like a miniature of a telephone antenna and affixes it to the pole, before getting down. Leaving the ladder in place, he returns to the van from where he calls Jose and asks him to translate.

'The signal's a little patchy, maybe because of interference, but I can pick up bits,' Jose tells him. 'They're talking about how Tabrez overreacted by deciding to flee the country. And . . . now they're referring to the CBI investigation and how nobody has any clue about who really was involved in the kidnapping plot. I think we have our men.'

Cyrus walks back to the wire pole and tells Mihir that they can remove the ladder. At the sight of them moving the ladder back to the van, Ravi indicates to the Examiner that they are good to go. They pull up right outside the building and slowly make their way up the staircase. Although it appears to be a relatively new building, it is a low-cost construction. The doors are made of thin PVC, which means they do not even have to bother knocking. With one swift kick, it crashes open, taking the men inside completely by surprise. Before they can even realize what is happening, they find themselves in handcuffs. Cyrus and Mihir enter soon after. Clad in gloves, they carefully collect weapons, cell phones, laptops, literature, etc., into large plastic bags that are then sealed off. The whole operation, from arrival to departure, lasts only three hours. Of that, more than two hours could be attributed to Bangalore traffic!

* * *

Immediately after Ravi confirms that the operation in Bangalore has been a success, Sarita requests an appointment with the home minister. When the minister's personal secretary informs her that the minister's schedule is full for the next few days, she asks for an opportunity to speak to the minister directly. 'A matter of national security, far beyond your clearance,' she tells the personal secretary. The home minister agrees to meet her that afternoon.

'Sarita, this better be important. I had to cancel a few important meetings for this. You know how it is, with elections coming up next year, There's so much work to do . . . selecting candidates, chalking out campaign strategies, raising funds, it never ends. And the demands of governance aren't going to go away just because elections are coming up. To add to all this, there's the mess that your man Ravi has created with the whole Kishan Jadhav saga. Anyway, please sit down and tell me. What did you want to talk to me about?'

Sarita takes her seat and a moment to focus her thoughts.

'Yes sir, I understand you're busy. I'll get to the point straightaway. Around nine months ago, the prime minister asked us all a question the night Mumbai was attacked—"What do I tell our fellow countrymen?" I'm sure you remember you were there. I believe I have an answer. And you might not like it, but it is my duty to inform you. The prime minister can tell our fellow countrymen that months of extremely meticulous work put in by some of our finest officers to nab the perpetrators of that attack and all else that followed was nearly derailed by their own government.'

The home minister is outraged by Sarita's bold insinuations.

'What are you trying to suggest, Sarita?'

'Only the truth, sir. To put it simply, with specific reference to recent events, you needn't worry about the mess that my man Ravi has created. Because it wasn't his doing. We have video footage of the entire encounter. Something we did, just in case Pakistan tried at some point in the future to rake up controversy over the detention of their citizens. The video shows clearly that the police acted on their own accord and shot at three unarmed men who were handcuffed. They also shot intentionally at Jagriti Saha. This video has been in Ravi's possession from the very beginning.'

The minister shakes his head in disbelief.

'That is most unfortunate. I can't believe it myself. But you can't be seriously suggesting that the government is to be held responsible. It was, in fact, a few police officers who claimed that Ravi had issued the orders to fire. Needless to say, they will be severely punished, and Ravi will be exonerated. But why didn't he attempt to deny those allegations? If he had the video with him all along, why didn't he come to us?'

'Because it would have completely jeopardized the task that had been entrusted to him all those months ago, a task with severe ramifications for the integrity and safety of our country. He put his head down and swallowed the bizarre allegations against him. Nevertheless, because the killing of those men was all over the news, the mastermind of these attacks . . . the commander-in-chief of the LeH slipped away before Ravi could get to him. The men actually responsible for the encounter will, of course, pay. But I'm not so sure that the buck stops there. To be clear, I am not in any way accusing you or the government of anything. But it could clearly be made to look that way, especially because no heed was paid to the fact that the man who the CBI embarked on a witch-hunt against was working on a matter of national security. Surely, the government can't feign ignorance on that.'

'That is all true, but you have to trust me, Sarita. The government or I had nothing to do with it. You know how these things take on a life of their own.'

'Precisely my point, sir. These things take on a life of their own. Because somebody, I'm not pointing fingers, but somebody has gone to such a great extent to frame Ravi, I can think of any number of ways in which it could now be spun. A massive cover-up, even a conspiracy on the part of the ruling party to eliminate its most vocal critic . . . basically, all the things that Ravi has been accused of masterminding in collusion with Kishan Jadhav, except for one crucial difference. With this version of events, there is solid irrefutable evidence. But I wouldn't dare release the video, sir. I wouldn't stoop to such lows, despite the gross injustice that has been meted out to my officers. Which is why I am coming to you, and which is why Ravi at no point even entertained the thought of going to the media. I do not care how you do it, but Ravi and his officers will have to be exonerated of all charges and their innocence proclaimed just as loudly as their presumed guilt.'

The minister is somewhat relieved at hearing this and wipes the sweat off his face.

'Thank you, Sarita. I appreciate your loyalty.'

'With all due respect, sir, this has nothing to do with loyalty. I speak on behalf of Ravi here. It was his decision not to release the video, and I am merely the messenger. He wished to convey that his continuing silence on the matter has and will have nothing to do with loyalty or any desire to earn favours of any kind. It stems from a fervent commitment to the dignity of the institution we serve, a commitment to steering absolutely clear of partisan politics. He intends to keep it that way, even at a steep personal cost.

'But please do not mistake this dignity for weakness. Ravi is an exception. Anyone else in his place, including myself, would have fought back with fervour. No government can keep turning its back on its own people and continue to expect servitude and cordial fraternity. At some point, things will give way. Again, I'm not suggesting anything deliberate, nor is Ravi. But just the perception that your own government is acting against you can do great damage. And something similar is responsible for the spurt in terrorism. There is a growing anxiety amidst sections of the Islamic community that they are second-rate citizens in their own country. It might not be true; in fact, I don't think it's true. But then again, it's the perception that counts ultimately. And the perception alone can create the right conditions for our enemies to take advantage and incite internal strife. Unless the perception is corrected, organizations like the LeH will keep springing up. And the solution can only be political.'

* * *

On the flight back to Delhi, Ravi tries interrogating the men in custody.

They say nothing at first, and Ravi doesn't press them any further. He remains silent for the next twenty minutes or so, merely observing them. It soon becomes clear to Ravi that one among them, a man identified as Shafeeq Rizwan, is bursting to speak out but is holding himself back. Ravi asks the rest of his team to escort the other suspects to the front of the plane and continue interrogating them. He remains alone with Shafeeq at the rear.

As soon as they're gone, Shafeeq bursts into tears, 'Sir, you have to let me go. Please. I had no interest in any of this, and I still don't. Somebody from your own department put me on this job. I was just a small-time drug dealer. And then, somebody came to me and said that they would have all my charges cleared and also take care of my mother's expensive treatment if I agreed to do all this. I even gave information, sir.'

Ravi's interest is piqued.

'I see. And who might this somebody be?'

'I can't tell you, sir. It was part of the deal. Even if I were to be caught, I had to remain silent on that person's identity. He would find out anyway and have me freed.'

'Fair enough, that is how we do things. I'm impressed by your commitment to upholding the terms of your agreement. But it was you who told us about the men who were sent to attack the Parliament in Delhi, wasn't it? In feeding us wrong information, where did your commitment disappear?'

Shafeeq's sobs grow louder, causing Ravi's men at the front to turn back. Ravi goes up to them and asks them to focus on their task and returns to find Shafeeq still struggling to keep his emotions in check.

'It wasn't my intention, sir. Believe me. But our commander, Tabrez, he found out, and I thought he would kill me. I would have still figured a way out, but when I found out that none of the promises that had been made to me were kept up . . . my drug charges still remained, and my mother passed away alone without the medicines that would have saved her . . . I saw no reason to continue putting my life at risk. And I became a double agent. I would feed my contact wrong information on Tabrez's instructions. What else could I do, sir? I was trapped.'

Ravi listens with genuine sympathy and consoles Shafeeq with a gentle pat on his shoulder.

'I'll be honest with you, what fate awaits you is beyond my control. But if you want any mercy, any help from me, you will have to be completely honest about everything. I have some questions for you, right now. We don't have much time, so you don't have to go into detail. Quick answers are what I expect. Firstly, where is Tabrez?'

'By now, Tabrez should be somewhere in Pakistan, sir. He fled as soon as you arrested our computer man in Mumbai.'

'You mean to say he found out immediately? Who told him?'

'Yes, sir. He found out immediately. I don't know who told him, but he has his ways of finding out.'

'Fine. Tell me this, are there more from your organization still out there, on Indian soil?'

'I don't know how many more are out there, and where they are, but there are definitely many others you haven't been caught yet. Iqbal, for instance. He's the second-in-command. Before fleeing, Tabrez handed the reins to him. And then there's Rukhsana, Tabrez's wife. I have never met her. In fact, very few people have seen her. She was never with us at any point, but we all know that she's been an integral part of Tabrez's plans from the very beginning.'

'Who exactly were the men you led us to in Delhi? What was the plan?'

'They were real terrorists, sir, people working with us. But the plan wasn't to have them killed, merely arrested. They had deliberately been fed false information by Tabrez, so that you would be thrown off the trail. And then we were going to list their release as one of our demands after kidnapping Kishan Jadhav. But neither of those two plans . . .'

The pilot announces that the flight is being prepared for landing. He requests the passengers on board to fasten their seatbelts.

'One final question, for now. Who told you about Qasim Khan?'

'I heard from my contact in your agency. When I was hesitant about taking up the job, he told me that there were several Muslims who had risen to great heights within the agency and that I had a bright future ahead. He mentioned a few names, just to assure me. Among them was Qasim Khan, working out of Mumbai. When it became clear that Basharat had been captured, having last been seen entering the mosque, Tabrez immediately connected the dots. I have never seen anybody as sharp or intelligent as him, sir. Please don't underestimate him. There's a reason why so many men are ready to die at his command. It doesn't matter how many of us you arrest. As long as he is out there, you haven't won.'

Epilogue

As he steps out on the verandah of the forest guest house where he and Rita are staying, Ravi takes in the magnificent sight that greets him—snow-clad mountain peaks that shimmer in the golden hues of early morning sunlight. Although it is officially the dawn of summer across most parts of the country, Manali at this time is still steeped in the cool breezy charms of late spring. Ravi is silently expressing his gratitude for the opportunity to escape the sweltering heat of Delhi when Ranger leaps out to join him. Clutching on to a frisbee with his jaws, Ranger wags his tail excitedly, almost as if to say, 'Enough contemplating, now come play with me.'

Ravi takes the frisbee and flings it as far as he can. He watches in delight as Ranger makes a mad dash and returns with it in no time. The game of fetch goes on for a while. Ranger is just as tireless in his pursuit of the frisbee as Ravi is in his pursuit of the country's enemies. The game comes to a premature end when the caretaker of the guesthouse brings tea and biscuits. Rita steps out clad in a red Angami Naga shawl and bearing her favourite book, *Autobiography of a Yogi*. She instructs the caretaker to keep the tea on the veranda table.

Ranger is annoyed at the abrupt end to playtime but decides to bide his time in a corner while his masters go about their business.

'Such a beautiful morning, isn't it? I don't think I've ever seen an azure blue sky in Delhi,' Rita remarks to Ravi.

'Absolutely. It's the perfect day for trout fishing. I'm planning on heading out immediately after tea,' he responds.

Rita looks at him with consternation, vigorously shaking her head in disbelief.

'What?' he asks, not quite sure what he has done this time to incur her displeasure.

'Three days a year, that's all we have completely to ourselves. And we didn't get even that last year. I've waited so long for this vacation and here you are talking about going off on a mission to hunt agents.'

Ravi bursts out laughing.

'No, no. I really mean it. Trout stands for plain and simple trout. I have made arrangements for a moonlit dinner on the banks of the Beas. Your favourite Chardonnay has already been arranged for, and I was hoping to make it extra special with some barbecued trout, freshly caught by yours truly.'

Rita looks at him with affection.

'Riverside moonlit dinner with chardonnay and barbecued trout. How quaint! Trying to emulate James Bond on the romantic front as well, I see.'

Ravi smiles with a hint of mischief.

'What can I say? I try my best. After all, my task is so much more challenging than Bond's.'

'What do you mean?'

'Well, the lady in my life is far harder to impress than all the Bond ladies put together.'

With that, Ravi reclines into his seat and shifts his gaze towards the mountains. After a few moments, he turns towards her again, 'Now that you've mentioned it, perhaps it wouldn't be the worst of ideas to name my next agent "trout". What do you reckon?'

Rita chuckles, 'Why not? Octopus must be all alone, out in the water. I was thinking last night while reading that you too should write a book.'

'Autobiography of a sleuth?'

'No. Autobiography of an animal farm keeper. You can have chapters titled Octopus, Takshak, Falcon, Scorpion, maybe Trout . . .'

They both erupt into laughter, after which Ravi sinks back into his chair. The silken warmth of the sun, coupled with the cool Manali breeze, makes him drowsy. His eyes unwittingly close, and his thoughts drift towards what Rita had described as his animal farm.

Octopus was a veteran of the Afghan war. He belonged to the anti-Taliban faction, and nursed a deep grudge against the ISI. After losing everything he held dear—family, friends, home—he had fled to India in a wounded condition. That is when Ravi had met him. He had gradually nudged Octopus towards joining hands against their shared enemy, an offer he had readily accepted. If not for Octopus and the information he had dispatched all those months ago, they would have made no progress in their pursuit of the LeH. Only a few weeks ago, he had heard from the Afghan field office that Octopus had succumbed to his injuries in a factional war.

Takshak was a timid Sikh, with a great love for cooking, who had found himself embroiled in the separatist schemes of the much-dreaded Babbar Khalsa organization. He was nothing like anybody else in the organization. The mere prospect of being slapped made him shudder. Ravi often wondered why he had decided to name him Takshak, after the mythical cobra. He was more like a panda, adorable and entirely harmless. Perhaps it was because he turned out to be a Takshak for the terrorists he had infiltrated and played a significant role in neutralizing. Towards the end of the Khalistan movement, Ravi had helped him settle down in France and pursue his culinary ambitions. Even to this day, he sends cards on Ravi's birthday and anniversary, inviting Ravi and Rita to join him in Monte Carlo, where he runs a Michelin-starred restaurant.

There were so many like them, nameless and faceless, who had helped the country tide over some of its greatest crises. Some, like Octopus, had been martyred. Others, like Takshak, had managed to flee and settle into the lives they truly deserved. With the Manali sun gently beating down on his face, Ravi tries hard to recall their names, their lives, their stories. Some of it returns to him in flashes, some of it is forever lost.

* * *

Sullu lies in her hospital bed, watching the news. She is still reeling from the effects of anaesthesia, but nothing can come in the way of her and the news. As has been the case for the past several weeks, every channel has its focus turned towards the tragic death of their beloved colleague, Jagriti Saha. Every single twist has been reported with unsparing diligence, given the unprecedented nature of the case. Much attention, in the last week, has been paid to the botched-up investigation of the CBI. Despite the government's best attempts to cover it up, media houses lap up the revelations that tumble out with every passing day. Sensational footage of police officers being led away in handcuffs dominate the airwaves. Ravi Kumar, Mihir Kaul, Cyrus Bandookwallah, and Jose Cherian are revealed to have played a singularly important role in neutralizing the dreaded militant outfit responsible for the spate of terror attacks that had left the country reeling.

Even as she slips in and out of consciousness, drifting from the news to a dreamless slumber, a nurse walks in with Madhav. In his arms is their child, a baby boy. Tears flow down her cheeks as she holds his tender body in her arms.

'Have you arrived at a name?' Madhav asks her.

'Yes,' Sullu replies, 'We will name him Ravi. Another Ravi has been a ray of sunlight for the entire country. Our Ravi will be a ray of sunlight in our lives.'

As she utters those words, Sullu feels as if a heavy weight has been lifted off of her chest. Just as inexplicably as it had arrived, it fades away. Only those who are now being celebrated as heroes—including her newborn son's namesake—know that dark clouds continue to obscure the rays of the sun. The threat of darkness continues to loom large.

Acknowledgements

The thought of writing this book would have remained in the realm of idea had it not been for the guidance of Sanjay Routray and his wife, Dikssha, who not only pushed for the fruition of the thought but arranged the required logistics too. Nikhil Ravishankar, a young copywriter in Sanjay's company, Matchbox Pictures, helped with his masterful skills, which he has acquired at a young age. I am grateful to Matchbox Pictures for having agreed to adapt the story for an OTT serial.